Also by Kate Cross

The Clockwork Agents Novels
Heart of Brass
Touch of Steel

BREATH of IRON

A NOVEL OF THE CLOCKWORK AGENTS

KATE CROSS

A SIGNET ECLIPSE BOOK

SIGNET ECLIPSE
Published by the Penguin Group
Penguin Group (USA) Inc., 375 Hudson Street,
New York, New York 10014, USA

USA | Canada | UK | Ireland | Australia | New Zealand | India | South Africa | China

Penguin Books Ltd., Registered Offices: 80 Strand, London WC2R 0RL, England
For more information about the Penguin Group visit penguin.com.

First published by Signet Eclipse, an imprint of New American Library,
a division of Penguin Group (USA) Inc.

First Printing, August 2013

ISBN 978-0-451-24006-4

Printed in the United States of America
10 9 8 7 6 5 4 3 2 1

PUBLISHER'S NOTE
This is a work of fiction. Names, characters, places, and incidents either are the product of the author's imagination or are used fictitiously, and any resemblance to actual persons, living or dead, business establishments, events, or locales is entirely coincidental.

The publisher does not have any control over and does not assume any responsibility for author or third-party Web sites or their content.

If you purchased this book without a cover you should be aware that this book is stolen property. It was reported as "unsold and destroyed" to the publisher and neither the author nor the publisher has received any payment for this "stripped book."

This book is for all the punks,

steam and otherwise, who unashamedly believe in love.

In the hull of this ship, there's a home that we've built
Myself and each soul of this crew.
And 'most every night by the oil lamp light,
I still think of you.

Steady as she goes.
There are those that stay with us through each ebb and
    flow.
They are the ones we call home.
Steady as she goes.

—from "Steady" by Eli August

Chapter 1

Evelyn Stone literally held a man's heart in her hands before tossing it into a bucket at her feet. She would examine it and its defects later. Right now she had a patient to fix.

The young surgeon assisting her watched in fascination as she took the mechanical heart he offered and introduced it into the gaping chest cavity. She had very little time to put the device in place and connect it to the circulatory system before the man would die.

It would not look good for her, or for the Wardens of the Realm, if the director of Germany's Schatten Ritters (S.R.), or "Shadow Knights," died in her care while under the protection of Austrian agents. She was supposed to be the best in her field.

She was also pretty much the *only* one in her field, except for some bloke in America. No one else in Europe that she knew of had made quite the same strides as she where organ replacement was concerned.

Quickly, Evelyn attached the man's remaining tissue to the mechanical pump and checked the seals. She set aside the part that would fit over the front of his chest like a shield, not only protecting the artificial organ, but providing a convenient port for maintenance.

Once the heart was in place, she could relax a little. That was the hardest part. Still, she worked as fast and efficiently as she could, and when the man's new heart began to beat in a steady rhythm, she breathed a sigh of relief. A person's heart could be stopped for only so long before lack of circulation did irreparable damage to the brain and tissue.

Above her head she could hear the polite but enthusiastic applause of her audience. This was the first time she'd performed this sort of operation with spectators watching her every move, evaluating and assessing.

She set her patient's chest back to rights and fitted the panel for his new heart in place. Later she showed the young surgeon, Dr. Franz Adler, how to properly care for the device, ensuring that it—and the man in possession of it—continued to function at optimum capacity for many years to come.

After the demonstration, Dr. Adler asked her to dinner, just as she expected he might.

He began talking about the surgery, the work they did within their respective agencies, and about himself, also as she thought he might, but after a couple of bottles of good German wine, he began to rhapsodize about her "exotic looks," "considerable intellect" and finally the beauty of her eyes. That was when she knew it was time to take him home.

"I have never seen anything like that," Adler told her much later as they lay in bed. "You are a genius. An artist. Your gift is squandered with the Wardens."

Evelyn smiled. He was handsome and fit and had a delicious accent that she loved to listen to as he complimented her. Of course, he seemed rather enamored of the sound of his voice as well, but she was sated and such languidness of muscle and spirit gave her patience. Normally she avoided such encounters with peers, especially those also in service to their country, but she'd accomplished something extraordinary that day and she needed to celebrate.

If she weren't enjoying Franz's company, she would be alone, probably reliving every last detail of the first organ replacement she had performed. She'd no doubt be very deep in her cups as well, vomiting red wine into the toilet's porcelain bowl. Sex was so much more relaxing and usually required less cleanup—and didn't leave behind a taste that made her wonder whether something had died in her mouth.

"I cannot believe you are going to leave in a few days," Franz lamented with a charming pout that emphasized his full lower lip. He was gorgeous, blond and blue-eyed, with a body that ought to be immortalized in marble. He was seven years her junior and had the stamina to go with his youth. She could have done much worse.

She *had* done worse.

"I have to return to London," she explained. "Besides, you are going to be very busy now that you are taking over the S.R.'s medical department."

Long, nimble fingers trailed over her bare arm. "You could always stay and we could run it together."

Of course, with the understanding that he would be the one in charge. No, thank you. "The Wardens would be lost without me. I cannot turn my back on them." That was only half bravado. The Wardens would miss her, but that wasn't what made her go back. What made her go back was that she was good at her job—very good at it—and she wanted to perform it where she could do the most good. And, if she admitted it to no one but herself, she wanted to be where she could occasionally hear the latest account of Captain Mac's daring adventures.

She had no business wanting to hear about him. She had given up that right. She didn't remain in London just for him; that would be pathetic. She had friends there, a home and a cat. She was important to the Wardens. She would not be so important to handsome Franz, and she refused to be mistress to a man's career. She had tried that once and it had ended badly.

If she was honest, she would acknowledge that most men would come second to her own work. She really couldn't fault Franz for a similar mind-set.

"Bah," he said. "The Wardens have no idea how fortunate they are to have such an angel in their employ."

Now he was being grandiose. Perhaps she should give his mouth a new occupation so he would stop talking. Or . . .

"I should go," she said, throwing back the blankets and slipping out of the bed naked. She had no shame for her body, but neither was she overly proud. She had long, strong legs, a soft belly, good hips and full breasts that, while not gravity defying, still managed a good degree of pertness. Most men found her appealing because of her mixed heritage. She'd been born in Jamaica, several months after her wealthy Irish-Canadian father had begun courting the granddaughter of a woman who had been a slave and the man who had bought her freedom. He'd brought them back to England with him, where he then proceeded to do his duty and marry an English virgin.

"Where are you going?" Franz demanded, sliding out of bed. The French safe she made him use—despite having a small pregnancy-preventing device implanted in her cervix—dangled from his flaccid penis like a little handkerchief poised to wave in surrender. "It is still dark."

"I'm returning to my hotel," she told him, pulling on her trousers. "I want to check on your director in the morning and I'm having a breakfast meeting with an old school friend." It was such a familiar lie that it rolled easily off her tongue. Although this time it was partially true. She was meeting an old friend, just not from school.

"Surely you can stay a little longer?" He graced her with a seductive smile, reaching out to stroke her bare breast.

Evie grimaced. That cajoling tone might work on some naive chit straight out of the nursery, but not with her. He should know the polite and honorable way to play this game. This was why she often went to the homes of her chosen partners rather than taking them back to her rooms. She had learned some time ago that it was easier to do the leaving than to try to show a stubborn lover the door.

She pulled on her shirt, knocking his hand away from her. "No, I can't." She tucked the tail into her trousers.

Franz blinked. "But I want you to stay."

"And I told you I can't." She shrugged into her corseted waistcoat. "Thank you for a lovely evening." She kissed his cheek as an added gesture.

The younger man raked a hand through his already disheveled hair. "Unbelievable. So we make love and now you leave like I am a whore."

He was difficult to take seriously when he was naked and had a safe hanging from his limp cock. She sat down on a nearby trunk to pull on her boots. "I'm sorry—did I mislead you into thinking I wanted something else? Did you hope that tonight would be the beginning of a long and loving relationship? Do you want to marry me?"

"No, of course not." Too late he realized his mistake, and his distaste quickly turned to panic. "I mean, I had hoped that we could enjoy each other's company for a little while longer and see how things develop."

She had two choices—roll her eyes or smile sympathetically. She chose the smile. "That's very sweet, and please don't think that I don't appreciate the sentiment, but I really do have to go." With that, she grabbed her coat and rose to her feet.

Franz chuckled humorlessly. "I'd heard you were a cold bitch, and now I believe it."

Evie didn't pause. She shoved her arm into one coat sleeve. "What's the matter? Angry I'm leaving before you have the chance to kick me out? I'm assuming you wouldn't want to risk your mother seeing me when she gets up in the morning."

A dull flush suffused his cheeks beneath the golden stubble of his beard. "My landlady is a woman of discretion."

She fastened a button. "Your landlady is your mother. Did you think I wouldn't see the photographs and portraits of you as a child when we came in? Did you think I was so enamored of you I wouldn't notice the note left on your dresser reminding you to give her your soiled laundry? She signed it 'Love, Mother,' for heaven's sake."

He stared at her with a mixture of horror and humiliation. "Get out."

"It's about damn time," she retorted, and yanked open the bedroom door. "And take that safe off. You look ridiculous."

"Bitch."

"Give your mother my best."

Evelyn closed the door behind her and made her way down the stairs, not caring if she was seen or not. She didn't care if by tomorrow afternoon Franz— and his mother—had told everyone in Germany what a whore she was. That would only make it easier to meet another man next time she traveled there on Warden business. Her reputation as a surgeon had nothing to do with her reputation as a woman. She would always be in demand because she was an expert at what she did, and she would always find a lover because she was an attractive, confident woman. Those three traits drew some people to her and repelled others at the same rate. Life was too short to worry about the ones who turned up their noses and looked down on her.

Mac had taught her that. The bastard.

She stepped outside into the waning hours of a beautiful September night. Perfect for a walk, even though there were plenty of steam hacks in the vicinity. This neighborhood wasn't far from the airfield where the dirigibles arrived and departed. Consequently, Evelyn's hotel was within close distance.

She paused on the walk, feeling eyes on her back. She glanced up and saw Franz in a window. She waved. He made a rude gesture that made her laugh. She truly was a bitch. She hadn't meant to hurt his pride, but if she was truthful, she'd really only been thinking of herself and her own wants and needs.

Regardless, she wouldn't see Franz again for a long

time, if ever. His ambition meant he wouldn't be content to stay with the Ritters for long. She would enjoy telling this story to Claire and Arden when she returned to London. Perhaps it wouldn't be a good idea to share it with their husbands, though. Men were oddly sensitive about such things, the babies.

Her boot heels clicked on the walk, echoing softly among the sounds of passing carriages and noise from the nearby airfield. Evelyn kept a cautious gaze on her surroundings. She could still feel eyes on her. Surely Franz had left his window by now?

Footsteps behind her. Light, but purposeful. She sped up, fingers slipping inside her coat for the weapon concealed there. It might be just another pedestrian, but years at W.O.R. had taught her that paranoia was a virtue.

Do not panic. What would Claire do in such a situation? Or Arden? Dhanya? They were smart, capable women, each of whom would keep her wits and be prepared just in case. She would do the same.

The footsteps behind her quickened, matching her own. No question now whether she was being followed. She clasped her blade, pulling it free of the sheath as fingers wrapped around her arm.

She whirled around, using her attacker's momentum to drive herself forward so that the edge of her knife came to settle at the base of a long, smooth throat.

Hands came up. One of them was metal—etched brass. "Jesus on the cross, Evie! Are you trying to kill me?"

Evelyn froze. "Nell?" She hadn't seen the woman in years, but there was no denying her braided gray hair and bright blue eyes, fanned by pale squint lines in her otherwise tanned face. She grinned, revealing unexpectedly straight white teeth.

"I knew you wouldn't forget me!" The tall, handsome woman came in to hug her, and Evelyn flipped her blade, moving it out of the way so Nell didn't slit her own throat. She hugged her back. The feel of those metal fingers—so much like bones—against her back was both familiar and unsettling.

"Nell, what are you doing in Vienna?" She looked over the woman's shoulder, expecting to see another familiar face—one wearing a smirk—but there was no one there. That shouldn't be as disappointing as it was, damn it.

"Picking up," her old friend replied, releasing her. "You?"

"The usual." She wasn't at liberty to discuss her assignment with non-Wardens. Not even former ones.

"Understood." Nell adjusted the handkerchief that covered the top of her head and was anchored by her braids. "You all done or still working?"

That was something of an odd question, but Evelyn supposed her old friend asked because she had catching up on her mind. It was late—very late—but she wasn't tired, and it was good to see Nell.

And Nell could tell her all about Mac and rip those old wounds open again. Maybe throw a little salt in for good measure.

"I'm pretty much done. Just a lecture planned for tomorrow and then back to England. You?"

"We're to set sail before dawn." Nell began to walk, so Evelyn fell into step beside her. "I'll walk you back to your lodgings. Where are you staying?"

Evelyn told her. Her German was atrocious, but she attempted it regardless. *"Der Lowe und Der Lamm."* The Lion and the Lamb. It wasn't a W.O.R. hotel, or even one sanctioned by the Schatten Ritters. It was the hotel she and Mac once stayed in. The same room as well. She told herself she had requested it because of the view.

It truly was an astonishing view.

"Is that place still standing?" Nell chuckled. "No accounting for people's tastes, I suppose."

Evie didn't respond. The hotel was a beautiful old stone thing and she loved it, but she wasn't about to say so in case her companion decided to share that information with her captain. Just the fact that she was staying there revealed more than she'd ever want him to know.

Instead she asked, "How is everyone? Did Barker get those new teeth he wanted?" The memory brought a smile to her lips.

Nell snorted and nodded. "He did. Can't get him to stop smiling now. McNamara's become a grandfather, and Esther and Dirty Joe finally jumped the anvil."

This was news indeed! "I thought he said he'd never marry her."

"He did. Then she decided that maybe she wouldn't marry him. That changed up his mind right quick."

"Yes, I imagine it would," Evie replied with a grin of her own.

"I suppose you wouldn't have heard that we lost Good Jock."

The grin slid from her face. Jock's real name had been Jacques le Bon, hence the foolish but suitable nickname. During their brief acquaintance he had taught her many of his grandmother's natural cures and remedies, some of which she often used. One had led to the discovery of the accelerated healing liquid she kept in the medical facility at Warden headquarters.

"No," she murmured. "I hadn't heard. How did it happen?"

"Garroted by one of those Bear Bastards." "Bears" was what most agents in Europe called their Russian counterparts.

"I'm so sorry. I know how much Ma . . . you all loved him."

Nell nodded, obviously ignoring her near slip. Mac would hear about that, too, no doubt.

God, she couldn't seem to stop thinking about him—even before Nell found her. Maybe it was this city, where they'd made such bittersweet memories, or maybe it was the fact that every time she slept with a different man she was all the more aware that he was not the man she wanted. Nell's appearance was definitely a stick poking an infected wound.

Shouldn't it have healed by now? It had been years. She should be over him rather than pining for him as her mother had pined for her English lover.

Nell continued to talk about other crew members, but not the one Evelyn really wanted to hear about. She listened raptly, laughing and tearing up in tandem as she heard about their triumphs and sorrows.

She looked up and saw her hotel in the near distance. Soon this meeting would be at an end. It would have to be. If Nell came into the building with her, there was a good chance the older woman would be recognized and more than likely delivered into Warden custody. The Wardens didn't much care for pirates, and after Evie left Mac, that was exactly what he and his crew had become, turning their backs on Crown and country.

"You'll tell Mac how sorry I am about Jock, won't you?" Evelyn asked, finally allowing herself to say his name.

Nell stopped walking, so she stopped as well. "You can tell him yourself."

Surely she hadn't heard that correctly. Her heart was beating so loud it was hard to tell. "What did you say?"

The other woman's expression turned sympathetic. "I'm sorry, Evie. I need you to know I was against this from the start."

Cold settled in Evelyn's chest. Claire would have had a weapon in hand by now; so would've Arden. She just stood there, stupid. "Against what, Nell?"

Out of the dark alley just behind Nell emerged two more familiar faces—Barker and Wells. Barker with his leathery face and kind brown eyes. Wells with her hair so red it looked to be on fire and eyes bluer than the waters around Jamaica. They didn't look happy.

Two more came up from behind her. She couldn't tell if she knew them or not. So someone had been watching her. It just hadn't been Franz.

Sloppy, Evie, she told herself.

"If it's ransom you want, you know the Wardens won't pay it."

"We don't want money, my girl."

Then what? Evelyn pulled her blade free once more. She couldn't take them all, but she could wound a couple of them badly enough that they'd feel it for the rest of their sorry lives. She'd start with Nell, her betrayer.

Evelyn lunged with her dagger but barely made it two steps before she felt a sharp sting in her side, followed by a jolt that dropped her to her knees on the cobblestones. They'd shocked her. She couldn't speak, couldn't really think. Couldn't do anything but twitch. At least she hadn't soiled herself.

Nell's face loomed over hers. "I'm really sorry, darlin'. I mean it." She pressed a white cloth over Evelyn's face.

Chloroform. Bloody brilliant. She'd have someone's head for this. Maybe his heart, too. Or his spleen. She'd remove them while he was still conscious. She'd—

She woke up with a mouth that felt as though it were lined with cotton wool and muscles that pinged as though they'd been denied blood. At least she was on a bed and her limbs weren't bound.

Evelyn moved her head on the soft pillow. It smelled delicious—vanilla and sandalwood. Some of her favorite memories involved a man with that exact scent. Often he'd join her in bed, his skin tanned yet smooth, hair damp from the bath, and she'd bury her face in the hollow between his neck and shoulder and take a deep, intoxicating breath.

She was in the middle of just such a breath when the reality of the situation struck her. She was on a bed that smelled of Mac. Beneath the pounding of her heart she could hear engines—a gentle *whump, whump* that never failed to lull her into slumber.

Bloody hell, she was on the *Queen V*!

Her attempt to launch herself off the bed ended with her strengthless carcass being dumped on the rug. Her muscles were still twitchy from being electrocuted. She spat out dog fur and cursed herself for giving him that overgrown mutt. Then she gathered all her willpower and pushed herself to her knees. Using the side of the bed helped her make it to her feet.

She grasped the edge of a window and peered out. The muscles in her thighs trembled, but held.

Clouds. Not fog but clouds. They were in the bloody sky. She knew it. She just knew it!

Closing her eyes, she swore silently until she ran out of foul words. It took three languages for her to pull herself together. She should have known that meeting Nell wasn't just a coincidence. It never was.

Why did they put her in this room, though? Of all the rooms about this vessel, why did she have to wake up on the bed she'd slept in for months during one of the happiest times of her life? Everywhere she turned, there was something of his—a discarded shirt, a pair of shiny brown leather boots, a straight razor with a pearl handle she'd held in her own hand more times than she could remember.

That was a lie. If put to the test, she could probably recall every damn one.

Her knees trembled, but she'd be tarred and feathered if she'd touch that bed again. Slowly she made her way to the desk. The room was large for one on a ship, but still small enough that there was a place for everything and everything in its place. The ship hit a pocket of wind and bucked, tossing Evie into the captain's chair with graceless ease. Thank God it was bolted to the floor.

No sooner had she righted herself than the door opened. No knock, no inquiry as to her state of decency. There was only one person it could be. She drew a deep breath.

Please let him be fat and pockmarked. And bald. His hair had always been his vanity.

God was obviously not in a mind to favor her today. The door swung open to reveal shoulders almost the same width as the frame in a cream linen shirt and narrow hips in snug brown trousers. She was on eye level with his crotch—not that she minded, but it wasn't very dignified.

She raised her gaze and wished she hadn't. The

last few years had been kind to Gavin MacRae. He was a tall man with long legs. His back was as straight and proud as ever. His stubbled jaw was just as firm, and his chin still had that shallow cleft. His mouth was wide and slim, bracketed by smile lines. They fanned out from the corners of his eyes, too, like faint scars in the tan of his face. Only, those blue eyes didn't sparkle at the sight of her as they'd once done.

She dropped her gaze, chest pinching. It had to be because of the current still tormenting her body. His nose . . .

"Did you break that poor thing again?" she blurted.

He didn't have to ask. His hand went immediately to the center of his face. Even his hands were as she remembered—long and strong.

"No," he replied, quickly dropping his fingers. "Someone else did it for me."

His mouth was as smart as ever as well. And he still possessed that drawl of a voice that sounded almost completely without accent except for a little Texas with a hint of Scotland—he'd grown up in both places and considered them equally as his home.

Or at least he had at one time.

Bloody hell but it was good to see him. Painful, too, like pressing on a bruise. He seemed healthy and hale—the lawless life obviously suited him. At least he was alive, which meant he'd survived a lot longer than she ever expected.

"You look good," he said, nodding his head in her

direction as he crossed his arms over the width of his chest. His shirt strained at the shoulders.

Evelyn looked down at herself. Her clothes were dirty and she'd been wearing them for almost a full twenty-four hours, she calculated, given the look of the sky outside. If he thought this was good, then his taste certainly hadn't improved.

"So do you." How calm she sounded—as if they were having tea. As if she hadn't broken his heart and her own in the process. "What Nell told me about Jock—was it true?"

His features tightened. "Yeah. It's true. We lost him two years ago."

Just a year after she'd walked out on him. "That must have been hard for you."

"Been through worse." The edge in his usually smooth voice said more than any words ever could. She hadn't been forgiven. Odd then that he'd had her brought aboard his ship unconscious.

"What's this all about, Mac?" she asked wearily. Despite a forced nap, she was tired. Exhausted even.

"Worn out after your night of unbridled rutting?"

Under different circumstances she would have smiled at his jealousy. He rarely ever used coarse language in front of women. "Rutting" was as rude as he was likely to get. She didn't smile, however; she rubbed her forehead and hoped the look she gave him was more disinterested than remorseful.

"If you wanted to talk, you could have come to my hotel. There was no need to grab me off the street." Wait, was that her luggage in the corner by the armoire?

He flashed that smirk she remembered so well and leaned one shoulder against the doorframe, arms still folded over his chest. "Talk? I don't want to talk. Darlin', this is an abduction. Consider yourself my prisoner."

Chapter 2

Perhaps he could have made the statement a little less gothic novel–style and a little more desperate, but Mac wasn't exactly in the frame of mind to give a damn how he sounded—especially not to Evelyn Stone.

She did look good, although a little grimy. More striking than he remembered. That was fate's way of buggering him good and hard. Long black hair spilled down her back in glossy waves, pins sticking out of it. Large whiskey and chocolate eyes framed by long sooty lashes glared at him. And that mouth . . .

If he wanted to talk. Christ on a rudder, did she think so much of her own appeal? "You're here because of your skills as a surgeon, not because I care for your company," he told her roughly. A little too roughly to sound sincere, but she didn't seem to notice. Her shoulders pulled back as her spine snapped defiantly straight. She had strong shoulders for a woman. Her entire body was strong. He remembered times with her legs and arms around him, holding him to her as if she'd never, ever let him go. He'd always admired the long, defined musculature beneath her soft café au lait skin. Always admired her.

And then she did let him go. Put him back together and tossed him carelessly to the wind as she seemed to do with every man since.

Yes, he'd kept tabs.

"Are you in need of some sort of . . . procedure?" she inquired, as though the thought of cutting into him gave her perverse pleasure. Obviously ripping out his heart three years ago hadn't been enough.

"Sorry to disappoint, Doc, but I'm not your patient."

"Pity. I warn you, I don't support piracy and I have no intention of stitching a pirate back together."

Yes, she despised pirates and all they stood for—it was part of the reason he'd taken on the profession. Every country in Europe that owned an air dock had heard of ballsy Captain Mac and his wily crew. "It's not a pirate, either." That was all he planned to tell her. "Get cleaned up and meet me on deck in fifteen minutes."

She arched a gently angled eyebrow. "And if I don't?"

"It's a long way to the ground." It was an empty threat. He needed her too badly to let her go.

"Surely this wreck of a ship has swallows on board?"

Every smart captain made sure his soaring girl had the small flying machines in case of emergency or necessity. "None that will be available to you. This isn't up for negotiation. Do what needs to be done and I'll deliver you safe and sound back to the Wardens' front door."

"And if I refuse?"

"Don't challenge me, Evie. And don't think for a minute our past makes one lick of difference. Twelve minutes." With that, he turned and closed the door behind him. He didn't lock it. At several thousand feet in the sky it didn't seem necessary.

Plus, Evie wouldn't try to escape. She'd do what needed to be done and then try to kill him in his sleep, or give a detailed report to W.O.R. when he dropped her off. Regardless, she'd remain on board if for no other reason than to make his life miserable. She was good at that.

His right hand splayed over his chest. His fingers didn't have to search for the faint ridge of scar tissue; they went there instinctively. Evie might have saved his life, but she'd marked him forever with that cut, though the wound to his pride had cut much deeper. His heart was still raw and inflamed—the memory of her was like an infection that refused to respond to treatment.

And Mac tried to find "treatment" in the arms of every obliging woman he could. He reckoned a long list of lovers was something he and Evie had in common.

He reached the end of the narrow corridor and the

stairs where he could climb up or descend to the lower levels where the galley, hold and crew quarters were. This floor had his rooms, Nell's and two cabins for passengers. Easiest money ever made was squiring people back and forth betwixt destinations they wanted to keep secret.

He climbed the stairs, the bright morning sunshine greeting him as he reached the deck. He blinked his watering eyes, squinted and stomped toward his first mate, who was at the wheel. Nell always had been the one who had the most common sense, and thus had a pair of tinted goggles over her eyes to protect them from the light. At her feet was a giant of a beast—almost as long as Mac was tall, and heavier. It was Napoleon—who had been a runt of a puppy when Evie brought him to the ship as a present.

The great, thick tail gave a hard thump on the deck. Mac squatted down to scratch behind floppy ears and get a warm, wet lick under his chin.

His second-most-trusted companion took her eye off the horizon long enough to shoot him an assessing glance. "You're still walking and in one piece, so I'll assume she didn't take it too badly."

Mac's own gaze went to the sky. He never got tired of the view. There were several ships like his soaring through the air over Austria—passenger vessels on their way north to Vienna, or perhaps southwest to Villach. Air traffic would start to thicken soon, as they moved farther east. Germany produced some of the best airships in the world, which made the country a hub for dirigible traffic, therefore cluttering the skies. People would transfer to other ships, and ships could often get serviced by some talented, mechanically minded buggers who always knew where a man like him could get some extra passengers or cargo.

There'd be no such side trip this time.

He rose to his feet—Napoleon went back to napping. "I haven't told her why she's here yet."

Nell snorted. "I don't know why you even have to tell her. Just get the gel patched up and we'll be on our way. Seems unnecessarily cruel to give her an explanation."

"I can't trust anyone, sis. You know that." He turned his gaze to the ground far below them, partially obscured by low, wispy clouds. Everything looked small from this far up, including his life.

"You trust me."

"You're an exception." She was his big sister, and despite a lifetime of kicking his arse, she'd also saved his arse six or a dozen times. He'd done the same for her.

"You telling me you don't trust Evie? Poseidon's hairy sac, Mac. She saved your life—twice."

"It takes saving my life five times for me to truly trust someone," he retorted with mock gravity.

"Don't you play that with me. I can still kick your skinny arse. Who broke your nose the first time?"

Mac tried not to smile. "You. I remember you got your arse slapped later by Ma."

"It was worth it," his sister shot back with absolutely no remorse. "I'm amazed you can even breathe through the damn thing now."

"You're just jealous because I'm so pretty. Has twelve minutes gone by yet?"

"You gave her a time limit? Good thing you're pretty, because there ain't a brain in your fool head."

"We don't have much time, Nelly. I'm already risking Imogen's safety giving Evie that long."

"It's been six minutes since you came up on deck."

"Damnation."

"Oh, for pity's sake, just go get her."

"I can't appear too desperate."

"You are desperate, remember?"

Mac's teeth ground together. He loved his sister, but there were times he wanted to pitch her over the side of the *Queen V* without a volans canopy to slow her fall. "The longer I can keep her in the dark, the better. You know how she feels about pirates. She may decide not to assist me on the principle of it." And that was something Mac couldn't risk.

"Are we still talking about Evie? Because I'm pretty sure that she is above that sort of shenanigans."

"She used to be." He'd like to believe she hadn't changed, but he wasn't keen on thinking too highly of her, either.

"I think she's still sweet on you."

He turned his head and locked his gaze with hers. "No, she's not. Even if she is, I'll be ruining all of that in a few minutes."

"She might understand."

"Are you sure we're talking about the same Evie? No matter how I play this, she won't understand it at all. It hardly matters."

"No," Nell agreed in that dry tone of hers. "I reckon not."

They stood in silence for a few moments. Finally Mac consulted his pocket watch for the fourth time and said, "Bugger this. I'm going to get her." Three minutes shouldn't make much of a difference. Hopefully the extra minutes Imogen had to wait hadn't made much of a difference to her condition.

"If I hear screaming, I'll bring a bucket of water."

"Who are you going to throw it on? Me? Or Evie?"

"Not certain. Whichever one of you I think will be most entertaining, no doubt."

Nell was right—he was desperate. Imogen's life depended on Evie's skill, and here he was, fretting and whining over a few moments. He shouldn't have given them to her to begin with. Damn stupid of him.

A few crew members passed him as he made his way belowdecks. They all smiled and acknowledged him with some form of respect. He wasn't much for standing on ceremony, but it was comforting knowing that his crew respected and trusted him.

Or at least most of them did. He had a sickening suspicion that at least one didn't share his crewmates' sentiment, but he wasn't going to think on that now, not when the only woman he'd ever die for—and almost had done so—was in his cabin. He didn't knock, the boy in him hoping for a glimpse of skin.

Alas, he was denied.

Evelyn had washed her face and, he assumed, the rest of her. She was clad in a fresh pair of trousers and a white shirt with a black corseted waistcoat, which was all the rage among ladies now. Her hair was twisted into a messy bun. Within an hour she would have little tendrils of curls slipping free around her face. He would have to watch that he didn't try to tuck them behind her ears as he always used to.

"You're early. I still have two minutes."

He didn't rise to the bait. "Come with me." When she didn't budge, he sighed in exasperation. "Please?"

"That's more like it. This life of debauchery has made sport of your manners."

"My manners are just fine. It's the people offended by them who are the problem." He stood sideways so she could slip through the door. Her hand brushed his thigh. He had steeled himself for contact, so he didn't jump three feet in the air and squeal like a little girl. He wasn't over her. He'd been aware of this for some time, but the realization of just how much power she had over him . . . well, it wasn't welcome.

"Second door on the left," he told her. Evelyn stood outside and waited for him to do the entering, which he did.

"They have this new thing now," she informed

him—rather peevishly, he thought. "It's called 'knocking.' Apparently it's all the rage. You should try it now and again."

"My ship. My doors." He held the heavy oak open with one arm. "After you." He wanted her where he could see her, and certainly not with access to his back. She'd already stabbed him there once.

The room was small but comfortable—as good as on any steamship. The shades had been opened to allow some sun into the room. The woman in the bed couldn't enjoy the sunshine—she was asleep. Sweat beaded her pale brow and pain furrowed it.

"Mac?" It was all Evie said when she discovered the woman.

"Her name's Imogen. She was shot yesterday. I thought it went right through, but I reckon it was scatter shot and some is still in her. She started running a fever a few hours ago." He didn't have to tell her how dangerous scatter shot could be, the tiny fragments breaking off to infiltrate organs and cause even more damage.

"This is why you shocked me and took me prisoner?" Evie turned a disbelieving gaze on him. "Bloody hell, Mac. You could have just asked."

Seriously? Yes, she meant it; there was none of the mockery she'd used before. She had to know he'd rather chew off his own arm than ask her for any favors. "We may not be friends, but at least this way you won't be lying when you tell your precious Wardens that I took you against your will."

"How very thoughtful of you."

"I also expect you'd only have said no if I asked politely." The woman could deny it if she wanted, but they both knew she'd rather chew off her own hand than help him.

She placed her hand on Imogen's forehead. "I don't say no when someone is injured." Then she put her fingers at the base of the other woman's throat. "She's fevered and her pulse is erratic. I'm going to have to take a look at her wound and clean it. Fetch my bag, will you? I'm sure you made certain it was brought with the rest of my things."

He had, and he didn't care that she gave him that pointed look that said she knew him so well. "I'll get it." He'd put it someplace she couldn't get to it—he wasn't about to risk her injecting him or his crew with some sort of drug that would make escape easy. He would let her go, but not until he knew Imogen was safe. She and Theo had been two of his closest friends, and Theo was dead. He wasn't going to lose her, too, not without a fight.

"She must be important for you to come to me."

Mac paused at the door and turned his head to regard her over his shoulder. "She is."

"Who is she?" Did he imagine the tension in her features? The false disinterest in her tone?

Evie had walked out on him. There was no reason for him to feel any guilt over what he was about to say, or to hope perversely that it might needle her, but he did.

"She's my wife."

*   *   *

Wife?

Evelyn had to grasp her hands in front of her to keep from pressing a palm over the sudden pain in her chest. Of course he would be married. He was too handsome, and too charming when it suited him, to still be unattached. He needed a woman to indulge and coddle him, to treat him like a dashing rogue.

The woman on the bed looked too mature for that sort of nonsense, but that meant nothing. Appearance was no honest indication of what lie beneath—a fact she knew very well.

She lifted her head. "Congrat—" Mac wasn't there. He'd gone to get her bag, leaving her alone with his wife.

His goddamn wife.

Her patient.

She had a duty and this woman needed her expertise. It didn't matter who she was; she needed medical care that only Evelyn could provide. That realization was what drove her to carry a stool over to the bedside and sit down on it.

She didn't pause to appraise the woman's prettiness, but peeled back the covers, and gently opened the front of the woman's chemise, which was held shut by tiny pink ribbons.

So feminine. Evelyn didn't own even one shift as pretty as this one. Soon, Mac's wife wouldn't, either; the bandages covering her ribs were stained with blood. It was a wonder the undergarment hadn't been destroyed already.

She needed to see the extent of the woman's injury,

but she couldn't do that without her bag. So she simply sat there and monitored the pulse of the woman who had finally gotten Gavin MacRae to the altar. Her other hand went to the woman's forehead. Her skin was clammy.

Poor Mac. He had to be half mad with worry. He might be a pirate, a daredevil, a charmer and the most reckless man she ever met, but when he offered his heart he didn't hold back. When he decided to trust you, it was a life-and-death sort of contract. He would die for those he loved, but he didn't know what to do when there was a chance they might be taken from him.

She had hurt him badly, and he would never forgive her for it. He wouldn't trust her any further than he could throw one of the ship's cannons.

The door opened and in he came, carrying her scuffed leather bag. She never traveled without some supplies. If only she'd thought to bring her healing compound, she could practically guarantee a full recovery, but without it . . . well, she wasn't going to go there yet.

Evie held out her hands, and he thrust the bag into her grasp. Immediately, she adjusted the small dials on the front to the correct positions to open the lock.

"I need hot water," she instructed. "I also need Listerine if you have it." She hadn't thought to bring that, either.

"I don't." He opened the top drawer in the little dresser and took out a bottle. "Will whiskey do?"

"Yes. I need to clean the wound." She pulled a pair of scissors from her bag.

He offered her the bottle. "I cleaned it earlier."

She raised her gaze to his as she took the whiskey from him. "Do I tell you how to steer this monstrosity?"

"Not since you've been on board this time, no."

Of course he would remember all the times she actually had. "Then you don't tell me how to treat a patient. If you knew the correct things to do, I wouldn't be here, would I?"

His jaw tightened. "No, you wouldn't."

Sometimes the truth stung, even when it was expected. "Then let me do what it is you want me to do for her." Their gazes locked and held.

Finally Mac gave a curt nod. "Do it."

She began to carefully cut through the bandages, which covered the woman from waist to breast. "If you're going to stay, take a seat over there. You're in my light."

"Actually I'm needed on deck. Just pull the cord by the door when you're done and I'll come back."

Evelyn glanced up. "I remember how to reach you on deck, Captain."

The pained expression that twisted his face could mean a variety of things, none of which she wished to ponder at that time. "Right." He spared both of them a prolonged awkward silence by opening the door and slipping out.

The room seemed bigger without him in it—quiet. Surprisingly she found it remarkably easy to ignore the rumble of the ship, just as she used to, so the only noise that made it through her filters was the slightly phlegmy sound of Mrs. MacRae's breathing.

Mac's wife was in very bad shape. Evie knew this before she peeled back the soiled bandage and looked at the wound. It was jagged, the flesh around it already becoming an ugly hue. Scatter shot was particularly nasty, not only because it was a son of a bitch to remove, but because it was notoriously prone to infection. It was intentionally filthy, which made it all the more dangerous. It was meant to kill—quickly or slowly and painfully.

Evelyn splashed a little whiskey on her hands before gently prodding around the ragged wound. Pus seeped out. She poured a bit of the whiskey onto the area before easing her finger inside. The woman stirred slightly, moaning in pain, but she didn't wake. Evelyn felt at least two jagged fragments. Based on her experience, there were anywhere between six and eight more in there depending on how many Mac had already removed.

It was a miracle the woman—Imogen—was even still alive. It was only because of luck, or because the shooter hadn't been very good at his/her job, that she hadn't died within an hour of being shot.

Why would anyone want to shoot her in the first place?

Evelyn removed her finger from the wound and wiped it on the old bandages. Had one of Mac's enemies done this as some sort of revenge, or had the woman been in the wrong place at the wrong time?

Of course, simply being with Mac could have been the wrong place. The man collected foes the way her nan collected porcelain dancing ladies.

Well, there was nothing for it. She needed assistance—she couldn't operate by herself, not without increasing the danger to Imogen's life. Evie rose from the bed and pulled the cord for the bell that would ring on the deck. Then she began removing the necessary equipment and supplies from her bag, setting them on the bedside table. She put on her special goggles with movable lenses that allowed her to magnify her work, and pushed the tiny arms over either side upward to allow her to see normally.

A soft knock sounded on the door a few moments later. "Come in, Nell," she said.

The door opened, and the older woman stepped in with a lopsided grin on her weathered face. "How'd you know it was me?"

"Your brother has an aversion to knocking. I'm glad it's you. Most men are useless when their spouse is being operated on."

"That so?" Nell shrugged. "Wouldn't know anything about that. What do you need me to do, my girl?"

Evie poured a measure of chloroform on a cloth and handed it to her. "Hold this over your sister-in-law's nose. It will keep her from waking up."

"Aye, I remember that from the last time."

That was not something Evie wanted to remember, even though it was far from the worst of the injuries Mac had suffered during their time together.

She didn't want to remember any of them, because they just made her all the angrier at him for what he'd put her through.

Nell did as instructed. Evie waited a few moments, counting down until she could be certain that the chloroform had done its job. Only then did she rinse her hands again with the whiskey, and clean her instruments with the liquid as well. With a small scalpel, she cut into the oozing, angry wound, mopping up the foul-smelling pus that rushed to the surface.

"Nasty stuff," Nell commented, but she didn't sound particularly bothered. Nell had seen a lot worse, Evelyn knew.

"Gunshot wounds are never pretty," she replied. "She's fortunate none of the fragments seem to have penetrated any vital organs."

"She's fortunate she's got you."

Evie set aside the scalpel and cleaned the wound some more. She smiled at the older woman. "I could argue, but I won't."

"You mad at me for nabbin' you?"

Selecting a pair of long tweezers, Evie slid two of the lenses over her eyes and turned her attention back to her patient. "I'm not mad at you. I'm mad at your brother."

"He had his back up against a wall; you know that."

"Yes." How to explain that was part of what made her so mad without giving too much away? She concentrated on extracting a piece of shot. "Can you move the lamp arm a little closer? How long have they been married?"

Light flooded the bloody flesh in front of her as Nell maneuvered the lamp. Evie deposited the shot into a bowl. It made a clinking sound.

"Four days."

She froze—just for a second—before remembering her task. "She was shot on her honeymoon?"

"They both were. She'd be dead if Gav hadn't got her out of the way."

Mac had been injured as well? Of course he wouldn't mention that. Her heart twisted—memories throwing themselves at the wall she put up around them. She would not think about that day when she'd had her hands inside his chest. "What happened?"

"Trouble."

That was all she'd get out of Nell. Mac's sister was loyal to a fault. Regardless, it was an apt answer. Trouble followed Mac, or perhaps he followed it.

And the people who loved him paid the price for it.

Clenching her jaw, Evie extracted another fragment. Four days married and Mac's recklessness had already gotten this woman shot. Hell, she had lasted six months before paying the price of being in Mac's life, and she'd gotten off lucky. Just a trio of slashes from man-made claws.

The rest of the procedure went on in silence. Evelyn removed seven pieces of shrapnel before she was satisfied that she'd gotten it all. Then she used yet more of Mac's whiskey on her patient, stitched the wound a bit and dressed it with fresh linen.

"That's the best I can do for now," she told Nell as she washed her hands at the basin. The water quickly turned pink, then red. "Hopefully it will prove good enough."

"I don't doubt it. I've seen you perform miracles before."

"Yes, well, that was in an operating theater, not a flying wreck of a ship." She reached for a towel. "Thank you for your assistance, Nell. Please tell your bother that I want to see this wound of his as well. He wanted me here, and now he has to pay the price for my company. We're still a day or two from London."

"Don't say that—you'll curse us."

She almost rolled her eyes, but didn't out of respect. Airmen (and airwomen, apparently) were even more superstitious at times than their seafaring counterparts. Talking about how close you were to the end of a journey was thought to anger the wind, or the clouds, or something, and bring about delays such as foul weather and equipment failure. There was no telling them that the weather was fickle, or that a rusty bucket of bolts was going to need repairs more often than not.

"All right, we'll get to London when we get there. I still want to see your brother." She began cleaning her instruments and looked up to find Nell watching her. "What?"

"Can I trust you not to hurt him, Evie?"

Her hurt him? He was the one who had kid-napped her, who chose this damn ship over her. What could she possibly do to him that was worse? Even if she stabbed him in the eye, it wouldn't heal the raw wound deep inside her.

They'd both hurt each other more than any scalpel ever could.

"I won't hurt him, Nell. I'm a doctor. It's my duty to heal, not to harm."

Nell didn't look as though she believed that, and probably with good reason. After all, she had seen Evelyn kill before.

"Do you want to take my bag with you? Will that make you feel safer?"

Her old friend scowled. "Don't be ridiculous. I'll go get him."

When she was gone, Evie released a breath she hadn't been aware of holding. She could hide away instruments with which to make an escape, but none of them would do her any good thousands of feet above the ground without even a volans canopy. Never mind that escape would leave her stranded on the Continent with little to no clothing, money or supplies.

Gavin MacRae was a man of his word. He would let her loose once they were in London, and London was exactly where she needed to be, so escape would be irrational. She'd only do it to piss off Mac, and that would leave his wife without proper care.

She ought to be glad this woman was Mrs. MacRae instead of her, or she could have been the one to get shot. Still, there was a small part of her that wanted to hate this woman for having what she'd once thought hers. Hell, she still thought of him as hers—sometimes.

The worst of it was that she was a respectable doctor with a job that paid incredibly well. She was reasonably attractive, and most modern men didn't mind that she was of mixed heritage. She had so much to recommend her, and yet she was still alone while a rogue like Mac, who called the entire sky his home and had nothing but danger to offer his spouse, was married.

He'd gotten over her, and that was the real twist in her knickers. She still compared every man to him, chose bedmates that often reminded her of him, and he'd gone off and married a goddamn blonde. She probably had blue eyes to go with that flawless complexion, too. She was like a little tea cake with pretty icing and Evie was a strong cup of coffee a few shades shy of bitter. Of course Mac would choose such a woman.

The door opened at the exact moment that self-pitying thought drifted through her mind with such dramatic poetry. Mac crossed the threshold, ducking slightly under the top of the doorframe. Most ships weren't built with tall people in mind.

His gaze immediately locked with hers. He didn't even glance at his wife. Perhaps he was afraid to for fear that her condition had worsened. Or perhaps he was looking for a fight.

"Nell said you wanted to see me."

"Yes. I want to see your wound."

"I don't have a wound."

"Your sister says otherwise. Shall we call her down here and see which one of you is lying?"

Mac swore—in Gaelic. She only recognized it because she'd heard it so many times before. His mama had taught him not to use such language in front of women, and he compensated by using a different language altogether.

"Not a word of this to anyone," he instructed as he pulled his shirt hem free of his trousers. "The crew can't know I'm injured, and they can't know about Imogen, either."

"Why not? Surely they know you're married."

"No, they don't. They think she's a passenger and that she's ill."

Evie's eyes narrowed. "Why the secrecy?"

"You know what they'd be like if they knew. They'd all be running about trying to take care of her and me, too. I need them all to be focused on their work, not asking me if she's all right every five minutes. Or worse, asking me if I am." He sighed and rubbed a hand over his face. "Look, I know I have no business asking any more favors from you after bringing you on board the way I did, but please, Evie. Not a word."

"Fine." It was obviously important because he wouldn't have asked otherwise. "What did you tell them to explain my presence?"

"That we had unfinished business. Most of them

know you. They're not surprised to see you again. In fact, they think it's funny."

"Funny?" Her brows came together low and hard. "It's funny to abduct someone off the street?"

"It is when she's the woman you swore you'd toss overboard if you ever saw her again." His lips lifted on one side. What was it with men and those damn lopsided grins? It seemed they all had one. "So yeah, it's funny when you then force that woman back onto your ship and lock her in your cabin. I've been taking a ribbing for it on deck. It was luck that the best doctor I know was so close by."

So he risked abduction charges from W.O.R., and allowed himself to look the fool, all for this oh-so-incredibly white and fragile woman on the bed. Mac wasn't above letting himself seem the fool—he always said it made people underestimate him, which was what he wanted in order to gain the upper hand. But to let his crew chuckle behind his back . . .

"You must love her very much." The words scoured her throat on the way out.

"She's very important to me."

"You've become such a romantic." Sarcasm, the balm for any hurt.

"I can't imagine what might have made me that way," he retorted, lifting his arms and peeling off his shirt. Evelyn just stood there and stared as exposed golden flesh pulled taut over his ribs. He tossed the shirt onto a chair by the wall, and stood before her, half-naked, hair mussed. It was as if three years hadn't passed at all, so familiar was this moment.

And then she saw the scars. He had them on his torso, his shoulders, his stomach. Little scars, long scars.

"The shot was cowardly," he said, and turned to present her with his back. There was a bandage high on his left shoulder—probably not much of a wound at all. Evelyn pressed her hand against her mouth as tears threatened.

His back was covered in crisscrossing scars. He'd been whipped—savagely so.

"Oh, Mac," she whispered. He glanced over his shoulder at her as hot, wet tears spilled over her lashes. "What did they do to you?"

Chapter 3

"Don't." It came out as a growl, but only because Mac's throat felt as though there were a giant hand wrapped around it, squeezing. "I don't want your pity."

Evie nodded, sniffed and wiped her eyes. Her hands seemed to wipe everything away, leaving no emotion behind whatsoever. "Then I'll give you none. Sit down, please, so I can examine your injury."

"It's nothing. Just a graze."

Dark eyes, the lashes made all the darker from that bit of wet, lifted. "Have you been to medical college since the last time I saw you?"

If her tone became any drier, he was going to need a camel just to have a conversation. "I've been wounded often enough to know when one requires attention and when it doesn't." Her tone was a bit uncalled for, given her reaction to his scars. Let her wince and get all weepy. She'd inflicted one of those scars herself, and a few others that existed below the skin, deep inside his soul.

"And I know enough about the wind to know in which direction it blows. That doesn't mean you're going to let me steer this bloody thing, does it? Now *sit down*."

Of course he did what she commanded, but only because he knew she wouldn't let up until she got her way. The woman brought new meaning to the word "stubborn." He didn't cuss when she removed the bandage, even though he felt the tug. The benefit to having as much scar tissue as he did on his back was that new wounds weren't as painful as they ought to be.

He reckoned that was just one more argument she'd make for wanting to poke his raw flesh. Maybe she planned to rub a little salt in as well, just for old times' sake.

"You're lucky the slug didn't go any deeper," she told him. He heard the slosh of liquid and knew she was going to pour some of his good whiskey on his shoulder. "Still, for a flesh wound it's fairly significant. You lost a good-sized chunk of flesh. I need to stitch this."

Mac gritted his teeth. Of course she needed to stitch it. She probably "needed" to stitch it with a needle as big as his arm and thread laced with poison. "Fine."

"I can give you something to help with the pain."

"Don't bother. It doesn't hurt much."

Her fingers were hesitant as they touched him. If

it weren't just the two of them, he wouldn't have thought it was her tending to him at all. Evie never hesitated when it came to touching him.

"Do what you have to do, Doc, and do it quick." Did she not feel the prickling tension? He wanted to be as far away from her as possible, and he certainly didn't want her touching him as though he were some sort of deformed monster.

"As you wish." Her voice was tight. Annoyed with him, was she? Good. That was better than pity. He didn't want her tears. Didn't want her sympathy. It was too late for that.

The needle jabbed his skin. Mac clenched both jaw and fist. All right, so it hurt more than he thought it would. No damn way was he going to let her know. Thankfully she worked quickly. Obviously she didn't plan to torture him for long.

"Who whipped you?"

And now she wanted conversation? "It was a long time ago."

Another jab. "I didn't ask when, I asked who."

Mac hissed. Thread burrowed through his punctured flesh like a worm. "What do you care?"

"Why are you being so difficult?"

"Because it doesn't matter."

"Someone hurt you—badly. Those sorts of wounds take a long time to heal, and it looks as though you were flayed to the bone."

Did she notice that her work had become more gentle? Or had he just gone numb? "Those tickled compared to what you did."

Hesitation—again. "That was a long time ago as well."

Touché, throwing his words back at him. "Not so interested in the scars you can't see, are you? Or maybe you're just interested in the ones you didn't make."

Her free hand slid over his shoulder like a striking snake, fingertips settling on the vertical ridge that began high up in the center of his chest. It was so faint—not much wider than the thread she'd used to close it.

For a second, Mac closed his eyes, savoring that familiar touch. Then reason returned. What the hell? He flung her hand away. The stitches in his shoulder tugged in protest. "Are you finished?"

"Almost." Evie's voice was little more than a whisper. He didn't care if he'd hurt her. Why should he? The woman had no heart, or very little of one. She'd put him back together and then walked away from him three years ago and never looked back. Oh, she'd told him it was because of the dangers he faced every day in his job with the Wardens. Spies didn't often live long lives. But he knew—or rather part of him suspected—she left because he was less of a man in her eyes.

And now she had the nerve to touch him as if she had some sort of claim on him. As though she had the right. As though she actually cared.

She didn't get to care, and just because she asked didn't mean he had to answer.

Mac could feel her knot the thread. Almost done.

"A French *ciel* admiral decided I would make a good example." Why the hell had he told her that?

"An example of what?" *Snip.* Finally.

Anger made the discomfort bearable.

"Of what happens to pirates caught in French skies." That wasn't the total truth, but close enough that it hardly mattered. He jumped up from the chair and reached for his shirt.

"Ah." That sound—it wasn't even a word, for Christ's sake—said so much. Mac yanked the shirt over his head. So much for her pity, so much for sorrow. Did she think he deserved fifty lashes and then another fifty more once the first had begun to heal?

"You're so goddamn judgmental," he accused, turning to face her as he jammed the hem into the waist of his trousers. Evie's eyes widened at his profanity. "You judged me from the day we met. I was the one expected to make all the changes—be who you wanted me to be, because what I was wasn't good enough for Dr. Evelyn Stone. Lady, I've seen you do things even Christ wouldn't absolve, and you stand there with your lips all pinched up like you're better than me. To hell with you."

For a moment she actually looked stricken, and then her eyebrows lowered into a frown. "I'm not the one who stoops to kidnapping."

"You're also not the one who woke up after almost dying to find out that the woman you love moved all of her things off your ship while you were unconscious. You weren't the one told that she couldn't be

with you anymore because it was too painful." He
made a face. "Painful, my arse."

"What ought I have done, Mac?"

"You should have let me die." He didn't shout it.
He said it so calmly, and so matter-of-factly he surprised even himself. "If you save my life just to de-
stroy it, you should have just let me go. Instead you
patched me up and sent me out into the world with
nothing to live for. That was cruel, Evie. Crueler than
the scars on my back."

Then he turned and left the room because her silence was worse than her pity.

"So the crew believes I'm back in Mac's bed?" Incredulous as she sounded, Evelyn knew she really
shouldn't be surprised.

"Oh, I wouldn't say that," Nell informed her with
a grin. They were in Mac's cabin. The older woman
had come to collect her for dinner. "But they certainly think he's tryin'."

Evelyn ran a brush through her hair. "Have they
started wagering on it?"

"You know it." Nell leaned against the wardrobe.
"You want in?"

"Ten pounds says he fails fantastically."

"Not exactly fair sport when you control the out-
come, though, is it?"

"That will teach them to bet against me in the future." As soon as she said it, she wished she hadn't.
It sounded as though she meant to stick around, and
she had no intention of that at all. Once they arrived

in London she had no intention of ever seeing Mac, his sister or any of his crew ever again.

"You have the blunt on you, or do you need me to spot you for it?"

Twisting her hair into a low knot, Evelyn reached for a pin on the dresser. "Helena MacRae, did you instigate this wager?"

Nell winked. "All my money's on you, girl."

She laughed. "You'd think the crew would be wise to you by now. You never make any wager you don't plan to win."

"Bah. That lot keeps hoping they'll get lucky. Every one of 'em hopes he'll be the one to best me."

Hair neat and secure, Evelyn put her hands on her hips. She hadn't changed for dinner and it felt odd, but here it would be stranger still if she got all fancied up to sit around a table with a crew who viewed laundry as a luxury.

"Nell, what's going on here?"

Was it her imagination, or did the older woman cross her arms a little tighter over her chest? "What's on your mind?"

"Why doesn't the crew know about Mac's wife? He fed me some cock-and-bull about not wanting them to fuss over him, but I think there's more to it."

"Like what?"

"You tell me."

"Nothing to tell. To be honest, I don't know much about it myself. I got the feeling there might have been another man involved, but beyond that your guess is as good as mine. All I know is that they've known each other a long time, met up in Warsaw and decided to get hitched."

"Surely he didn't marry her without you present?" Nell was all the family Mac had and vice versa. The two of them were very close.

Nell shot her a dry glance. "Course he didn't. Nobody'd believe him if I wasn't there as a witness. You know he always said he didn't want to get married."

"Yes." Bloody hell, she sounded like a frog with that croak. "I remember. She must be very special indeed."

"Don't be like that, now. You had your chance and you let him go."

As though she needed to be reminded! That moment was forever burned into her memory, right along with the stark betrayal on Mac's face when she ended their relationship.

He hadn't really expected her to spend the rest of her life wondering if every flight would be his last, had he? The man courted danger the way a fortune hunter did debutantes.

"I know what I said, Nell," she replied tartly. "And if you'll recall, I had good reason to say it."

"Oh, aye. My brother almost died and you tossed him over."

Evie's temper spiked. She prided herself on being levelheaded—sometimes even mule-headed—but she had her limits. "I saved his sorry life! The two of you seem to forget how many times I patched him—

both of you—up just so you could go out and tempt death again. I've never met anyone with less regard for life than a bloody MacRae!"

"I wouldn't say we have no regard for life—" Nell blustered.

"Of course you wouldn't!" Evie threw her hands into the air. "That's because you're all as mad as a bag of Bedlam-born cats!"

The two of them stared at each other a moment and then burst out laughing. Which one of them started it didn't matter. The tension between them disappeared as quickly as it had come.

Nell sighed, her strong shoulders slumping. "I know why you left him, my dear, and I know 'twas a good reason, but he's my baby brother and all I've got in this world. Can you blame me for wanting to break both of those talented hands of yours even though I understood?"

"I don't blame you, Nell. I made my decision and I'm the one who must live with it. I think it's safe to say that I will end my life with more regrets than Mac. He's always listened to his heart."

"While you've always listened to your head." Her voice and expression were so full of understanding and sympathy that Evie had to look away. She checked her hair in the mirror affixed to the wall.

"Well, I look as good as I'm going to, not that anyone will be impressed." She managed a smile. "Shall we?"

Nell consulted her pocket watch. "We'd best if we

hope to dine on more than scraps the vultures leave behind."

They left Mac's cabin together, and Evie was glad to be out of it. At least out here she could smell something other than him. See things that didn't necessarily bring back memories, good or bad.

Napoleon came flying down the stairs almost as soon as the door clicked shut. Evelyn barely had time to prepare before the huge dog jumped up, front paws hitting her square in the shoulders and knocking her back against the doorframe. Hot doggy breath assaulted her, as did a huge, wet tongue. She screwed up her face, held her breath and tried not to laugh.

Of course, that would be the moment Mac stepped out of his wife's cabin and joined them in the narrow corridor.

"Get down, runt," he said, as calmly as if asking for sugar in his tea. Evie took the folded square of fabric he offered. The glossy black dog immediately lowered his front paws and sat on one of Evie's feet, panting and tail wagging. She patted him.

There wasn't room for the four of them in the narrow space, but Mac didn't seem to be the least bit concerned about how close they were. It was only she who twitched when wiping dog slobber from her face with his handkerchief.

He locked the door of the cabin and handed her the key. "Only you and I are to enter this room. Nell, too, if necessary."

Evelyn took the large, tarnished key from him as

she pocketed the damp linen. "Trying to keep people out or someone in?"

"Both," he replied with a cheeky grin. Was he serious or making sport of her? There wasn't much of a difference where he was concerned.

She tucked the metal into her trouser pocket. "How is she?" She had to take a step closer to him to let Nell pass. The older woman left them alone without a word or backward glance.

"Asleep. She's still fevered, but she seems more restful."

"It will take a little while for the infection to run its course. We should see a drastic improvement over the next couple of days. Regardless, I'll check on her after dinner."

She turned to leave, but Mac stopped her with a hand on her shoulder. She closed her eyes as the warmth from his fingers burned through the fabric of her shirt. His touch was like being bombarded by every pleasant childhood memory she'd ever had all at once.

"Evie . . ." His hand dropped away as she turned her head toward him. God, but it was a chore just to look him in the eye. "Thank you."

She nodded. "You're welcome."

"I want to apologize for the things I said earlier. It was uncharitable of me, not to mention overly dramatic."

One of the things she always admired about him was his clear sense of self. Sometimes it took him a while, but he would admit when he was wrong. He wasn't above laughing at himself if it was necessary, nor would he hesitate to list his own faults. He could do all of this without any shame. That was why she couldn't help smiling.

"I always said you should have been an actor."

"I thought you said that because I'm so ruggedly handsome."

"And the fact that you can lie with a straight face."

Now he was the one who smiled. "I never lie. I only—"

"Embellish the truth," she said at the same time he did.

He offered her his arm. "May I escort you to dinner, madam?"

Evie slipped her arm through his, feeling the warm, solid strength beneath her hand. He was incredibly well built and strong for a man without physical augmentation. Yes, he had a few "improvements" made, but his bones were the bones of a regular man, not reinforced like Lucas Grey's or Alastair Payne's. Mac's talents lay in things more covert than physical strength.

And he possessed so many talents.

The dining hall was at the opposite end of the corridor and down another flight of stairs. Stern side, it was on the same floor as the crew's quarters. If things were as they always had been, Nell's cabin was on the same floor as Mac's, along with a couple of extra little rooms for any guests they happened to take on. Sometimes pirates made more money off passengers than they did off plundering.

From what she'd heard of Mac's exploits over the years, money was not something he needed to fret over. He was rumored to be incredibly wealthy. With any luck he'd live to be old enough to enjoy it.

The crew was already around the table when Evie and Mac entered the hall, which really wasn't a hall at all, but on a ship, one didn't let the size of the quarters dictate its title, else she'd be in a room called the "vittles closet" or something similar.

All but two of the faces gathered around the table were familiar to her, and lit up at her appearance.

"Say your prayers, lads, we've an angel on board." It was Pliny who spoke—a great barrel of a man with a head of wiry gray hair and more toes than teeth. He rose to his feet and danced around the table to catch her up in a fierce hug, sweeping her into a little jig.

Evelyn laughed and let herself be swept around. A couple of turns was all it took to make her head spin when she was set back on her own feet. The others had stood as well, and now gathered to be hugged in turn. The last of whom was Eli, a slight man with a pleasant face, bushy sideburns and a faded red shirt that had been mended so many times it was almost patchwork. He was the cook, the doctor, the entertainer and the launderer. He could also climb a mast with the speed and grace of a monkey up a tree. Rumor had it that he was wanted for murder in Canada, but Evelyn never believed it. However, he did make the best potatoes she'd ever eaten, and she was part Irish.

"I've got something special for you, Miss Evie," he said, ducking into the small kitchen space to the right of the room. There was a pantry off there as well. He returned just as she was sitting down and placed a green bottle on the table in front of her.

"Ginger beer!" She laughed as the crisp, spicy scent reached her nose. "I haven't had it in ages."

"I'll wager what you did have wasn't nearly as good as this. Brewed it myself."

Eagerly she lifted the bottle to her mouth and took a deep swallow. Her entire mouth came alive as sharp flavor filled it. It burned just the way she liked it, was just the right temperature, the right amount of ginger and the right amount of sweetness.

Eli waited on her judgment.

"That is by the far the best ginger beer I've ever tasted," she informed him, and took another swig to back it up. She belched as delicately as she could—which wasn't very—and roused a chorus of cheers from them all.

Mac introduced her to the newer crew members, both of whom seemed friendly enough. One was a man from Jamaica with whom she enjoyed chatting. She hadn't been back to Jamaica in a long time. In fact, the last time had been with Mac.

Lord, but it felt comfortable sitting at that table, talking to those people. It was like . . . seeing family after a long journey. She could almost forget that Mac had abducted her.

That he had married another woman.

Nell was right. She had no business being peevish,

not when she'd turned him down. And if she had someone lovely waiting for her in London, it wouldn't smart nearly so much, but all she had in London other than a few close friends—most of whom were happily married—was a very fat cat named Norman. While he was a lovely boy, it wasn't quite the same.

Eli kept her in ginger beer as they dined on his splendid potatoes, roast beef and vegetables. Conversation continued on nonstop, punctuated by laughter and eager interruptions to tell another side of the tale. She heard of new adventures, revisited old ones and remembered old friends—Jock in particular.

"Remember that time in Crete when Jock took a shine to that handsome barmaid?" Eli asked, chuckling at the memory.

"Aye," Nell replied. "Handsome is the right word—she turned out to be a man."

Evelyn remembered that night. She'd been there with them, and poor Jock had been just drunk enough and just dear enough that the fact that the object of his affection wasn't really a woman didn't really matter. He still let her sit on his lap and sang bawdy songs to her.

She mused, "At the end of the night, he gave her a rose and a kiss on the hand. She said no one had ever treated her like such a lady."

Those of them who had known Jock shared a bittersweet smile around the table.

Mac raised his tankard, half-full of ale. "To Jock. Too rotten for heaven, too good for hell, may his rest be anything but peaceful."

All other cups, bottles and tankards rose. "To Jock!"

Evie drank, then lowered her bottle to the table. Silence descended over their gathering—an unsolicited moment of quiet for the friend they'd lost.

The moment was broken when the bell in the corner of the ceiling began to clang violently. Evelyn's spine snapped straight. She looked at Mac, then at Nell, both of whom were looking at each other. Evelyn didn't need them to acknowledge her, or even speak. They all knew what that bell meant.

It meant trouble.

"I'll check," Eli offered, jumping out of his chair.

Everyone else exchanged glances. Everyone, that was, except for Mac. He sat at the head of the table and took a drink of ale, looking as calm and collected as a saint in church.

A few minutes later there was a distant thump and the frantic thudding of boots on wooden stairs. Eli raced into the dining hall, eyes wide, cheeks pale beneath his impressive facial hair.

"Captain! You're needed on deck, sir." His face was grim. "We've got trouble."

Chapter 4

The absolute last thing Mac needed was an encounter with pirates, especially bloodthirsty, rival pirates who saw the *Queen V* as a threat to their pillaging and killing. As a general rule, pirates were not nice people.

"Get eyes on them, Nell," he commanded as he watched the small ship approach. It was a dark craft, almost imperceptible in the night. Frankly he was amazed anyone had spotted it so early. They had time to prepare.

The *Queen V* was not equipped for full-out war, though she was heavily armed and fortified. The old girl had a few surprises on her that would even the field of play.

His sister scampered up the ladder to the crow's nest with the speed and agility of someone half her age, and with twice the ease. She was born to sail the skies, Nell was. He never would have taken command of his first ship, and certainly wouldn't have found a crew for it, if not for her. And he wouldn't have survived very long without her, either, especially not after Evie tossed him over.

"Looks like the *Dark Wing*," she called down. "No colors."

Damnation. The *Dark Wing* wasn't as agile and sleek as the *Queen V*, but it was a relentless beast, well manned and fully gunned with long-range Hephaestus cannons that shot balls of flaming iron at her foes. No colors indicated the ship was not under contract to any organization or country, which meant that it was out for blood and spoils.

Wonderful.

"All hands man stations!" he yelled. "I want the Forde engine on fire and the Aether cannons lined up."

Around him his small but capable crew ran about doing as he commanded. There wasn't one of them that took his time or appeared to be anything but one hundred percent on his side. How could there be a traitor on his boat? Among his friends?

"Got a message, sir!" Pliny ran up, gray hair streaming behind him. "From Harrigan."

"Iron Hand" Harrigan was the captain of the *Dark Wing*. He fancied himself something of a pirate prince, or king even. The skies were his domain, and he'd kill anyone who didn't swear fealty.

Mac was the reason he was called "Iron Hand," because Mac had cut off the flesh-and-bone one the pirate had previously owned. Needless to say they weren't friends. They weren't even acquaintances.

They were out-and-out enemies, and if Harrigan got within firing range, he'd aim for Mac's head.

Was it a coincidence that Harrigan just happened to be a hundred miles outside his usual territory and just happened to stumble upon the *Queen V* while she was undergunned and had Imogen on board?

No, it wasn't. Harrigan was a pirate, but he was also a mercenary. He was in the same airspace because someone had hired him to find Mac—find him and kill him, and anyone else who might know all the secrets tucked away inside Imogen's mind. If it was someone else suggesting it, he'd call them paranoid, but the information Imogen carried had already been responsible for the death of one person, possibly two, and if Mac didn't figure out what it was, it just might kill him. Kill all of them.

They had to get out of there. Imogen had to live. Evie had to live. There'd be no death on his ship, not this night.

"What's going on?" Evie appeared at his elbow, dark brows knitted together.

He glanced at her, arms folded over his chest. "You shouldn't scowl. It will give you lines."

She turned that frown on him. "Be serious, will you? Just answer the question."

"I thought I had. You asked what was going on, and you were scowling. You know scowling all the harder won't make it any better."

"There are times I wish looks really could kill."

"You wound me. Doesn't that go against your vows as a doctor? You're supposed to heal, not kill."

"For you I'm sure even Hippocrates would make an exception. Are you going to tell me what's going on or not?"

"Iron Hand Harrigan is stalking us."

"The pirate?"

"Do you know anyone else that goes by the name of Iron Hand?" Surely she remembered the man.

She looked as though she truly could kill him. Oddly enough, that made him feel better. If Evie was scratching for a fight, then all was well with the world. It was nice to know he could still rile her, and comforting to realize that she let him because she knew he was concerned.

"What did you do to piss him off?" she asked, her tone so dry there must be sand in her teeth.

"Nothing. Well, there was that time I cut off his hand, but other than that he's got no reason to come gunning."

Her expression spoke volumes. Let her think the worst of him if it kept her from wondering if there was more to Imogen's wound than being in the wrong place at the wrong time with the wrong man. Once upon a time he had trusted Evie with his life. He trusted her with Imogen's, but she was a Warden, and he would not jeopardize everything by risking her sending a message to the director. He knew what he was doing, and he didn't need Evie trying to take over.

"You need to go below," he told her, all trace of teasing gone from his voice.

She jerked back. "What?"

"Go below. It's safer for you."

"When did you become concerned for my safety?"

"Right around the time I realized you still think you're smarter than me."

The scowl was back. She really was going to get a line. "I've never said that."

"Didn't say you did. I said you think it. You always have."

"That's not true."

He shrugged. "Hardly matters now. My boat, my rules. Please go below, Dr. Stone. I don't want the Wardens kicking my balls for getting their precious healer shot."

Evie looked as though she'd like to kick his balls for being an ass. Fine by him. He owed her nothing. If they got Imogen to London in one piece and still breathing, then he'd try to repay her in some way, but not one second before. He didn't care if it was petty. She'd broken his heart, and on this ship he was captain. His word was law.

"I can have one of the men escort you below if you insist," he added when she remained silent.

"You're an ass."

"I know." He unfastened the leather sheath that was tied to his belt and handed it and the dagger within to her. "Lock the door, and use this if you have to."

"A dagger? I don't get a gun?"

"I've seen what you can do with a blade, woman. Still have the scar. Go."

She wasn't pleased, but at least she didn't argue

anymore. He shouldn't have brought up the scar. Maybe he did owe her for something after all. But saving his life only to walk out of it hardly seemed the kind of thing he ought to be thankful for.

And it wasn't what he should be thinking about with Harrigan breathing down his neck.

How had the pirate found them? Mac had set up a snare to catch any Aetheric transmissions sent from the ship, so unless the traitor could hide his transmissions, he would have to have been one of the few who went ashore when they nabbed Evelyn.

Or perhaps the traitor was someone higher up— not on the ship at all, but aware of who he was and what sort of work he did. What sort of cargo he had on board.

Or perhaps he'd better get his arse moving before Harrigan shot it off.

Evelyn had returned to Imogen's bedside, so that was one less thing he had to worry about. Now he just had to keep the bastard from getting ahold of his ship.

The *Queen V* was a fast old girl, nimble and able to get out of a tight spot in a hurry. That was great when flying into a mountainous area with a full crew. They weren't over any mountains; they were over a series of villages—some of which were going to get hurt if Harrigan started tossing cannon balls about, which the pirate was known to do.

Idiot thought of himself as a high-seas pirate of yore; otherwise he'd embrace Aether cannons that blasted energy, not iron and newer forms of warfare.

These were weapons that kept nonengaged casualties to a minimum.

"Harrigan's gaining on us, Mac," his sister yelled above his head. He didn't have to look up to know that she had both eyes pressed against the viewing lenses of the binocoscope, which would give her a close-up look at their pursuers. "Looks like they're readying their gulls."

Gulls were named after seagulls, because they fired groups of ammunition rather than solitary balls, and they made people duck and cover, hoping to dodge the shit. Looked as though Harrigan had made some improvements after all. Gulls weren't very useful on sea ships, but they were terribly effective against aircrafts as they punctured balloons and sails with alarming ease.

"Pliny, get the starboard wing up!" Mac yelled as he ran toward the other mechanism. The older man was already there, pulling free the chain that would grind the gears into motion. Mac opened the panel on the inside wall and did the same. A three-inch compartment that ran the entire length of the ship opened along the rail. Out of it rose the clatter of metal scales attached to thin, jointed scaffolding. It was all attached to a center arm, which rose out of the side of the ship and then out to the side. There was a click, and a blanket of metal fell over the top half of the wooden body of the ship. A series of clanks and twangs loosened the upward stack. Mac and Pliny stomped on the pedals to release the coil of metal at each end of the ship. There was a sharp *thwang* and a wall of tiny joined metal plates shot upward, curving on the frame as it knitted itself together to shape itself around the balloon-sails that kept the ship in the sky.

But it wasn't quite fast enough. Harrigan had already fired. It wasn't a big shot, but it was just enough to whizz overtop of the expanding wing. A series of pops exploded above Mac's head—seemingly louder than the blast of the cannons that fired them.

"We're hit!" he shouted. He could open one of the metal pieces to check on their attackers, but there wasn't any point. He heard another cannon fire, but this time they were ready and the shots bounced off the wing, like a bucket of marbles hitting the nursery floor.

"Eli!"

The smaller man appeared. "I've got it, Captain." Without another word, Eli unwound a length of rope from the coil on the side of the ship and scampered up it. There were other similar coils around, thick rope that would allow a man to climb up into the balloon.

"Return fire," Mac yelled. "Make it count!" They hadn't much, but there was something to be said for determination and sheer bullheadedness. Plus, he had made a promise to Theo, and he kept his promises.

Most of them. Those that really meant something.

Nearby he heard the increasing whine of the Aether cannon as it charged to fire upon the *Dark Wing*. Another barrage struck the wing, but the metal shield held.

Eli slid down the rope. "They got us good. I can patch some of the smaller ones, but the wing caught a couple of the holes on the way up and tore them even wider."

Mac swore—properly swore. His mother would box his ears for such language, especially in mixed company, but Nell didn't count and Evie was belowdecks, and the harsh, guttural words felt good on his tongue. "So we're going down."

Eli nodded, somber eyes peering over the wire rim of his spectacles. "We can deploy the volans canopies if we start to lose air too quickly."

"Not while Harrigan is on our arse." He'd shoot those down as well, and there were no shields for those safety canopies. The swallows were out. The tiny flying machines would be blown out of the sky like fireworks on Guy Fawkes Day.

He rubbed a hand over his face. "How long?"

"I'd say thirty minutes at the most. We're already starting to lose altitude."

Now would be a perfect time for more swearing. "I want everything we have locked on to that ship."

Eli's eyes widened. "Mac?"

Usually he went the heroic route—taking prisoners and saving victims—but not today. Not with Imogen so frail, not with Evie on board. He would not leave the two of them and his sister at the mercy of Harrigan and his crew.

Mac looked his friend in the eye. This was not open for discussion. "Do it."

Eli ran off, barking orders as soon as he was in

earshot of the others. Mac turned and stomped off toward the wheel.

They'd been in the air for some time now; they had to be near Frankfurt. Little wind made the journey slower than he liked, and because of Imogen they'd had to take a bit of a detour. It was a gamble— one he wouldn't have taken if they hadn't gotten Evie.

There were times when he hated her with a passion, and times when he loved her equally so, but she was brilliant. If anyone could save Imogen, it was her. It had nothing to do with him; he was smart enough and self-deprecating enough to know that. That was why she was there.

He checked the compass on the console above the wheel. There were various other gauges, levers and switches there as well. Right now he was only concerned with where they were and how long it would be before they were forced to land.

Mac did the math in his head. He'd never been much for school, but put him in the air and all that stuff made perfect sense. As he'd suspected, they were close to Frankfurt. They were also dropping as Eli had said. It was going to be close. He had friends in Frankfurt. More important, he had people he trusted. People who would be able to get them back in the sky as quickly as possible.

He opened a drawer and withdrew a portable telegraph machine. He was slow as molasses trying to use the blasted keyboard, so he kept his message short and succinct: *Falling. Pursued. You owe me.*

The reply came as he changed the coordinates within the *Queen V*'s guidance system. He'd be taking her down manually—some things machines and logic engines just couldn't do with the same precision human hands could. He took his eyes off the dimming horizon long enough to check the response:

Bastard. See you soon.

Mac shut the drawer with his knee. At least something was working out as he'd hoped. Grimly he maneuvered his ship toward Frankfurt.

"They've got a net, Mac!" his sister yelled.

Of course they did. Nets were woven from fine fibers and draped over ships like gossamer—they also repelled Aether blasts.

"They're not returning fire." Nell's tone was rich with confusion. "They're following but not firing."

Mac's jaw tightened. That meant Harrigan hadn't wanted to blast them to bits. He wanted to ground them. The bastard wanted to make certain Imogen was dead—and probably him as well. He—

Hell and damnation.

Mac stared at the small machine anchored to his ship portside. How he had missed it until now was a mystery, but he had, and so had everyone else in the confusion. It was a sparrow and it wasn't one of his.

Iron Hand Harrigan was on his ship.

Evie.

Mac's heart jumped into his throat. "Somebody take the damn wheel!"

*   *   *

Evelyn was checking Imogen's pulse, trying to ignore the firing overhead, when she heard a creak outside the door. Mac? No, he would have barged in by now. Nell? Possibly, but why hadn't she knocked?

Then the knob turned and caught. She'd locked the door from the inside as Mac instructed. It certainly wasn't him. If he'd forgotten his key, he would tell her. Nell would have announced herself as well.

It could be a member of the crew, but she doubted it. They were too busy fending off attackers. That left only one other option as something scratched at the lock. She could be wrong, but usually her instincts were right in such cases. Quietly she rose from the side of the bed and moved to the wall so that the door would shield her. She wrapped her fingers around the handle of the knife Mac had given her and pulled it from the sheath.

The lock gave with a click, and this time when the knob turned, the door opened with the faintest of groans. A man slunk in—and slunk really was the only word she could think to describe it. He wore tall leather boots with flat soles, a soiled poufy shirt and a scarf around his head. He couldn't look more stereotypically pirate if he popped right out of the pages of *Treasure Island*.

Around the edge of the door, she watched as he approached the bed. He looked down at Mac's wife for a few moments, then ran the backs of his fingers along her pale cheek. It was when he stroked her breast that Evelyn changed her grip on the knife so that it would slice and carve as she wanted.

The pirate stopped fondling the unconscious woman long enough to wrap both hands around her neck and squeeze.

Strangling? That was how he was going to kill her? It seemed a terribly personal way to dispatch someone. Those who employed it were usually the sort who enjoyed the kill, and liked to be up close to watch the life drain from someone's eyes. And Imogen's eyes snapped open wide as she began gasping for breath.

Evie struck fast. She wasn't as well trained as her friend Claire, but she knew what to do and, more important, had the determination to do it. It wouldn't be the first time she'd fought to save herself or someone else, and it probably wouldn't be the last.

He spied her out of the corner of his eye as she moved, but that was all right. He let go of Imogen and pivoted his body to confront Evelyn. She grabbed him about the waist and hauled herself in real tight, the edge of her blade poised snugly between his thighs.

"One wrong move," she murmured. "One twitch, and you'll either end up a eunuch or bleed to death in very few minutes, so I suggest you stay very, very still."

He held his arms out very carefully. "Easy, luv."

"I'm not your love. What are you doing here, Harrigan?" As soon as she'd seen his left hand around Imogen's throat, she recognized him. The dark metal appendage set with jewels could belong to only one man—Iron Hand Harrigan. Mac had cut off the pirate's hand, and Evie had made certain he didn't bleed out before the authorities arrived. Why wasn't he rotting in a jail somewhere?

"I know you," he rasped. His voice was like rusted gears grinding together, and his breath smelled of spiced rum. Usually that odor was somewhat pleasant, but not when mixed with poor oral hygiene.

"Mm, we go way back. How's your mum?" Lord, she sounded just like Mac. Speaking of whom, she needed to get some help down here. She could feel the ship slowly sinking, and knew they'd been hit. Once they were on the ground, there was nothing to stop Harrigan's crew from overpowering them. Why couldn't Mac have a larger crew? He had, what, maybe twelve or thirteen on board? Harrigan probably had twice that.

"You're MacRae's doxy."

"Was," she corrected, noting out of the corner of her eye that Imogen watched them with a wide, slightly unfocused gaze. "I'm not his anything anymore."

"Right." Harrigan grinned—that sort of overly confident grin that she found so very annoying. Did he not remember that she had a blade to his balls? "But here you are, defending the little bird."

Imogen reached for the bell pull beside the bed. Evie shifted a little so that Harrigan was forced to turn his back on the injured woman completely. "Yes, well, I took an oath, you see."

Suddenly the door flew open and Mac was there, Napoleon at his side, growling so fiercely Evie thought he might rip the pirate's throat out. Harrigan moved like a striking cobra, grabbing Evie's wrist in his metal grip. Cold iron cut into her skin, ground against her bones. "Back off, MacRae—you and the dog—or I break your doctor's fucking hand."

Mac froze. Lifting his hands, he moved closer to the bed, putting himself between Harrigan and his wife—what any good husband would do—but he didn't spare a glance at Imogen; his gaze was fixed on Evie and the pirate. "Don't be stupid, Harrigan."

"Yeah, Harrigan," Evelyn jumped in, slipping her left hand into her pocket. "Don't be stupid." This time she whipped out a scalpel and shoved the sharp tip against his jugular. "Let go of my hand. *Now*."

Slowly Harrigan did as she commanded. It was all she could do not to sigh in relief when blood flow resumed to her fingers, and she found that she could move them without pain. If he'd made it difficult for her to perform surgery, she'd make sure the only thing his cock was good for was the occasional piss.

Evelyn pressed a little harder on the scalpel, drawing a drop of blood. "Mac, you'd better take him into custody before I decide to finish him."

"Don't do that, my dear," Mac said happily, coming toward them. "I've got plans for him." Then he grabbed the pirate by the shoulder and turned him around, hauling one arm behind his back. He snapped a pair of manacles onto one wrist, then pulled the other back and did the same.

"Walk," he commanded, and pushed Harrigan

forward. When that didn't immediately get results, Napoleon growled and gave the intruder a nudge with his broad head.

Evie followed them, but first she stopped to check her patient. "Are you all right?" she asked.

Imogen nodded, weakly, grimacing in pain. "My husband . . . ?"

"Will be in to see you as soon as he can."

Her eyes, glazed as they were, lit up. "Good."

"Try to rest. You need it. Here, this is for the pain." She gave her a measure of laudanum sweetened with a little honey to make it more palatable. Then, once she was certain her patient was resting, she went after Mac.

By the time she arrived on deck, Harrigan had been strapped into a volans canopy, his hands now shackled in front of him.

"Are you doing what I think you're doing?" she asked.

Mac nodded and held up a small bit of metal. Evie recognized it as a small auditory transmitter, similar to what W.O.R. agents used to communicate with one another. Harrigan must have had one to talk to his ship.

"Your captain is about to take a little trip," Mac said into the device. You might want to make sure your hatchling makes it safely back to the nest." And then the wing shield they'd put up began to lower back into its bin.

"Give me a hand, Ryan," Mac said to a large red-headed man, who scooped Harrigan up by the feet as Mac took his shoulders. Evie noted the pirate didn't look the least bit concerned.

"I'm going to kill you for this, MacRae," he said.

"You say that every time, Harrigan," Mac replied conversationally as they carried him to the rail. "Maybe someday you'll actually get your chance." And then with a nod to Ryan, the two of them lifted the pirate and tossed him over the side.

"Man overboard!" Mac yelled before tossing the transmitter after its owner.

Evelyn rushed forward and peered over. Harrigan plummeted toward the ground, and then there was a plume of silk as he deployed the canopy and slowly drifted downward.

"Steer her a few degrees south, Nell," Mac ordered. "It will take Harrigan's crew a while to collect him and get back into the air, but I don't want to make it easy for them to track us."

Evelyn raised her attention to him. He wore the self-satisfied smile that she'd fallen in love with years earlier. Cocky bastard. As his sister took the wheel, Mac's gaze slowly slid to hers. Of course he didn't seem surprised to find her staring. "Good work, Doc."

She shrugged, even though his praise warmed her. She smiled. "You're the one who taught me to always have a backup plan—or weapon."

His expression changed as they gazed at each other. Evie knew what that darkening of his eyes meant, that slight lowering of his lashes. He was a charmer and a rogue, but he always got this hint of vulnerability to him every time he ever kissed her. He was looking at her like that now, as though weighing the consequences, wondering if she'd reject him.

She wouldn't. And just as she could see the intent in his eyes, she knew he could see the answer in hers. He leaned toward her. . . .

"Your wife wants to see you," she blurted before he came any closer, jerking back. "I told her you'd come as soon as you could." Then she turned on her heel and escaped belowdecks, but the only room she had to hide in was his, and that didn't feel like escape at all.

It felt like delaying the inevitable.

Chapter 5

Your wife.

It was a simple enough phrase—one Mac expected to hear many times during the course of his life.

Of course, he assumed he actually would be married at the time.

He could have gotten himself in a heap of trouble. What had he been thinking almost kissing Evie? He hadn't been thinking. He'd been acting on instinct, giddy with besting Harrigan, and overwhelmingly relieved to find Evie safe and sound.

And Imogen, too. He couldn't forget her. She was everything.

Everything except his wife.

If he knew Evelyn—and there was no doubt that he did—then she would have run off to hide somewhere. The only place to go was his cabin, unless she went to the galley or Nell's room. She wouldn't invade someone else's space, though. She was too considerate. So she would go to his quarters because they'd once been hers as well. And she'd pace back and forth, convinced that he was a cad.

So Mac avoided his cabin and went to sit with Imogen instead, since she'd be alone. He had promised her real husband, Theo, that he'd look out for her, and he'd done a sorry job of it thus far.

Nell promised to guide the *Queen V* safely to ground. They had the wind at their back, and he'd had Pliny and Heath, one of the newer crew members, fire up the turbines—large whirling blades that extended from the sides of the ship, sucked air in and blew it, propelling the craft forward with an extra burst of speed. Normally they were used only on calm days when there wasn't much wind to ride on, but in this case they were used to put as much distance between them and Harrigan as they could.

The bastard refused to give up who'd hired him. Mac hadn't expected to get any information. Pirates weren't exactly known for their loyalty, but every good pirate was loyal to one thing. For most, that one thing was money. A pirate who wanted to live a long life did not betray those who paid for his services. To do so was bad for business and bad for one's health.

No one on his crew objected to tossing Harrigan over. No one even blinked. How was Mac to find the traitor when they all seemed so bloody faithful? It was almost enough to make him second-guess his suspicions, but then he remembered how warm

Theo's brains were as they splattered his face, and all doubt was eradicated.

He sat down on the side of Imogen's bed after shutting the door behind him. A few seconds later, her eyes fluttered open—not much, but it was better than nothing at all. She was still quite flushed, but her skin seemed cooler than it had been. If she survived this, it would be all because of Evie.

"You should be sleeping," he murmured.

"Hurts," she replied. "Shot?"

He nodded. "Are you too warm?"

"No. Not warm enough."

There was a quilt at the foot of her bed. Mac pulled it up over her. "I'll have some bricks heated for you if you want."

"Tha . . . that would be lovely. Thanks. Water?"

He got up and poured some water from the pitcher on the dresser into a shallow glass. He held her head up as she took a sip. Her sigh of pleasure made him smile.

"Better." And then, as he set the glass on the bedside table, "Where's Theo? That . . . the woman said he . . . was here. I want . . . I want to see him."

Aw, hell. He should've jumped over the side after Harrigan. He should have realized this would happen when Evie told him that his wife wanted to see him. Imogen didn't remember the attack, or at least not the part where her husband was killed. Then again, she'd already been shot herself at that point.

"Theo's on board." That wasn't a lie. His body was on ice in the cargo hold. Mac hadn't been about to leave him behind. "He was shot, too, Genny. You'll have to wait to see him." He hated bending the truth, but doing otherwise would make it all too easy for her to give up and die herself, and everything she knew would go with her. Then Theo's sacrifice and his own efforts would have been in vain. He would not allow his friend to be left with such a legacy.

Theo Hardiston was going to be remembered as a hero if it was the last thing Mac did.

"The doctor. That's her, isn't it?" Her eyelids began to flutter, as though the sheer effort to keep them open was becoming too much for her. "Your *Queen V*."

"Yes." His lips lifted into a smile despite himself. He knew he never should have told her about Evie, but he'd been drunk at the time. Other than Nell, Imogen was the only person to know that his ship—his most prized possession—was named for the woman who broke his heart. He'd "acquired" the ship at a poker game shortly after meeting Evelyn, and as soon as he saw her, he knew there could be no other name for her. Sleek, proud and gorgeous: Those words described the ship just as aptly as her namesake.

Imogen licked her lips. "Don't . . . let her get . . . away this time."

"Don't you worry about me." Mac forced a light tone, even though it felt as though his ribs were crushing in on his insides. "Now stop jabbering and get some sleep, or I'll put you to work peeling potatoes."

She was already out. Thank Christ. His shoulders slumped as he planted his face in both hands and rubbed. He needed some sleep soon as well. It felt as if he'd gotten only a handful of rest since the attack. The last thing he needed was to become slow and weak.

But sleep would have to wait, at least for a little while longer. Once they were on the ground in Frankfurt, he needed to rendezvous with Dash and get some new balloon-sails installed. Then they needed to be airborne again as soon as possible. In London Imogen would be taken to the Warden compound, where she would be cared for by Evie and her staff, and then Evie would learn the truth.

Not that it mattered. She didn't want him any more now than she had wanted him three years ago. He was the one who couldn't let it die.

Once he was certain Imogen was asleep and likely to remain that way, Mac got up and left the room, locking the door behind him. He might have worried that the traitor knew who Imogen really was and what cabin she was in, but the door to Nell's room had been open when he came down, and his sister never left her door open—she was too afraid that they might have picked up a rat somewhere along the way and it, or them, would get into her room and crawl over her at night.

He really oughtn't have locked her in their rat-infested cellar when they were children. Their mother had tanned his hide good for that. Regardless, Harrigan hadn't known where to look, which meant the traitor wasn't certain about anything. There was still hope.

Mac rose to his feet with a silent but huge yawn that made his ears pop. They were losing air. He needed to be on deck. He opened the door to find Napoleon waiting there with a large bone in his mouth. He'd taken to keeping watch over Imogen— a trait his master admired.

"Go on, then," he instructed, standing back so the beast could enter. He padded to the foot of the bed and flopped down on the floor. He'd sleep there for quite a while before Mac had to let him out, and there was water in the basin if he needed a drink. Mac left him happily gnawing on his treat.

In the corridor, Mac paused for a moment and turned to face the door to his own quarters. She was in there—the woman who haunted him like a shipwreck. She was amongst his things, getting her scent all over the place. Her perfume would linger for days after he left her in London. He would have to make certain the rum was well stocked before they took flight again; otherwise she'd take over his dreams.

He really should hate her for making him so weak. He did, to an extent. But if he walked into that room, she'd only have to look at him and he'd take her to bed and keep her there—everything else be damned.

"You all right?"

Mac whirled around. His sister was on the stairs, peering down at him with an odd expression on her face. "What?"

"You're rubbing your scar. Are you all right?"

He dropped his hand. Of course he'd been rubbing the damn thing—he always did when he thought of

Evie. As usual, as the realization struck him, he drew a deep breath. It didn't feel any different than it ever had, but it had been three years since he'd drawn air into his lungs. Three years since he had lungs.

"I'm fine." His tone was clipped. "Throwing Harrigan over the side was exactly what I needed. Were you looking for me?"

She nodded. She knew he was lying, but she never pushed—he loved that about her. "We're close. Thought you'd want to take us in."

"I do. Thanks." He started up the stairs.

Nell stopped him with a hand on his arm as he tried to pass her. "It's good having her on board again, isn't it?"

Mac didn't insult either of them by playing dumb. "No," he said. "It's really not."

"Bad luck having a woman on board," he said in the aftermath of the attack.

"Didn't have any trouble till the doctor came on." This was what he said when the rest of the crew got antsy the closer they came to ground.

"Shoulda let Iron Hand take her." That was his response when some speculated that the pirate had wanted the doctor. What else did they have of value?

He had to give it to MacRae; he had his idiot crew eating out of the palm of his hand. No one ever questioned the great Captain Mac.

Bollocks.

He kept to the stern as the *Queen V* glided toward the ground, buildings and trees coming up to greet them. Landing made him want to puke, always had. Christ, he'd be glad when all of this was over and he could go back to his old life, his old job. If he could just get rid of that damn doctor, he could kill the spy MacRae protected and be on his way. He was tired of this life. He wanted to go back to Russia, back to his family. Wanted to speak his own language with his own people. These English and American mongrels annoyed him with their strange accents and their insistence that their way of life was the right way.

If they were so right, then why was every other agency in the world out to bend them over?

A grinding noise rose over the engines—the sound of the landing gear being lowered. Ships like this were brought in by magnets or by anchor. Because of the condition of the balloon and the impromptu landing, MacRae was using the anchor, which would be caught by a mechanism that would then slowly pull them into a dock.

If Harrigan had done his damn job, they would have been forced to land in the countryside, where the crew and the cargo would have been easy pickings, but no. Harrigan's crew was as much shit as their captain. Who failed when attempting to kill a woman? If she'd been a Russian woman, he might be more sympathetic, but Harrigan was an imbecile. Hopefully the man got caught in a tree on his way to the ground. Buzzards should pick out his stupid eyes and tongue.

But it was useless to rage about the pirate. His

agency should have known better than to hire outside their ranks. He could be whipped for expressing
such an opinion out loud, but there was no one to
hear inside his mind.

So now it was all on his shoulders. Sometime between now and London, he would have to find a
way to get to the spy, and if he had to kill the pretty
doctor to achieve his goal, so be it. And then he
would hope to God that MacRae didn't find him out,
because as stupid as the man might be, he was a
ruthless son of a bitch.

The man was not afraid to die, but Gavin MacRae
would make certain death was a long and painful
time coming.

Evelyn hadn't been to Frankfurt in a long time. The
last time had been with Mac, and it had been a much
more romantic trip than her current voyage. She
probably wasn't going to get to see much of the city
at all before they were airborne once more.

"You going to leave us now?" Nell asked. The two
of them were on the deck, watching Mac and Pliny
descend the landing platform stairs to the ground,
Napoleon sauntering along behind them. Under the
bright lights they were met by a very handsome,
roguish sort of fellow who looked as though he'd
like to punch Mac in the jaw.

He should get in line.

"I should," Evelyn replied. "It would serve him
right if I did, but I'm not going to walk away from
someone who needs medical attention." How very

professional, how magnanimous of her. Too bad it wasn't true. No, she wouldn't turn her back on someone who needed her care, but neither was she ready to walk away from Mac again. Not yet.

Lord, part of her hoped he might try to kiss her again. She wanted to kiss him, even though she knew it was so very, very wrong. He was married. Worse, his wife was her patient. She wouldn't kiss him, but she could think about it. And if he kissed her, she would know that he was a cad.

He was obviously worried about the woman, but it didn't strike her as the all-encompassing obsession of a man who feared he might lose the most important woman in his life. Recently her friend Arden had given birth to a baby boy. It hadn't been a particularly difficult birth, but Arden's husband, Lucas, had paced and fretted and basically driven himself mad with worry until he knew both mother and child were fine.

Mac was not a heartless man. There was no way she'd believe he had become one, nor would she take credit if he had. He was not cruel, and he wouldn't leave the side of someone he loved, especially not when that loved one was so injured. Was their marriage one of convenience? It didn't matter, because vows were vows. Never mind that her father had never adhered to his, she would not be the "other" woman, not after seeing how every betrayal had broken her mother's heart.

Nell smiled at her. "Mac will be happy to hear

you're staying on. Having you look after Imogen has given him peace of mind."

"Yes," she replied drily. "He's overjoyed to have me along for the journey." She frowned as one of the crew shot her an odd look. Fabulous. They thought the attack was her fault—bad luck to have a woman on board and all that nonsense. They always had a woman on board. Or did Nell not count? Superstitious fools.

Nell's smile lingered. "Well, I for one am glad to have you along. I've missed you."

Even if Evie had been able to think of a suitable response, she'd never have vocalized it around the lump in her throat. Her old friend seemed to sense her emotional distress, and turned her attention elsewhere. "That Dash is one fine example of God's handiwork, don't you think?"

"Dash?"

"The man who's going to get us airborne again." She pointed at the man talking to Mac. "The one who looks like he'd gladly knock my brother's teeth out."

Oh, *him*. Evie nodded. "I could probably spend a few hours looking at him."

"I could do a lot more than look, but all right."

Evelyn grinned. Nell had always talked as if she had scores of lovers, but Evie had seen her with only three men, and one had been her fiancé, who died almost four years ago. The other two were men she met in port when the need for a little physical connection got to be too much. She made Evie look like a whore, not that she would ever apply such a label to herself. Liking sex didn't make her a whore.

It was having sex with men who weren't worth the privilege that made one a whore. Even Franz, despite his immaturity, had treated her body like a gift.

Mac had always treated her body like a possession. He knew just how to touch her, when and where. He would ruthlessly draw a response from her no matter how tired or angry she might be. The slightest brush of stubble as he kissed the small of her back, or a faint scrape of teeth against her neck, was often all it took to make her want him. He would tease and toy, cajole and caress relentlessly until finally sliding inside her, her body so attuned to his that they came together in dizzy delight.

It was as though her body was made for his, and she had never found that same feeling with another man.

Maybe it was prideful of her, but she'd wager a full year's salary that he hadn't found it with anyone else, either. But then, he was the one who was married, wasn't he? It occurred to her then that regardless of the circumstances, he had asked that woman to be his wife. That was something he had never asked her. They had talked about it, she was certain. They'd discussed their future and made jokes about what to name their children, but he'd never actually gotten around to proposing. It was just as well, of course, given that she'd left him, but the realization left her feeling raw, a hatred for the feverish woman belowdecks squirming in her belly.

Jealousy was an ugly, bitter emotion, and not one she found at all attractive in herself, but as she turned her gaze toward the small group of people gathered near the boarding stairs of the ship, something deep inside her reacted to the sight of Mac, something primal and possessive. He was hers, and marriage to another woman wouldn't stop her from feeling that way.

Maybe she should leave now. Mac's wife would be fine. He'd be fine. Evelyn might go to her maker regretting the day she let him go, but she was going to have to let him go again. He wasn't hers, no matter how much her heart insisted otherwise. Her feelings were meaningless. He was the same man he'd been three years ago when his lungs had been destroyed during an attack by the Company, a rival agency that supported chaos and discord in the world.

She had saved him then, but almost losing him, realizing he was as mortal as any other man, had shaken her so deeply she had nightmares of his death. She felt the loss of him as though it had already happened, even though he was alive and recovered from the ordeal. The bellows she'd fashioned for oxygenating his blood worked just as well as his lungs had, if not better, and he went back to the sky good as new.

Except for that broken heart.

He had asked her to come with him, told her he

needed her with him. Had that been his idea of a proposal, or was she grasping at straws so she didn't have to play second to that delicate, English, oh-so-milky-white woman whose life rested in her hands?

Cold bitch.

It had nothing to do with her mixed blood, and she knew it. Very few people seemed to care that she was not one hundred percent English. Mac certainly hadn't. Yes, his wife was the quintessential English rose with her golden hair and cornflower eyes, but it went beyond that as well. Imogen MacRae was everything Evie was not. Why, she'd wager she'd been a virgin on their wedding night.

And the thought of that wedding night turned the knife in her gut a little harder, like those claws that had scarred her during the encounter when Mac's lungs were destroyed. She was not a good woman, not by most measures. She was a good doctor. Hell, she was a brilliant doctor, but as a person she often fell short of expectations. She liked to drink and swear, wear trousers and sometimes smoke a cigarillo, even though she knew that smoke couldn't be good for her.

She liked to screw, rolled her eyes at the term "making love" and believed every woman should have an electro-vibration machine in her bedroom. She was selfish at times, would lie to protect herself— though the truth was a weapon she often brandished with cutthroat skill—and often thought a back-handed slap was an effective way to get someone's attention.

But she wasn't strong enough to give herself to

Mac heart and soul knowing that he could be taken away at any moment. Imogen obviously had no problem with that. That made her a braver woman than Evie would ever be.

And Mac, the bastard, didn't seem the least bit worried that he might lose his wife, which made him either terribly confident in her abilities, incredibly willing to give up control or not nearly as good a man as she had once thought.

She was going for the latter, because he'd replaced her with a delicate little flower who had no business getting shot. Damn it, if anyone was going to take a bullet for him—if he was going to shield anyone from harm—it should be her. If for no other reason than that she could be justified in shooting him her- self once she recovered.

Wait one bloody moment. Had she actually just felt jealousy toward a woman who had been shot? Honestly? She pressed a hand to her forehead. This was ridiculous.

Oh, Arden and Claire would give her *such* a rib- bing for this. Where were they when she needed them? Back in England with their gorgeous hus- bands having babies and getting shagged as often as they liked without having to deal with pompous surgeons or kidnapping ex-lovers. They would tell her what to do.

And knowing the two of them, it would involve some kind of mechanical device or weapon—perhaps both. Preferably something she could use on Mac. A little jolt of electricity might be just what he needed.

However, if she was fair, she would have to admit that he must have swallowed practically every drop of pride he had when he decided he needed her help. He wouldn't blink at kidnapping, but coming within a hundred yards of her had to annoy him.

She *hoped* it annoyed him. She had to take something away from this when it was all over. Had to have some manner of validation. If ever she needed a reminder that leaving Mac had been the right thing to do, she need only unlock the door to the room belowdecks and check his wife's wounds. If she and Mac had stayed together, they might have had children by now—not that she thought of herself as much of a motherly type. Hell, she could have been the woman who'd been shot.

No wonder she was jealous, she thought. If she could roll her eyes at herself, she would. The question was—*why* was she shot? Evelyn had seen that wound. She'd listen to the song and dance that the woman had taken a bullet meant for Mac, but that wasn't true. That wound was a gut shot just a life-saving fraction off the mark—or a chest shot coming in low. Scatter shot was meant to turn insides into ground meat.

"I think I'll take myself to land," Nell remarked, jerking Evie out of her thoughts. "You coming?"

She shook her head. "No. I'm going to check on my patient. She's resting, but I don't want to leave her." Actually she'd rather be anywhere else, but her conscience wouldn't let her run.

Nell smiled. "You're a good doctor, Evie."

A tight smile was all the response she could muster as her old friend left her. What the hell? The woman was Nell's sister-in-law. If Evie had married Mac and ended up in the same situation, she'd like to think Nell wouldn't leave her to go flirt with some unsavory—albeit gorgeous—character.

Something was not right, and thinking about Imogen's wound made it all the more suspect.

Mac's shoulder wound was from different ammunition than what had struck his wife. If that first shot had been meant for him, why hadn't the second been the same?

Because it hadn't been meant for him. If it had been, it would have struck his wife much higher than it had.

No, it wasn't Mac someone had tried to kill. Imogen had been the intended target. She was much more than Mac's wife, wasn't she?

Evelyn's temper rose. If Mac abducted her to save the life of some outlaw . . . it didn't matter. Her spine relaxed as quickly as it had stiffened. Saving lives was her duty. Judging them belonged to someone else. She'd repaired people far worse and sent them back on their way in the name of the Empire.

As she turned on her heel and started for the stairs to take her below, everything began to fall into a pattern she could believe. Mac and that woman might very well have been involved in some fashion, but it wasn't love. He'd married her for reasons that were his own—and Evelyn didn't care to know them. The why didn't change the fact that they were husband

and wife. Still, it explained why he wasn't hovering, why Nell wasn't a mess. It explained that ruffian who sneaked on board; he'd come with the express purpose of killing Imogen. The woman was in danger, and completely defenseless. Someone had to protect her.

And if it wasn't going to be her husband, it was going to have to be Evelyn.

Chapter 6

Dashiell Evans was a lunatic, a born killer and made the best pie Mac had ever tasted. They went straight to a building marked OFFICE and sat down at the rough-hewn table in a back room that was part of Dash's living space when he was in town.

"You're lucky I was even here," Dash informed him, setting a plate with a large slice of apple pie in front of him, and two more in front of Pliny and Nell. He'd given a plate of scraps to Napoleon, who was nosily gulping them down. "I was supposed to head out to Portugal today, but things got complicated."

That normally meant that someone got killed, calling for a change of plan. "I appreciate you helping us out," Mac replied.

Dash scowled. Women seemed to find him handsome, but Mac couldn't see it. To him, the man always looked angry. "As if I had a choice." He pointed a silver serving knife at him. "This makes us even, Mac. No more favors. I almost got shot last time."

Mac made a face. "That Aether blast missed you by at least six inches. That's not 'almost.' Regardless, I expect you'll end up in my debt again someday, my friend."

"I'm not certain I want to be your friend."

"Not many are." Mac cut off a bite of pie with his fork and lifted it to his mouth. He chewed and swallowed. "Damnation, but you make a fine pie."

The compliment took the edge off Dash's frown, just as Mac knew it would. They'd been "friends" a long time—long enough to be able to count on each other for help. It wasn't that they particularly liked each other, but that they both knew the worth of having someone owe them a favor.

"Can I have a slice to take back to the ship?" he heard himself ask around a mouthful of sweet cinnamon apple and flaky crust.

"Getting a bit greedy, aren't you?"

"It's not for me."

Dash rested his forearms on the table. The man could probably break walnuts in the crook of his elbow. "Got a lady on board, do you? Is she pretty?"

Now Mac was the one scowling. "No."

Dash laughed. "She is! Maybe I should take the pie to her myself."

The last thing Mac needed—wanted—was for Dash and Evie to meet. The universe would probably implode. "That's not going to happen."

The bastard actually chuckled. "Oh, this is brilliant."

"She's an old friend," Nell jumped in. Mac could have hugged her. "And she's spoken for."

Make that a punch instead of a hug, especially with that look she shot him.

"Then I will resist putting temptation in front of her." Dash grinned. "I guess you're stuck with me, Nell, my darling."

His sister arched a brow. "Only if you make it worth my while, ducks."

"Oh, I'm sure I can make it worth your while."

"I bet you say that to every woman."

"Only the ones who have the power to steal my heart."

"How long is it going to take to fix my ship?" Mac cut in, not bothering to hide his annoyance. "Once the two of you are done flirting, I mean."

Dash leaned back in his chair. The leather gave a soft moan—must be female, Mac thought drily. "Flirting is one of the greatest pleasures life has to offer. If you tried it on a female other than your boat, you might not be so peevish."

Mac clenched his jaw. "My. Ship."

"I've got a few lads coming in. We should have you on your way by mid- to late morning."

Well, shit. "No way you could do it sooner?"

Dash gestured to the window beside the table. "In case you haven't noticed, it's nighttime. I don't have a full crew on at the moment, and the lights aren't high enough to work by. Sorry, Mac. It's the best I can do."

Mac nodded. "I know." That didn't make it easier to accept, though. He ate the last bite of pie. "I suppose it might be best to stay out of sight for a bit."

"You're welcome to use the facilities if you like," the other man offered. "I'll be upstairs. We'll get you back in the sky as soon as we can."

A small—but genuine—smile tugged on one corner of his mouth. "And off your hands."

"That, too," Dash agreed with a little grin. Then he cut another piece of pie and plopped it onto a plate. "I want that back in the morning."

As if Mac would have need for a delicate china plate.

"Oh," Dash began almost as an afterthought. "When my shipment arrives you're not to go anywhere near it—understood? It will be in the cargo bay for the next dock, but stay as far away from it as you can."

"What is it?" Nell asked. Mac knew better.

"You don't want to know." When Dash Evans said those words, they were meant in all sincerity. He was part of the Irregular Transpirations, or I.T., division of the Wardens. They dealt with those sometimes wonderful, sometimes terrible but always unusual happenings that tended to have science at their root.

"You have my word that none of my crew will venture close." Mac rose to his feet and extended his hand, which Dash accepted. "Thanks for the pie."

"If she likes it, tell her there's plenty more where that came from."

Even though he knew he was being made sport of, Mac was nevertheless tempted to shove the plate of delicious pastry into the other man's smirking face.

The four of them—he'd almost forgotten about Pliny since he was so quiet—returned to the ship, where they found the rest of the crew gathering on deck for some music and entertainment. Now was the time of night when, if things were quiet, Eli would grab his guitar and Charlie would bring out his violin, or fiddle as he called it, and they'd play so the others could sing along or dance as if they were on a bed of hot coals barefoot.

"Perhaps we ought to have invited Evans up here after all," Nell suggested with a sly grin.

Mac didn't take the bait. "You can go fetch him if you want, sis. I'm going to take this pie to Evie and then I'm going to pass the hell out."

The teasing smile faded. "That was nice of you to think of her."

"Really? Most times when I think of her, it's anything but pleasant."

His sibling shook her head. "So flippant. You think that wit of yours hides the fact that you're as vulnerable as anyone else, but it doesn't. Not to me."

"You're not the one it's meant for," he replied honestly. "I don't want to discuss it, all right? Once we're back in the air, we'll be that much closer to England, and then she and I will go our separate ways again. It doesn't matter what I do or say. That won't change."

"If you'd just—"

"Don't." He held up a hand. He was so tired he could go to sleep on the deck. "Not now. Go have fun. I'll see you in the morning."

He left her standing there and slowly made his way belowdecks. His boots clomped heavily on the stairs. His legs felt as though they were made of lead. He could sleep for a week and still be exhausted. Even his bones felt tired.

It took every ounce of strength he had to move quietly past Imogen's room. He didn't want to disturb her or Evie. Nell told him that Doc had stayed behind to look after her patient. He owed her such a huge debt for this—not just him, but a whole batch of people owed her. Would she ever know just what she had done by saving Imogen's life?

Probably not.

He entered his quarters to find it lit by the gentle glow of a lamp. Just stepping into the familiar surroundings eased the tension in his neck and shoulders. He set the pie on the nightstand before removing his jacket. He flung it onto the foot of the bed, and began unbuttoning his shirt. Should he take off his boots or just fall on top of the quilt with them on?

He pulled his shirt over his head, throwing it into the basket to be laundered. Then he stretched, linking his fingers and lifting his arms high over his head. His spine popped in a couple of places, the scars on his back and Evie's stitches pulled, but it felt so good.

"Ahem."

"What the—!" Mac whirled around, Aether pistol in his hand. Evelyn rose from the stool in front of his shaving/toiletry table. "Doc. What the hell are you doing here?"

"Could you point that someplace else? Thank you. Apparently this is where I'm to sleep, although that's going to be an issue if you intend to sleep here as well."

He hadn't even thought of that. Some part of his brain had assumed it was only natural that they share a bed, as though he'd forgotten that she dropped him like a hot stone.

Her hair was down, and she was obviously dressed for bed, a velvet robe wrapped around her curvaceous frame. God, she had beautiful hair. Thick and dark. He remembered how it used to feel in his hands, or draped across his chest. "I forgot. Don't worry, I'll sleep with Imogen." He meant in the same room as Imogen, but from the tightening of her lips that wasn't how Evelyn heard it.

Jealousy was not an emotion she had a right to. If she hadn't been such a coward, they could have slept in the same bed almost every night for the past three years. What pissed him off was knowing that she'd only have to say the word and he'd take her into his bed again without so much as a blink.

She'd best stop staring at his chest if that wasn't what she wanted to happen. Mac holstered the pistol, retrieved his shirt and pulled it over his head once more. "I'll get out of your way." So much for a comfortable bed. He'd be sleeping on the floor or in a chair. He should have put a cot in Imogen's room and had Evie sleep there. "Dash sent you pie."

"Mac, I'd like to ask you something."

He was at the door, stopped and turned. The lamplight made auburn highlights in her hair. "Yeah?"

Her chin lifted. "Why is someone trying to kill your wife?"

Just concentrate on his face. Don't look anywhere else.

God, he has beautiful eyes.

Inwardly, Evelyn gave herself a shake. She was not a love-struck girl and he was not a prince out of a fairy tale. She was a mature woman who had had her fair share of lovers. No man should have the power to reduce her to mush, especially not one who had chosen a life of danger over a life with her.

When he remained silent, she pushed harder. "I know she didn't take a bullet meant for you, and I know that ruffian sneaked onto this ship with the express purpose of killing your wife." *I also know that you're not much of a husband.* She didn't add that. Mostly because it was a topic she didn't wish to discuss.

"Why does it matter?" he asked.

She folded her arms over her chest, mimicking his stance. "I'd like to know if you've gotten me involved in something unsavory."

"Unsavory?" He laughed. "Woman, I remember when Trouble was your middle name."

"You gave me that knife knowing full well someone might come aboard, so that I would protect your wife. I've saved her life twice now. Isn't that worth a little truth?"

He glanced away. Ah, she'd struck a nerve. Good. She simply wanted to know what was going on, so she could be prepared. Not because she suspected his marriage to this woman was in name only.

As though it mattered. Trouble might have been her middle name, but Stupidly Reckless was his. There was no future for them regardless of whether his marriage was real. And even if he wasn't married, they'd still be the same two completely ill-suited individuals that they'd always been.

"Imogen has something others would like to have."

That was his explanation? "Did you steal something from those pirates?"

"No. They were just hired to get her."

Hired mercenaries? "Good God, Mac. What sort of trouble have you gotten her into?"

It was the wrong thing to ask. Evelyn knew this even before his back stiffened and his eyes lit from within with a familiar brightness that meant he was good and pissed off.

"That just has to be it, doesn't it?" he demanded, hands going to his lean hips. "If something's wrong it's all my fault. You think I got her shot? I was supposed to be the goddamn cavalry, Evie. I lost a good friend that day, and barely managed to get Imogen on board without getting my own brains blown out. I didn't get her into anything, but I sure as hell got her out of it."

She stared at him. He wasn't just angry, he was hurt. Mac's code of honor wasn't exactly heroic, but it was one he refused to break. She'd impugned that by implying he was responsible for his wife's wounds.

"I'm sorry. I should have known you would never intentionally put anyone in harm's way."

He scowled at her, annoyed. "Stop it. I've put plenty in harm's way, but I always make sure I get them out again."

"Like me?"

"Like you."

And that was obviously all the apology she was going to get for being plunked down in the middle of whatever this intrigue was. He probably thought she owed him for the way she left him. Maybe she did, but hadn't saving his fool life been worth something? She guessed not if he was still pulling the same reckless stunts three years later. Working with the Wardens had taught her that some people thrived on danger. Mac was obviously one such person, while she was the person often tasked with putting the ones like him back together when they got themselves broken.

It seemed Imogen was a lot like Mac. They'd probably have a short and blissfully happy life together.

So why did that thought make her want to punch him in the nose? Not as though she could damage it any more than it already had been.

"I need to send a telegram," she told him brusquely.

"I was supposed to meet a friend of mine in Vienna. She'll worry when she can't find me."

He nodded. "There's a machine on the desk."

She knew that. She'd walked around for almost an entire day with part of it imprinted on her backside after they'd had sex on his desk. "Thank you."

Mac didn't say anything. He simply grabbed a blanket off the foot of the bed and went to the door. Evelyn moved behind the desk, seating herself in the chair bolted to the floor.

"Doc?"

She looked up, surprised to find him still in the room. "Yes?"

"I'm sorry."

It was like a kick to the chest. "For what?" Did it matter?

He smiled that little lopsided smile of his, but it didn't reach his eyes. "Pretty much all of it."

"Oh." That was all she had a chance to say before he walked out and closed the door.

Imogen stirred when Mac and Napoleon entered the room. Mac winced as the floorboards groaned beneath his boots. How was it that his bloody dog could weigh more than him but be as quiet as a mouse?

"Theo?" Her voice was faint and rough from disuse and medication.

The blade of guilt lodged between his ribs twisted. "It's Mac, Genny."

"Oh. I woke up . . . no one here . . . hurts . . . scared."

Ah, another turn of the knife. "I'm with you now. No one's going to hurt you."

"I know . . . always count on you . . ."

She'd drifted off again, thankfully. Mac took a book from the nearby shelf and slumped into a reasonably comfortable chair beneath the window. The lamp on the table burned with just enough light for him to move around without banging into anything, but it would be more than ample to read by.

After that exchange with Evie, he was going to need something to lull him into a relaxed state. Why couldn't he know more than one doctor? More than one brilliant doctor whom he could trust to save a life? One who he hadn't slept with, preferably, and one who did not have the power to turn him to a raving lunatic.

How was it possible to be both attracted to and repulsed by the same person? Wanting her made as much sense as drinking a bottle of lye—it was going to end badly if he gave in. Yet he wanted to do it— just to see what would happen. Just to grab a bit of that old happiness that he knew was as substantial as a dream.

From what he heard over the years, she collected lovers the way he collected scars. No man wanted to know that he'd been but one of many. He'd like to think that she'd been trying to forget him, but that was something a boy would think, not a grown man whose entire adult life seemed to have been spent with spies and pirates. Evie was a passionate woman, and it would be naive to think she wouldn't have other men. He'd been with other women.

Other dusky-skinned, dark-eyed women, who bore a certain passing resemblance after a few drinks and in the right light.

God, they hadn't all been reminders of her, had they? That was too pathetic—too obsessive—even for him.

Evie wouldn't even mock him for it. She'd probably pat him on the head and say how sorry she was that he'd never been able to get over the sheer marvel that was her.

He opened the book. *Jane Eyre*. Damn, he should have brought a bottle of whiskey with him. He remembered Nell rhapsodizing about this story when they were younger. At least he could pretend that the madwoman in the attic was Evelyn.

She'd only been on his ship not quite a full twenty-four hours and already she was asking the wrong questions. It was his own fault that she didn't believe his marriage to Imogen was a love match. She was really going to get curious if she found out it was a hair away from being an illegal sham.

Imogen knew what Theo knew, and Theo was dead. Only Imogen knew where and what the information was. It was amongst her belongings; that was all Mac knew. He also knew that if Genny died, her effects would go to her next of kin and get tied up in all manner of probates and such. The information she had was crucial now. So Mac had done the only thing he could; he made Nell temporary captain and had her marry them while he did his best to keep Genny alive, her dead husband but a few feet away, where Mac had dropped his body on the deck. Somehow they managed to get all the blood out of the wood before the crew returned to duty.

The marriage was as tenuous as a spiderweb, but the Wardens could make it hold up, at least long enough for him to go through Genny's things and find the intelligence she and Theo had gathered.

If she survived—and thanks to Evie she probably would—they'd pretend the marriage never happened. It wasn't as though they'd signed anything. Hell, the bride hadn't even been conscious! Well, she had wakened long enough for him to get her to say yes, but even then it hadn't been at the right spot. Worst-case scenario, they'd get an annulment.

Right now he had to worry about keeping her alive to make it back to England and deliver her into Warden hands. And he had to keep curious Evie from asking more questions. The more she knew, the more danger she was in, and if she asked the wrong person the right questions . . . well, the traitor on his ship would quickly catch on.

As it was he'd barely managed to conceal what Iron Hand Harrigan had been doing on his ship. He told the crew it had been a planned coup and that he'd caught the scoundrel trying to molest Evie. At least she wouldn't dispute that, knowing that Imogen was in danger.

He had an injured spy on his boat, her dead husband in the ice chest, his ex-lover in his cabin and a traitor in his crew. Just another day aboard the *Queen V*. He'd never thought there would come a day when he would tire of this life, but he was beyond tired. He was bloody exhausted. He was too old, too tired and not nearly as full of piss as he'd once been.

The wind in his hair just didn't feel the way it used to. And the gorgeous wide-openness of the sky, in all her forms, wasn't so breathtaking without someone to share it with. He didn't necessarily need a wife, just a change of scenery, or at least a different vantage point. After fifteen years in the sky, Mac was ready to look up at the clouds rather than through them.

He opened the book. *There was no possibility of taking a walk that day.*

"Welcome to my world, Miss Eyre," he muttered around a yawn. He propped his elbow on the table and leaned his head against the palm of his head. Hopefully he wouldn't fall asleep in this position— sleeping sitting up wasn't as merciful on a body in its thirties as it was on one in its twenties. There were mornings when he ached in places he didn't even know the name of.

He began to read. It was a better story than he'd expected, and he found himself having a fair bit of sympathy for the young heroine, even if she was determined to end up with her scowling, brooding employer.

"Oh, Rochester," Mac murmured. "You beautiful cad." Why did women always seem to fall for the rogues and the cads? Probably he shouldn't question it and just be glad they did.

A knock at the door made him lift his head just as

he was starting to nod off. He jerked upright, the muscles in his neck spasming in a manner that set his teeth on edge. Slowly he rose to his feet and crossed to the door.

"It's me," whispered a voice on the other side.

Nell. He opened the door and peered out. "What is it?"

His sister's gaze raked over his face. "You look like hell. When's the last time you slept?"

Mac shrugged. "I reckon it was the last time I went to bed."

Her lips pursed. "When was that?"

"Dunno, but I was awfully close until you woke me up." He had to keep his voice low so as not to wake Genny. "What do you want?"

"It's Dash. There's been trouble with his delivery. He needs you and Evie."

If Dash needed someone with more medical skills than his own, it was bad news indeed.

Mac managed a grim smile. "Sleep is for babies and corpses. Rouse Doc, Nelly. I need you to sit with Genny until I return." He could leave her with Napoleon as sole guard, but if there was trouble afoot, he'd prefer to have his sister keeping watch as well.

"Of course." She left him to go knock on the door of his cabin. Mac placed the back of his fingers against Imogen's forehead. She was still warm, but not as hot as before. That had to be a good sign.

He closed the door behind him as he left the room, leaving it unlocked for his sister. Then he hauled himself upstairs.

The night had taken on a chill—the crisp, bracing kind that spoke of changing leaves and mulled cider. It also backhanded the need to sleep right out of him. He jogged down the plank, to a faintly lit loading dock a ways down from where they were berthed. There were several men gathered around—a few of whom were even standing.

Mac glanced around. Some of the men on the ground didn't look so good—like the dead kind of not good.

Dash appeared out of the dark, battered and bloody, but not dangerously so. He thrust an Aether rifle into Mac's hands.

"Orders?" Mac asked.

The other man wiped a trickle of blood from above his eye. "Shoot to kill—if you can."

"If I—?" Mac looked up at the ship. On the deck there were even more bodies strewn about—some that weren't entirely intact. And in the middle of them was a very large crate with iron bars around it—bars that had been bent like hairpins. And behind that was a very large hole in the crate where something had busted its way out. A *very large* something.

Mac's shoulders slumped. "Aw, hell."

Chapter 7

Evelyn was sitting at Mac's desk in her smallclothes with a canister of nitrous oxide when Nell entered the room.

"What is this aversion your family has to knocking?" she demanded. She was tired, hungry and embarrassed to have been caught with a canister of "laughing gas," as it was often called. It was very popular at parties, but took on a slightly pathetic cast when used by oneself. In fact, it seemed rather desperate.

"Sorry, Evie girl, but you gotta come quick."

Her heart jumped into her throat. She yanked her legs off the desk and leaped to her feet. "Is it her?"

"No, it's Dash and Mac. Something's gotten loose. He's got a lot of men in need of medical attention."

She was already pulling on her trousers. "Be a love and fetch my bag, Nell." She tossed her the canister. "Throw this in if you don't mind." It wasn't her first choice, but it made patients much more comfortable during minor procedures.

The older woman ducked out, shutting the door behind her. Next time Evelyn would know to lock it if she wanted any degree of privacy. She jammed the tail of her shirt into her trousers, pulled on her boots and laced up a corseted waistcoat. Her hair she pulled back in a loose plait. She had nothing to secure it close at hand, so she let the end hang free. It would unravel eventually, but it would do for now.

She grabbed a coat—one of Mac's because she was not getting blood on hers—and tore from the room. She met Nell at the stairs.

"Your bag, Doctor."

Evie forced a smile. It wasn't that she didn't love Nell, just that stress tended to rob her of any sense of humor. She knew for most people humor helped dispel anxiety and other mental ailments, but she wasn't one of those. Unless, of course, she was the one trying to ease the tension.

She took the heavy leather bag and quickly made her way to the deck and down the steps to the dock. The landing bays were partially covered to give some protection from the elements, but other than that it was very much like the sort of dock used for seafaring vessels with a wide-open approach so that all ships circled the central hub that had a small tavern/inn and sold repair equipment. There was usually an engineer or two on hand to take care of serious repair matters, and a smattering of people looking to obtain transportation to various ports in Europe, generally in a secretive fashion.

Tonight, however, this particular section of the facility property was closed to travelers and other ships. Only the *Queen V* and one other were docked there. As soon as the night breeze found her downwind, Evie knew that was for the best.

She smelled blood and shit—and lots of it. It was the kind of smell one either became accustomed to or at least learned not to gag at it. It was the smell of a violent death. A massive one.

"What the hell happened here, Nell?" she demanded.

The older woman kept pace beside her. "Dunno. Dash came to the ship in a fine mess, looking for you and Mac. Told everyone else to stay on board."

Evie came to an abrupt stop. "Then why are you with me, Nell?"

Rounded brows rose, crinkling Nell's forehead. "Because I want to help."

"Mac left you in charge of the ship, didn't he?"

"Yeah, but—"

"No." Evelyn fixed her with a direct stare. It was the one she used to intimidate Warden agents, and stubborn men. It was one that most people found quite threatening. Nell, as thickheaded as her brother, smiled.

"C'mon, Evie! You can't expect me to let both you and Mac run headlong into trouble."

"I expect you to do what your captain ordered you to do. I expect you to get back on that ship, disengage the stairwell and be ready to fly the hell out of here should things get serious." As if they weren't serious already.

Nell drew back, spine stiffening. For a moment, Evie expected her to put up a fight, but Nell wasn't dumb, just protective. "You've got to look after the rest of the crew, my friend. They're your responsibility now, as is your brother's wife."

The older woman nodded. "You're right."

Evie smiled gently—it was the smile she used when reassuring patients just before surgery. It wasn't false or forced, but rather came from that part of her that refused to believe anything might go wrong. "Of course I am. Go."

"At least let me tell Mac you're coming. It might be dangerous."

Now would be a good time to roll her eyes, but she didn't. Never mind that she had been the one to force Iron Hand Harrigan to surrender. She stood by quietly while Nell pulled a small device that resembled a tuning fork from her coat and struck it against the railing of the steps leading up to the ship. As the device vibrated, she spoke into it. Evelyn had seen Arden use such a device before, as well as other Wardens. It was an effective way to send a message to someone wearing the appropriate receiver, but not so great for conducting a give-and-take conversation.

Nell put the fork back into her coat. "There's Mac now. Be careful, Evie."

Of Mac or whatever monster had created that stench? "I will."

"Take care of my little brother."

Oh, dear lord. That was not a responsibility she wanted! Yet her chest clenched at the thought of anything happening to Mac. "I will."

Nell gave her shoulder a squeeze—the woman had incredibly strong hands—and began climbing the stairs to the ship. Evie tightened her grip on her bag and set off toward where Mac stood at the end of the platform. He wasn't covered in gore, nor did he appear to be injured, but his face was pale and his expression grim.

When Mac took a situation seriously, it was time to worry.

"What is it?" she asked, when she was close enough to speak without raising her voice.

"I have no idea," he replied, ever-keen gaze watchful. "Dash tells me it once was a man. Dash, this is Evie. Evie, meet Dash. Don't think we need to be formal at the moment."

"Indeed," she replied, lifting her chin in greeting when the other man, who was kneeling on the deck, nodded at her.

Behind Mac and slightly off to the side, she saw bodies on the ground. Two appeared to be alive. Dash was tending to one of them. He had a claymore beside him, within reach. If a blade that big was necessary, then they were in very big trouble.

Evie immediately went to the other living victim. The poor man was of Chinese birth. When he saw her he began to talk in his native tongue with great emotion and velocity.

"He says it was a devil," Mac translated. "A black devil."

In her experience most things people called devils or monsters were naturally occurring. She'd yet to have a true paranormal experience, and never expected to. "Are you inclined to believe him?"

"Damned if I'm not tempted." Mac turned in a slow circle, searching the shadows.

"Could you please tell him that I'm going to clean and bandage his wounds? Anything requiring stitches will have to wait until all the survivors have been moved to safety."

"These are all the survivors," Dash informed her as Mac spoke to Evie's patient. "At least that we know of."

Sweet God. "How many dead?"

"Twenty-three, give or take." Mac's tone was just a twitch too pointed to be matter-of-fact.

"Then we'd best get these two to safety fast."

A roar cut through the night, seemed to reverberate through her entire body. It was a sound of hunger, of anger and primal blood lust.

Mac raised his rifle. "Doc, I want you back on the ship. Now."

Dash rose to his feet. His hands and clothes were stained with blood. "We need her in case there are more survivors."

"Then we'd best ensure that she survives as well." Mac's head turned toward her, fixing her with a stare that made her want to do exactly as he told her. When he got like this, he was a force of nature. "Go."

"I would like nothing more," she told him, throat suddenly dry. "But I don't think that's a viable option at this time." Slowly she inclined her head to his right. Her palms prickled as blood rushed to her feet.

Her companions looked where she gestured. Standing—at least she thought it was standing—at the edge of the shadows was a huge bipedal creature. The ability to stand upright was about all it visibly had in common with humans. It had to be close to eight feet tall, with shoulders twice as wide as any man's. Its head resembled that of a bull, with a broad, short snout and long, curled horns extending out from the top sides of its skull. Its skin, or pelt, was black as ink. It should have blended effortlessly into the dark except that its fur or skin had such a sheen to it that light danced over every angle of its form.

It had cloven hooves, on legs that were shaped like those of a horse, only thicker and heavier. Its arms were incredibly long and sported hands that were a mix of paws and talons.

In short, it was the sort of thing that did not occur in nature, but in a laboratory. It was a monster in every sense of the word. An abomination of science.

"Where did it come from?" she asked, shifting her weight so that she might easily leap to her feet if necessary.

"Greece," Dash replied as he reached for his sword.

"You have got to be having me on." Greece? Really? "Is it the Minotaur, then?"

"I assume that would have been the model, yes."

"I don't suppose you have a spare labyrinth lying about, do you?"

Mac flicked the switch to power up his pistol. "Got one in the cargo hold."

She shot him a scowl. "If it began as a scientific experiment, then it stands to reason the creature began its life as human."

"Pretty obvious it's become something else, Doc."

"But it is of flesh and blood. If it has a heart, it can be killed."

He looked at her. "Any thought as to how, oh sage one?"

She shrugged. "Theseus cut off its head."

"Sounds like a sound plan to me," Dash tossed in, hoisting the claymore. "Goddamn the Brass Market for importing shit like this."

So not only were some Greeks paying a fortune to make this monster, but there were those who would pay an even heftier amount to control the bloody thing.

Based on the carnage it left in its wake, she'd say that controlling it was not going to be an option. Nor was mercy. The thing might very well have been human once, but science had stolen every last drop of its humanity. It was a mindless killer—or perhaps it knew quite well what it was doing. Either way, it had to be stopped. There was no hope of helping it, defending it.

"What would be the purpose of engineering such a creature?" she asked.

"Killing machine, I wager," Dash replied.

"What an amazingly brilliant job they did of it."

"All for the betterment of science," Mac added, staring at the creature down the length of his arm. "On three. One . . . two . . . three."

He pulled the trigger.

The blast hit the Minotaur in the center of its chest. The smell of burned fur and flesh flooded the docks. The creature's cries of pain echoed so loudly, Evelyn knew her ears would ring for at least several hours.

That is, if she lived through the next several hours.

The bull-man ran toward her in a very exaggerated human gait. Why in the name of all that was holy did it choose her? Mac was the one who shot it. There were lots of women out there with glossy, languid eyes, looking for a partner to go home with. Have fun in and out of bed with a man who had at least one other bull-like appendage than just his head. She giggled at the thought.

Perhaps the "laughing gas" hadn't been such a grand idea.

"Evie, get out of the way!" Mac shouted.

The Minotaur pounded toward her, drawing closer and closer as its awkward "hooves" struck the ground. What had they done to the poor thing's feet? She could see that they'd started out human, but were now pulled up tight, the heel bent toward the back of the leg so it was forced to run on the balls of its feet, which had metal riveted to them, making them resemble a more bovine model.

This was cruelty at its finest. Killing this poor creature would be a mercy.

As it bore down upon her, she could see where its face had been altered, where the bull nose and mouth replaced the human. They would have had to alter the skull as well. How had the original person even survived the process? How had they managed to make it so terribly strong? How could animal and human be combined in such a manner when they were so very different in form and function?

"Evie!"

She glanced at Mac. "Stop screaming. I hear you." She withdrew the canister of gas as the creature drew so close she could see where they'd grafted horns to its head. She'd taken an oath not to do any harm. Surely it didn't apply in this circumstance.

Just as she raised the canister, preparing to get as much into the creature as she could, she heard the unmistakable whine of an Aether gun.

"No!" she cried, but it was too late. Mac's shot hit the creature at the base of one horn. A little lower and it would have a nasty hole in its brain. As it was, one of its horns was now considerably shorter than the other, singed and stinking.

The Minotaur screamed and pivoted on one hoof. It lowered its head and leaped toward Mac. Good Lord, it was fast.

Mac raised the pistol and fired again. The creature dodged. The blast struck it on the shoulder, filling the air with the smell of charred fur and flesh and burned blood. Another scream rent the air—part human, mostly monster. It was a horrible, spine-trembling sound.

It struck Mac, driving one horn deep into his side, lifting him inches off the ground, and shaking him like a rag doll. It was going to kill him.

She leaped into action at the same time Dash did, but she got to them first, throwing herself high onto the creature's back, forcing it to bow further. It was just enough for Mac to push himself free. He fell to the ground with a grunt, hands instantly going to the wound. Blood dripped over his fingers.

Evie shoved the mask of the canister over the beast's nose and let the gas flow as quickly as it could. Bovine-bent human legs buckled. Dash yelled and she jumped off, landing near Mac as Dash swung the massive sword. She looked up just in time to see the Minotaur's head sail from its body before turning her attention to Mac.

Blood bubbled on his lips. "Evie?"

Inside, Evie knew that she wanted to cry, but the tears were not allowed to come. A part of her screamed in rage and pain, while another took over with unfeeling practicality.

"No one gets to kill you but me, MacRae." She slipped one hand beneath him to cover the wound and the other over the entrance wound. She pressed hard. "Mr. Evans, I'm in need of every medical treatment and device you have."

There followed the unmistakable clank of a claymore hitting ground, followed by running footsteps.

"Why didn't you move?" Mac rasped. Blood trickled from the corner of his mouth.

"Why didn't you trust me?" she shot back. She would not allow him to blame her for this! He couldn't die. He just couldn't!

He wouldn't. She wouldn't allow it. She'd cheated death once for him and she would do it again, damn it.

She snagged her bag—she'd dropped it when she leaped for the creature—with the toe of her boot and dragged it closer. She had to have something in there that would help. If only they were in London, she could get him to the Warden infirmary. She didn't care if he was a pirate; let W.O.R. try to stop her from fixing him.

A wad of muslin would help a bit. She had to take her hand from beneath him long enough to grab the cloth and shove it under his back. That would apply pressure and help slow the bleeding.

Where the hell was Dash?

Mac's glassy gaze met hers. "I think this might be it, Doc."

"No. It's not. Say that again, I'll end you myself."

His hand curved over the one pressing against his side. "Worst thing I ever did was let you walk away."

The burning she'd tried so hard to contain rose hot and wet behind her eyes. "Don't talk." *Don't say things you might not mean.*

"It's true. Should have dragged you back kicking and screaming. Never should have let you go. Never loved anyone else. I want you to know that."

Oh, damn. A tear slid down her cheek and there was nothing she could do to stop it. Mac's hand left hers and touched her cheek, wiping away the tear, leaving a smear of blood in its place—she could feel it warm and sticky. "Shouldn't cry for me."

And that made it all the worse. "You son of a bitch. Don't you do this to me!" She slapped his face hard when his eyes started to close. His lids jerked back open. "Don't you dare die. You don't get to leave me, Mac. Not this time."

His brow furrowed as he looked at her. Could he even see her? His gaze had lost focus. "You're the one who left, woman, after patching me up and sending me out on my own. It would serve you right if I died on you. I'm going to haunt you, too. Next . . . next time you take a bath I'm going to be perched on the towel warmer watching."

It was a strange thing, smiling and crying at the same time. "I'll be sure to put on a show." He was slipping away. All her training and technology—all her intelligence—and she couldn't save him. Could fate surely be so cruel as to throw them together once again only to have it end like this?

Perhaps this was the way it was meant to end. Perhaps she'd only bought him extra time when she gave him new lungs. Perhaps this was God's way of telling her to stay the hell out of His territory.

"Make sure Imogen gets to London," Mac's voice was little more than a whisper. "Evie, promise me you'll take her to Dhanya."

"Dhanya?" She couldn't have been more surprised if he'd asked her to take his wife to see Father Christmas. "What does Dhanya—?"

She was cut off by the arrival of Dash, who came running back, slamming to his knees beside her. With him he had transfusion equipment, surgical instruments, bandages and a bottle filled with a viscous, slight pink fluid, the sight of which made Evie's heart skip a beat.

Of course he would have some of her healing elixir. He was a Warden. When she discovered the formula, Dhanya had made certain it was delivered into the hands of other Warden medical officers. Did she laugh, cry or rage in response?

She did none of those, but she grabbed the bottle from his hand, ripped the cork out with her teeth and then poured the entire contents directly into Mac's wound.

"Damnation!" he cried, eyes wide. "What the hell?"

Obviously he'd discovered swearing in English during their separation. "Be quiet," she commanded. "For once, just be quiet and let me help you."

"Like you helped me last time? Stitched me up and then tossed me aside like I wasn't worth spit."

The hurt in his tone struck a chord, but she wasn't going to have this conversation in front of a stranger, and especially not when she was trying to save the bastard's life! "Either that or bathe fully clothed from here on out."

He didn't seem to know what to say. No, that wasn't it. He'd passed out.

"Mac?" Panic welled in her chest.

No answer.

"Is he . . . ?" That was all Dash seemed to have to say.

Evie pressed her ear to Mac's chest, searching, praying for a heartbeat. Where the hell was his heartbeat? Why couldn't she hear the bellows sucking in air? No. No. *Nonononono*.

Other people had arrived—the crew. She ignored their panicked questions and shouts. Let Dash deal with them.

She hit Mac with the bottom of her fist hard in the chest. "You do not get to die!" she shouted. She hit him again. And when Dash tried to pull her away, she hit him, too, and then Mac a third time. She shoved Dash away, stumbling on her knees to fall hard on her palms, both of which were on either side of Mac's gorgeous, thick head.

"You come back to me," she ordered, giving his chest another thwack. "You come back to me *now*."

Mac's eyes flew open as his chest arched. He sucked in air with a ragged gasp, gaze darting about as though he didn't know what was happening. Then those beautiful eyes that were a mix of faded blue and hazel looked directly into hers.

"You got me back," he rasped. "Now what are you going to do with me?"

Chapter 8

She kissed him. Grabbed him by the lapels and hauled his shoulders off the ground just enough to plant a solid, closed-lipped, joyous smack on his wisecracking mouth. He groaned, but she didn't fool herself into thinking it was out of pleasure.

The cheering of the crew made her let him go. Evie didn't look at him, but rather rose to her knees and addressed his shipmates. "Get him to his cabin. And for God's sake, be gentle with him."

McNamara, Pliny and Eli came forward to assist their captain.

"The rest of you, back to the ship," Nell ordered. Then she turned to Evelyn. "You all right?"

No, she really wasn't. She nodded. "Fine. Go look after Mac. I'll be there in a tick."

Nell wasn't stupid; she knew when she was being asked to leave. She nodded, dipped her head at Dash and then jogged back to the ship.

That left Evie alone with Dash.

"Say or ask whatever's on your mind," he said, leaning on the hilt of his sword. The tip pressed into the dock, blood pooling around it. "But be quick about it. I put a call into I.T. This place will be crawling with investigators and disassembling crews very soon."

Disassemblers—people who came in and cleaned up the strange and bizarre so that most of the modern world could go on believing they lived in a safe and remarkable age. Science, for all its wonders, was every bit as dark as it was light.

Evie used her forearm to mop her brow. Her hands were covered in Mac's blood. She was numb inside—not even the decapitated monster affected her. "We can't get back into the air without those repairs."

"Don't worry; they'll get done."

She met his gaze with a direct one of her own. "Won't the Wardens arrest Mac?"

"You let me worry about the Wardens."

"I'd love to do just that, Mr. Evans, but you'll have to forgive me that I'm a bit skeptical about your ability to protect anyone."

He actually chuckled. "I see what he likes about you."

Didn't he mean "liked"? Past tense. "Please don't try to flatter me. I want to know what the hell happened here that resulted in so many deaths."

"Sabotage is what happened. That thing was locked up tighter than a—well, never mind what. The point is, it was secure."

She hadn't expected so exact or quick an answer. "I beg your pardon? Are you saying someone intentionally let that creature free?"

Dash nodded. "That's my meaning exactly. We don't do anything half-arsed in I.T., Miss Stone. If we lock something up, it stays that way."

"Doctor," she corrected.

His lips lifted in one of those damnable half smiles. Oh, if she wasn't shaking so badly she'd punch him in the face. Trembling and cold. Damn, she was in shock. "You're a ballsy woman, *Dr.* Stone. Some men find that an attractive trait."

"The same sort of men who think shameless flattery like that actually works, I suspect. Mr. Evans, why would someone want to let such a creature run loose?"

He leaned the sword up against the small building that obviously served as some sort of office and moved toward her. "I could ask you the same thing. I've seen some damn strange things in my life, especially as a member of I.T., and I've never had a creature get loose. That makes me think it was someone on the *Queen V.*"

Her spine snapped rigid. "That's absurd. Most of that crew's been with Mac for years. Surely there were people here who could be just as much to blame."

He held his hands out to his sides, palms up. "You see anyone else around who's still breathing? There was no one else here but me, and the crew of the ship that brought the thing here, and they're all dead, except for those two who could have been helped by that little pink bottle you emptied on the man you walked out on three years ago. Let me ask you, Doctor, why do you think it was let loose? It almost killed Mac, kept you distracted and just got three-quarters of the crew off the ship."

Blood rushed from Evelyn's head to her feet. The world, already tipsy, dipped and spun. She turned toward the ship, grabbed up her bag and ran. Was it Harrigan and his crew? Had they caught up with them so quickly? Her heart smashed against her ribs as panic set in.

Her boot heels struck hard as she ascended to the *Queen V*. The deck appeared deserted. Everyone was with their fallen captain, which meant no one was with his wife.

Something in the back of her mind made her skid to a halt at the top of the stairs leading belowdecks. It was as though her mind suddenly decided to catch up with her feet. She couldn't go tearing down there with the entire crew gathered at Mac's bedside. Most of them didn't know what was truly the matter with Mac's wife, and if she ran down there like a madwoman, they'd begin to wonder.

Slowly one foot preceded the other down the steps, each worn smooth by years of traffic. Instead of heading directly to Imogen's cabin, she joined the crowd in and around Mac's. The crew stepped back to clear a path for her—the magical woman who had saved their captain's hide a second time.

She should be heartily tired of saving the man's

pert arse, but for the life of her she couldn't summon the ire or indignation necessary. Evil had been defeated, Mac was alive and she had blood on her hands. All in all, it was a grand day and dawn was a mere suspicion on the horizon.

"How's the invalid?" she asked. The silence that had fallen at her arrival was deafening.

"He's sore," Mac replied, voice hoarse. "He feels like bees are buzzing under his skin, and he's in a very foul mood."

"Wouldn't be right if you weren't," she shot back. For a second—and only one—she allowed herself the bleak thought that she was the cause of his foul mood, that her kiss had angered him. But then she reminded herself that he had almost kissed her not long ago on deck, and hadn't anything like her excuse. She would have kissed anyone if she'd managed to bring them back from the brink—and she was going to take full credit for it seeing as how the pink goo she'd used was of her own invention for the Wardens. It was a miracle when it came to healing, forcing tissue to knit itself back together with incredible swiftness and renewing flesh at a cellular level.

On second thought, she wouldn't kiss just anyone. Dirty Joe was one whose lips she'd avoid—for obvious reasons. Pliny was another. He was a lovely man, but he smelled slightly of beets and bay rum—not the most pleasant of combinations, especially when mixed with sweat.

"I'm going to wash up," she told him. Obviously

there was no hiding the fact that she was covered in blood. "I'll be back to check on you in a bit."

"You don't have to fuss over me, Doc."

She knew that tone. She'd heard it a few times during the course of their relationship. It was his you-don't-have-to-humor-me and I'll-martyr-myself-if-I-want voice, which meant that he was quite uncomfortable and was going to let every-one know it with a series of growls, sighs and per-haps the odd profanity since he seemed to have developed a proclivity.

"That buzzing is from the accelerated healing pro-cess your body is experiencing at the moment. It will end soon enough. It should also take much of the soreness and discomfort you're experiencing with it. I can give you some laudanum if you need it."

He grimaced. Even flat on his back, back from the brink of death and covered in blood—some of which was actually his—he was completely in charge, the very picture of the ideal alpha male.

"I'm fine." His scowl declared him a liar. "Go wash that blood off yourself and then get back here as soon as possible. I need to be back on deck so we can leave as soon as the repairs are done."

"I'm not part of your crew, so I don't take orders from you, Captain." She said it with a smile, making the room chuckle. "I'll check in on you in a moment. Nell, might I have a word?"

The older woman didn't speak or change her ex-pression, but merely followed Evie out the door.

"I want you to come with me to check on Imogen," she whispered.

Nell's eyes widened. She was an intuitive woman, and would know that if Evie wanted her assistance, it must be serious.

The door to Imogen's room was unlocked.

"Damn," Nell swore. "I forgot to latch it. Didn't think I'd need to with Napoleon in there."

Evelyn turned the knob and opened the door, expecting the worst. Instead, she was greeted with the sight of a slumbering woman with a huge beast of a dog on the floor by her feet.

"Oh, thank God," she breathed. She and Nell stepped into the room and closed the door. Napoleon thumped his tale once, peering up at them from beneath his lashes. He was such a shameless flirt.

"I've got to wash my hands. My fingers are starting to stick together."

Nell made a face, her complexion going slightly gray as she looked at Evelyn's hands. "He almost died, didn't he?"

Evelyn went to the washstand and reached for the heavy brass pitcher nesting amongst coiled metal tubes upon which it rested. The tubes circulated steam, which heated them and then heated the pitcher and the water within it. A wooden handle kept it from burning any fingers that curled around it.

"Let me. You'll drop it with your hands so slick." Nell lifted the pitcher. "Put your hands over the basin."

Evie did as she was told, and her old friend
poured the just-shy-of-hot water over her hands. It
felt divine. She rubbed her hands over each other,
loosening the dried blood before reaching for the
soap. Once she had lathered and scrubbed, and used
a brush under nails, Nell poured more water for her.
Hands clean, she rinsed the soap and brush and put
them back in their respective places.

"I'll dump the basin," Nell told her.

The ship was equipped with a small water closet
and bath. Many of the crew often took baths in tin
tubs in the crew quarters, except for Nell, of course,
and the odd time one of the men wanted privacy.
Mac had a tiny shower bath and toilet in a space that
used to be a closet in his cabin. How the two of them
had ever managed to cohabit for any length of time
in that confined space, on this little ship, was a mystery to her, but it never felt like a sacrifice. She'd
loved the time she spent with the crew of the *Queen
V.* She even kind of loved the old girl.

While Nell was gone, Evelyn wiped down the
outside of her leather case and then her own face. A
glimpse in the mirror showed a faint amount of
blood. It didn't seem to matter what she did; she always ended up swimming in the stuff.

Mac had almost died.

Her fingers curved around the foot of the bed,
steadying her as the world dipped and swayed.
They weren't in the air, so she couldn't blame anything but her own emotions. She needed a drink.

And she needed absolution. She glanced at the

woman on the bed, guilt rippling down her spine. In her hand, Evie had held a vial of the incredible accelerated healing serum she'd discovered and used on Warden agents. She'd used practically the entirety of that vial on Mac, without a thought to his wife.

She could excuse herself by saying Mac's life was in more danger—though she could probably shoot that one down herself without really trying. He was doing everything in his power to save this woman and get her safely back to England, and Evelyn would toss her over the bow if it meant saving Mac.

That was not a good feeling to have as a doctor. She did not pick sides, nor decide who got to live and who must die. Her job—her sworn duty—was to ensure that everyone who crossed her path got the same chance at survival.

She'd tucked the bottle in her bag. She removed it now, lifting it to the light. There was a tiny little bit of pink pooled at the bottom. It would have to do.

She pulled back the blankets and removed the bandages around the woman's middle. The wound was still angry looking, but not as much as it had been. Imogen stirred, thick lashes fluttering open. "Doctor?"

Evie smiled. "Sorry to wake you. I'm just going to clean this up a bit, all right? I'll be done in no time. Are you in pain?"

Pale brow furrowed. "I am."

Evie withdrew a small bottle and a metal syringe from her bag. She drew a small amount of laudanum from the bottle into the syringe and then injected it into Imogen's arm. "There. You should feel better in a few moments. You just relax and try to go back to sleep."

"All right." Her eyelids were already drooping. "Why was the dog barking?"

"What?" Evie asked with a frown of her own, but she received no answer. It would do no good to try to rouse the woman and talk to her—not with just having injected her with an opiate. Her only option was to continue on as she'd intended.

First, she bathed the area in whiskey; then using her index finger, Evie scooped out as much of the slightly viscous liquid as she could and lightly spread it over the worst of the carnage that was Imogen's wound. Once she was certain she'd gotten all she could, she followed up with a layer of honey from the jar she kept in her bag. Honey would keep the bandages from absorbing the healing goo; plus it had healing properties of its own. She wiped her hands, reapplied bandages, discarded those that were soiled and used a little whiskey to clean her hands since Nell had yet to return.

Where was she? It didn't take that long to empty a basin of bloody water into the loo, did it? Of course, she was acting captain until Mac recovered, so perhaps she was needed elsewhere.

That left her with a little too much time on her hands. She didn't want to go check on Mac without having someone look after Imogen.

Speaking of guardians . . .

She turned to the other occupant of the cabin. If something had transpired in this room while everyone else was gone, he was the only witness. Had the circumstances been different, more commonplace, she would have felt foolish. It wasn't foolishness that had dread pooling in her belly.

"Here, boy." A pat on her thigh was all the encouragement the big Newfoundland needed. He rose slowly to his feet, and turned the few degrees necessary to plop his massive head onto her lap. Evelyn stroked his broad head.

There was blood on his muzzle—just a little. Again, under most circumstances she would assume he cut his lip or gums on a sharp piece of bone, but when he opened his great mouth to pant, she spied something caught around one of his bottom teeth. Napoleon had always been a very gentle dog, so she had no problem plucking the foreign matter from the drool pond that was his mouth. She'd had her hands in some pretty off-putting places, but something about sticking her hand in a mouth—be it human or animal—made her positively spleeny.

It was fabric. It looked to be part of a shirt, one that was faded, the cloth worn thin. The kind of shirt a man who spent most of the year on a ship and rarely got to a tailor might own.

Someone had come into this room while they were gone—just as she had feared—but they hadn't expected Napoleon to be there, and protective as the Newfoundland was, he put up a ruckus. When barking didn't work, he made a grab for the intruder.

Judging from the sodden fabric and the speckles of blood on his muzzle, Evie wagered he took a bite.

Had it been one of Mac's crew? No. They were as loyal as the day long. She doubted Napoleon would attack one of them. But if not crew, who? And maybe Napoleon only snapped to protect his master's wife.

He'd once bit Pliny on the backside because the crewman pretended that he was going to grab Evelyn. He'd been a pup at that point, but still a big enough dog that Pliny had trouble sitting for a few days.

"You're a good boy," she praised the dog, and got a face full of exuberant, hot canine breath in return. She was going to have to tell Mac about this, although she had the feeling he wasn't going to be surprised. He'd brought her into the middle of a very dangerous and secretive situation. Evelyn didn't like secrets, and didn't much care for danger. She was more on the side of prolonging life rather than risking it at every turn.

She wrapped the wet fabric in a small piece of cut bandage and tucked it into her pocket. It was time for her to check on her other patient.

He had some explaining to do.

The woman could have cowed Nelson—Wellington even. Hell, if she'd been alive at the time, *she* could have defeated Napoleon with nothing more than an arched eyebrow before the war even started.

Mac was on his back, propped up just enough against the few pillows he had on his bed so as not to feel like an invalid. Not that it mattered. As soon as Queen Evie stomped into his cabin and ordered everyone out, he felt particularly vulnerable—and not just because the confounding woman, who had tossed him aside like the contents of a chamber pot, seemed hell-bent on making certain he lived long enough to regret ever seeing her unforgettable face. When he finally did give up the ghost, she would be the last thing he thought about; he just knew it.

He waited until they were alone, the door shut, before speaking. "The last time I saw that expression on your face, you tore me apart for that Belgian fiasco."

"You almost got us both killed," she reminded him coolly.

"I also got us out of there, which is the most important part of the story."

"You were responsible for why we were there in the first place. Getting us out doesn't change that."

He smiled, because there was no real coldness to her tone. There were times when he knew she loved the danger as much as he had. Or perhaps he'd just wanted her to. Not that it mattered anymore. "What's the worry, Doc? Come to kick me for getting you involved with the I.T. monster? Take your best shot, but I think I paid for that one already."

Evie scowled. She was a decidedly fierce woman when frustrated or angry. He liked to think of her as perpetually irritable, better suited for dealing with as few people as possible, hence her placement deep within the bowels of Wardens of the Realm headquarters in London. She fixed people up if there was anything left to fix and then shipped them out again. She rarely ever saw violent death, or witnessed the horrendous injuries being inflicted. That kind of distance made it easy to forget that the damage had been intentionally dealt. She could deal with the bloodshed, but not be of the bloodshed.

When she tossed him over, she thought she'd never have to face him again. Had she really believed he would let her run away like a coward without rubbing it in her face when the opportunity arose? True, he wasn't painting himself as the great adventurer and hero that he'd hoped, but then again she wasn't exactly flawless, either.

She took something from her trouser pocket and offered it to him. It was a square of gauzy fabric—the kind used for bandages. He opened it and found another piece of fabric inside.

His nose wrinkled. "Why does this smell like dog breath?"

"Because it came out of Napoleon's mouth."

"He didn't eat something of yours, did he? I thought he'd grown out of that."

For a moment she looked completely surprised. "You haven't trained him not to do that yet? Mac, he's not a puppy. He's a four-year-old who doesn't know his own strength. He could eat my entire suitcase if he wanted. No, he did not eat anything. Not anything of mine."

He blinked. "Get to the point. I'm tired and I have to take a piss."

"I can help—"

"No, you certainly cannot." He spoke calmly, in a tone his mother often used to let him know the penalty for disobeying her would be a switch across the back of his legs. "You can tell me what the hell you're being so secretive about."

"I'm secretive?" Her eyes flashed onyx. "I don't think you've told me one scrap of truth since you abducted me."

"I didn't abduct you. I offered you a free flight home. W.O.R. should be ecstatic to save a bit of coin on your return trip."

"You brought me aboard this bird to save the life of your wife. I did that, and I didn't ask too many questions, but that changes now. Harrigan sneaked onto the ship to kill her. And now someone else has been in her room, whatever their intentions."

"Wait." Had he heard that correctly? His attention span wasn't quite what it ought to be with all the delicious medicine in his blood. He wasn't even capable of being as alarmed as he knew he should be. "Who was in her room?"

"A man who is missing a piece of his cuff," she replied—a little snottily in his opinion. "And a little chunk of himself, thanks to Napoleon. I understand you need to be . . . delicate with this, but, Mac, I need to know what's going on."

No, she really didn't. "The information she has is priceless. There are those who don't want it to make it to the Wardens."

"Well, yes. I deduced that for myself. Napoleon

took a bite of someone tonight. Someone who I assume wanted to hurt Imogen."

"A member of the crew," he supplied, filling in the blanks for her. "Why do you think I nabbed you, Doc? I needed the best doctor I could find, and I needed one I could trust not to gossip. I needed someone who knows my crew but also has a wider experience with the world. Someone who would notice suspicious behavior." That and the fact that he heard she was in Vienna and that she was sleeping with a younger man. If he wasn't having sex, then she wouldn't, either.

"So, what? You take her to London and hope the Wardens don't catch you as you deliver her into their hands?"

"I'm not wanted to give evidence or to stand trial. There's no reason for them to detain me other than to record my version of events. I'm not afraid of W.O.R., Evie. You should try it for yourself."

"I'm not afraid," she replied, scowling. "I'm afraid that you're going to get me into a situation I may not survive, or one that would make me have doubts concerning my career. *You're* the one who frightens me, not any of them."

He laughed—it hurt horribly. *Christ on the cross!* "Why?"

"Because you honestly believe that ignorance is the best way to keep those around you safe. It's not—it will get them killed."

He hadn't kept Theodore in ignorance. In fact, he'd been the one kept in the dark, and he was the only one involved in that scenario who made it out relatively unscathed. Theo was dead, and Mac had no idea what he'd died to protect.

"What would you like to know, Doc? Ask me any question and I'll answer it." He must still be floating on a morphine cloud to make such an offer. What difference did it make? They were over, and once they were in England she'd leave him again. Leaving was what she did.

But she could have left already. Dash would have gotten her home. Maybe she had plans to hand him over to the Wardens herself. She'd be in for a surprise then, wouldn't she?

She looked as though she didn't know where to start.

"I have one for you," he said. "Why are you still here? You could be halfway to London by now, or back to your boy in Vienna."

She snorted. "He wouldn't be worth the trip."

A little prodding was needed it seemed. "So why hang about?"

"You need me," she said bluntly. "A doctor, I mean."

"Of course." That wasn't what she meant at all, and he liked it.

She glared. "Wipe that smirk off your face. Once we're in London I'll no longer interfere in your suicide attempts."

Mac rolled his eyes. "That's a little dramatic, don't you think?"

"Not at all. You've always run headlong into danger. You'll fight anything for anybody—except me, of course."

Now, that was a lie. "I seem to remember a particularly burly man in Ireland who wanted to take you home with him. Didn't I convince him otherwise—eventually?" Now that he thought about it . . . "And that Amazon woman in Romania. She tried to skewer me when you told her that you were already involved with someone."

"That's not what I mean. You'll take on all comers, but you wouldn't fight for me. You wouldn't fight to keep me."

If she had chosen that moment to spontaneously shoot fireworks out her posterior, he couldn't have been more surprised. "I was in the hospital, learning how to breathe again! You walked away when I had very little fight in me, Evelyn. And you took most of what was left with you."

She glanced away—coward. "You have to be the hero, Mac. Always the hero."

"Are you mad? I'm not the hero, Evie. I never have been. I'm the one who gets the hero home. The one who drops him into a secret mission. Dash, he's a hero. You're a hero. I just keep you all in business."

"That's ridiculous. You love being the center of attention."

"Are you accusing me of being an attention whore? Because it takes one to know one, darlin'."

Her hands clenched into fists. "You love the notoriety. The excitement."

"I'm generally happy to escape a situation relatively unscathed, yes. A pat on the head never hurt anyone."

She could cheerfully strangle him; he could see it in her eyes. Her nose—straight and strong with a slight tilt—flared even more as she sucked in a breath. "I couldn't watch you risk your life anymore, knowing that someday I wouldn't be able to put you back together. It was selfish of you to expect it of me."

"Did it ever occur to you to ask me to give it up?"

"And have you despise me for it later? No, thank you. It was abundantly clear that you loved the danger more than you ever loved me."

Something snapped. It might have been his healing flesh, or maybe the resentment he'd carried for three years. "You destroyed my pride, left me so that the sky was all I had left." He clenched his jaw, but the words broke past. "You broke my fucking heart!"

Oh, if only he had some way to capture the expression on her face, but he hadn't any photographic equipment.

"Of course I didn't chase you, didn't fight for you. You saved my life and then robbed me of the only thing I had to live for—you."

Baring his soul was worth it when her eyes widened in horror.

"How could I fight *for* you, Evie, when I would have been fighting *you*?"

Chapter 9

Evie didn't know what to say. So, after a moment of silence, she said, "I need to check that wound."

Mac, gentleman that he wasn't, didn't let her off the hook so easily. "I'm afraid you'd have to crack me open—my heart is still on the inside."

"And in fine working order, I'll wager." Let him try to disconcert her. This was what he did, this tossing about of words until you were dizzy from just trying to catch up. He'd try to incite a riot of guilt inside her.

"What's the matter, Doc? Don't want to talk about it now that you've been given a share of the blame?"

"Perhaps I oughtn't have behaved as I did," she allowed, not meeting his gaze as she sorted through her bag. "But it wouldn't have mattered. You would have resented me forever for asking you to give up flying."

"Have you added divining the future to your list of talents?"

She made a face at him. "You know very well it's true."

Suddenly he looked very sad. "You don't know me at all."

She knew him better than he knew himself! She didn't say this, though. She was tired, and had obviously ended up in the middle of another dangerous situation with Mac. Once they were back in the sky, it would be only a matter of a couple of days before they reached England and her life went back to normal. Surely she could last a few days without dissolving into a raving harpy?

Evie sighed. "Just let me check your wound, Gavin. Then I'll leave you alone."

There was something in his expression that made her throat tight. "What?"

"You've never called me by my first name."

"Well, perhaps it's time I did." Perhaps, in order to move forward with her life, she had to stop thinking of and treating him as though he were the same man she had loved three years ago. Maybe that was the only way either of them could get past the hurt and the anger. Or maybe it was just something to tell herself so she didn't start thinking that leaving him had been the biggest mistake of her life.

As though she hadn't thought it countless times in the last one thousand, one hundred and sixty-two days.

She gently pulled back the blanket. Up until this

point she'd been able to ignore that he was shirtless because she was more concerned about his injury than his chest. Now she had to admit interest was pretty much even for both. He'd always been lean with broad shoulders and narrow hips, but he seemed . . . harder than he had before. Or maybe she just appreciated it more now that she couldn't touch him whenever she wanted.

Ugh. What romantic pap. She was too old to make up nonsense like that.

Her makeshift bandages were still in place. Someone had thought to put a towel over the bottom sheet so as not to get it bloody.

"Tell me if I hurt you," she said.

"Ow."

Sigh. *Count to ten.* She raised her gaze to his. "I haven't touched you yet."

He smiled coolly. "Thought I'd say it now in case you run away before I can say it later."

"You're an arse."

"And you're a coward."

Evie clenched her fists. "Shut up and let me do my job."

Mac held up his hands. "Go ahead. Wouldn't dream of stopping you, since it's your fault I got hurt in the first place."

"Excuse me? I saved your sorry life."

"If you had gotten out of the way, I would have been able to shoot the damn thing."

She could have hit him. Instead, she mourned the fact that he was less of a gentleman than he used to be. Swearing. What was next, kicking puppies? Never mind that she had a vocabulary that would make more sailors blush.

"I knew what I was doing."

"Yeah? Looked to me like *you* were playing the hero. Ow! Damn it, woman!"

Smiling, Evie held up the bandage she'd ripped away. Blood stuck to his skin and hair like thick glue. One of the aspects of the healing compound was that it made blood age and sometimes clot much faster than normal. "Sorry. Better to just rip these off." She tossed the soiled fabric onto the floor and reached for clean rags and the Listerine—which someone had gotten from Dash, she assumed, as there'd been nothing but whiskey to use before. She preferred the sterile fluid to spirits anyway. The more whiskey left in the bottle, the more she could drink.

He hissed slightly when she began to clean the wound. Of course the sound went straight to her imbecilic heart. His flesh was healing nicely already. That liquid was the best achievement of her medical career. Really, it was just a mixture of natural compounds that promoted healing put through a simple process that required an Aetherical charge before bottling.

The faint scar—not much thicker than the lead of a pencil—that ran from the top of his chest all the way to his navel caught her eye.

That was the crowning achievement of her career.

"Doc?"

She ignored him. Her hand moved without her permission, but with sure purpose. She prided herself on the stillness of her fingers—they rarely trembled. They trembled now, though. Just a little. She touched that thin ridge, her throat clenching at the contact. His skin was golden, lighter than her own. And that scar was even paler.

Memories of that day assaulted her mind, slamming down from all angles, each like a punch in the gut. She remembered little of the surgery—that had been done without her emotions present. She knew what to do and she shut everything else down so her hands could do it.

The accident. The terrible concave of his chest. The blood pouring from his mouth and nose as he slowly suffocated.

The realization that if he died she would want to die, too. And madness. She lost her mind for a little while, and that was good. Saving the life of the man you loved was so much easier when you didn't—couldn't—think about it.

Warm, slightly dirty fingers closed over hers. She'd have to wash her hands again before she redressed the wound. Mac squeezed her hand.

Don't look at him. Don't meet his gaze. Making demands of herself didn't work. She tore her attention away from their intertwined fingers. Were those hers pressed so hard against his chest, feeling the beat of his heart, the rise and fall of the lungs she had given him?

Her gaze met his.

Wham. Like slamming her head on the corner of the cupboard, only twice as painful.

It was all there in his lovely eyes: blame, regret, contrition, anger, sadness and a tenderness she thought she'd never see again. She had hurt him— terribly so. She hadn't really considered that when she left; she'd thought only of her own pain, and the certainty that he wouldn't live to see his next birth-day.

He'd had two since then. Two of which she had not been a part.

She leaned closer. What was she doing? She was going to kiss him if she didn't stop herself.

He was a *married* man.

That stopped her.

"I was certain you were going to get yourself killed," she whispered. The tightness in her throat would not allow for more. "It was too painful for me to stand by and wait for it to happen. I couldn't live like that anymore."

"You'd rather have a lifetime of regret than a few years of something wonderful?"

When put that way it sounded as though she was unhinged. She leaned closer. "I'd rather leave you than have you taken from me."

Mac blinked. Obviously he had not expected her to blurt out such a confession, but what did it matter now? It was over. Done. He was married to someone else.

Married to her *patient*.

That was a pot of cold piss tossed in her face. She

jerked back, refocusing on the task at hand. "It's already starting to heal."

"Dash always has the best medicine. I reckon W.O.R. supplies him."

"They do. The compound I used from his stock was an invention of my own. It speeds up a body's natural healing cycle." Why did she tell him that? She sounded as though she was bragging, or looking for a pat on the head.

"How is it you're friends with Evans even though he's a Warden?" she asked as she began to gently wipe away the dried blood from his skin. The wound might be healing, but she still had to be careful. No hurting him for sport now.

"I'd be a pretty sorry excuse for a friend if something like that mattered."

"He's sworn an oath to turn pirates in to the authorities. He could lose his position because of your friendship. Shouldn't that matter?"

She glanced up to find him smirking at her. "You think you know everything, don't you? Must be a lovely place, inside that mind of yours. All applause and accolades for the magnificent genius that is you."

It was an old argument. Being reckless and impulsive, he often mistook her voice of reason as judgment and censorship. She hadn't wanted to change him so much as make him think before he acted.

"Where you're concerned I'm right more often than I'm wrong," she informed him. And there had been times she wanted to be oh so very wrong.

"You aren't as smart as you think, Doc."

"Be glad I'm as smart as I am, MacRae, else you'd be long dead."

His smirk faded, replaced by something darker, spiked with hurt. "As long as you're alive to rub my face in it, how could I ever forget?"

He was the most annoying man she'd ever known. So why didn't she pull her hand from his? The beat of his heart was distracting. "I haven't seen you in three years. How—in the name of all that's good and holy—could I rub your face in anything?"

"Every time I heard someone praise you—or worse, ask about you—it was like being poked with a blade. Every time I encountered some dim-witted boy who bragged about shagging you, it was another slap."

"Someone bragged about going to bed with me?" It was the wrong question to ask, the wrong thing to focus on, but it was oddly flattering.

"More than one." A dangerous glint lit his eyes. "Took a few broken knuckles before I learned to stop punching each and every one of them."

How chivalrous of him. "I have not had enough bed partners for that statement to be the least bit truthful."

Mac shrugged. "None of my business, is it? Took me a while, but I eventually figured that out as well. *You* weren't my business."

"You poor, tormented man." She couldn't stop the sneer. "Do you think it was any easier for me hearing how you danced from one dangerous escapade to another? I'd done all I could to keep you from dying and still you courted death like an impoverished peer after an American heiress. I heard women talk about you, too. You don't think that was a slap in my face?"

"You don't get to be defensive, Evie. *You* left me."

She yanked her fingers free of his and went back to cleaning up his torn flesh. She was so tempted to jab the wound with her finger, just to make him miserable, but that would be dangerous, not to mention childish. "Because you didn't give me a choice."

"You didn't give me one, either."

Hadn't she? She thought she had. No, she *knew* she had. Right? "It doesn't matter anymore. I don't know why you insist on going on about it. It was years ago. It's over."

It was as though a door slammed between them. Evie couldn't pinpoint exactly what changed in his expression or posture because he was as still as a statue, but she felt it.

And she wished she could take it back.

"You're right," he said, clipped. "Hurry up, will you? I'm exhausted and I'd like to finally get some sleep. You should as well. Nell will check on Imogen if you want to sleep in her cabin."

Impulse told her to argue, but there was nothing to argue about. She was tired and needed to sleep. And if his suspicions were right about his crew, then Nell was the only person she could trust other than Mac himself.

"Do you want me to leave you some laudanum?" she asked, in her most doctorly of tones.

"No. I have some in the drawer." He nodded at his bedside table. "When you go, could you tell my sister to come in, please?"

"Of course." He'd asked fairly politely, given that his jaw was clenched. She could berate him, tell him how much he needed rest to finish healing, but there was no point in making a shrew of herself. He knew all these things. Plus, he looked as if he hadn't slept in days. If he wanted to talk to Nell, then she wasn't going to stop him. He most likely wanted to share Evie's suspicions with her, and instructions for getting the ship back in the air as soon as possible.

He said nothing more while she finished her task. Twice she heard him suck in a short breath, but he didn't complain and barely moved. If it weren't for the warmth of his skin, and the sheer beauty of the musculature beneath it, she'd think he wasn't real, or that he'd fainted. A quick glance confirmed that he was indeed awake.

He was watching her.

Once she was satisfied that the area around the wound was sufficiently clean, she covered the expanse of injured flesh with the same honey she'd used on his wife. She had taken care not to clean the inside of the wound, where the healing solution would still be working. She wiped the honey from her hands and then quickly applied pads of bandages to both entrance and exit wounds before wrapping a length of linen around his torso several times.

"Do not remove this dressing," she commanded. "It needs to stay on for at least six hours." No doubt he'd still be asleep when the six hours ran out. Every minute was extra healing, and he needed that most desperately. It made sense that the more serious the wound, the longer the medicine needed to work its magic.

"Fine." He yawned. "Are we done?"

God, he could be *such* a petulant bastard! She wanted to say *A long time ago*, but that seemed unnecessarily cruel. Not to mention that it was exactly what he could have said himself if anyone asked.

"Entirely," she replied, closing her bag. She rose to her feet. "Remember, you need to heal completely before you can return to work. Nothing strenuous for at least two or three days." She knew better than to order him to bed rest. He simply wouldn't do it. Being idle would drive him up the nearest tree, which in turn would make life difficult for the crew.

How could one of his assembled family betray him?

He saluted her with that damn smirk still on his lips. "Yes, Doctor."

She could force him to eat her bag and the contents of it, but again that was a schoolboy type of thought. She couldn't dismiss everything he said as blatant lies and concealed truths; she was ready for a break from it.

At the door, she paused. There was one thing she

could do: "Mac, I'm sorry for hurting you. I never meant to."

His gaze locked with hers. "I know. You didn't think of me at all."

Evie swallowed. It was true. She hadn't thought of how her leaving would affect him—not really. She knew he'd be hurt, but she had assumed he'd move on to his next adventure. She intentionally didn't think of how he would feel because all that mattered was protecting her own heart. She had been the one in danger of losing the person she loved, and in her selfishness she'd hurt them both. "I—"

"Close the door behind you, please, Doc." He closed his eyes and pulled the blankets up to his shoulders. "I don't want to be disturbed."

Lips tight, Evie left the room without another word.

"I want this damn ship in the air, *Dash*. Now." It had been seven hours since his . . . *discussion* with Evie, and Mac didn't feel any better about it. The sooner he got to London and rid of her, the better.

"They're working as diligently as they can, Mac. We'll have you in the sky before the cavalry arrives. You're going to have to grow some patience."

Mac gritted his teeth. They were in his cabin, each sitting on either side of his desk enjoying a glass of whiskey. "I've been shot, gored by a Minotaur and am trapped on what is essentially a floating cottage with my older sister, a bunch of men for whom bathing is a mystery and the woman responsible for my lack of a heart. I have plenty of patience, you bastard, and I'm at the end of it."

Dash—who really was a bastard, and a son of a bitch to boot—grinned at him. "A little conflict's good for a man. Keeps him on his toes. I wouldn't mind being trapped with the lovely doctor in such close quarters."

Lying on the floor beside the desk, Napoleon raised his huge head and chuffed. That was apparently all he had to say on the matter, as he immediately went back to sleep.

"You want her? Take her." He meant it, but he didn't. He'd kill anyone who tried to take her from him.

All the more reason to let her go. If it weren't for Imogen, he'd hand her over to Dash for transport back to London. The Wardens were going to want to talk to her about the Minotaur anyway. Irregular Transpirations was nothing if not thorough. But after she showed him the fabric she'd taken from Napoleon's teeth, he had no choice but to keep her close. Imogen's continued survival depended on it.

"She'd be safer with me," Dash remarked, green eyes narrowing thoughtfully. "Someone in your crew let that monster out."

Mac nodded. He'd known this conversation was going to happen. "I don't know who it is, but they don't want me to make it back to London."

"Is it you or the job?"

"Job. I think."

The other man nodded. He was in his early

thirties—about the same age as Mac, but his eyes seemed to belong to a man much older. It was a common trait amongst agents, both men and women, who had seen too much. His superiors at W.O.R. used to say what made Mac such a good operative was that his eyes didn't give him away.

He wondered if they did now.

"Anything I can do?" Dash asked.

Mac laughed—a sad attempt at humor. "And end up further in your debt? I'm going to owe you for the next five years after this carnage."

"Five?" He raised a brow. "Try ten."

"Not bloody likely." He might have genuinely grinned then were it not for the thought of all those people who had been killed because someone had targeted him. Logically he knew he couldn't blame himself for their deaths—he would have stopped them if he could have—but that didn't keep it from lying heavy on his conscience.

"I'll give the Wardens a full report," he added, even though it wasn't necessary. Dash knew he could depend on him; it was why they both cursed each other so often. They might never be friends, but they were already brothers of a sort.

"Be careful," Dash warned—unnecessarily. "If you're seen with W.O.R. agents, your façade as lawless renegade will be over."

Dash was one of the few people, other than Dhanya Withering, W.O.R. director, who knew that Mac was back in Crown employ. Of course, it was part of an agreement he'd made to keep Nell out of prison. She'd been taken into custody after a raid on one of their regular clients for whom they "exported" items into London.

Withering had approached him. Mac had planned to break Nell out and head for Italy, but he'd been offered a second chance at a life he thought long out of his reach.

It had also been Dhanya who first theorized that he had a traitor on his ship.

"I'll be careful." This close to the end, he had no intention of revealing himself. Evie accused him of trying to be a hero, but he wasn't. He was just exceptionally lucky. She'd always been something of a good luck charm for him—a fact further proved by the fact that she'd saved his life again.

"We'll have you in the air within the hour," Dash promised. "Can you wait that long?"

It would have to do. Thanks to Harrigan they were already way behind schedule. He needed to send word to Warden headquarters and update them on events. He didn't dare do that from the ship. Even with his portable telegraph, it was sometimes easy for people to intercept messages, especially if they were in close range with the right equipment. He would be stupid not to be paranoid.

In fact, he'd wonder if his room was "bugged" with auditory or viewing equipment if he didn't have a lovely gadget to ferret out those sorts of devices.

"Send word to the director for me?"

Dash nodded. "Of course. Just an update on your flight plan?"

"Yeah. For now I just need her to know we're on our way and our estimated arrival date. I've never been so eager to get back to England in my life." Not since the odd trip when he'd have to leave Evie behind. Having her on board used to make his life complete.

Rubbish.

He scribbled a brief list of things for Dash to say in his message to Dhanya, properly coded to save the other man the trouble.

"I can't remember my brother's birthday, but I can remember bloody ciphers and codes," Dash muttered with more than a hint of irony.

"One more reason to get out while we're still young enough." Mac folded the small sheet of paper and handed it to him.

Dash finished his drink and rose to his feet. "I'll go check on the men. It sounds as though they're done. We'll run a safety check and get you in the sky."

Mac also stood. He was a little stiff and battered from his ordeal with the Minotaur-man—the wound on his side itched and pulled annoyingly as it healed at a phenomenal rate—but it was better than the alternative. He offered his hand to the other man. "Thank you. I'm sorry for involving you in this."

"Not your fault. Fly safe, Mac." It wasn't just a trite saying.

"Come see me sometime you're in-country."

"You're really going to retire? Give all this up?"

"Happily."

Dash looked dubious, but he was respectful enough not to take it further. "I'll be sure to look you up."

He'd be surprised if that actually happened, but it was nice to hear it all the same. "Stay sharp."

After Dash left, Mac didn't remain at his desk. With a bottle of whiskey, there would be just too much temptation to keep drinking and wallowing—something he was not going to let himself do. There was no point. He appreciated Evie's apology, and that she finally seemed to realize how badly she'd behaved, so maybe now he'd move on. He had to move on, or he'd end up a bitter old man with nothing but regrets. He'd already seen his father end that way, and given that the man was a miserable bastard who didn't seem to care if his children liked him or not, Mac was determined not to let his life go in the same direction. Life was just too damn short.

Bracing his hands on the top of his desk, he pushed himself to his feet. Evie's elixir had done amazing work on the wound, but the rest of his body still felt as though it had been trampled. The stuff was in his blood now, though, and he could feel the aches and stiffness easing by slow degrees. He would probably be right as rain by evening.

God love science.

Slowly he made his way the short distance between his room and Imogen's. He unlocked the door and walked in to find his sister snoring softly in the chair by the bed.

Imogen was awake.

"Hello," he said. He tried not to frown at her strange expression. "Genny, are you all right?"

"No," she replied, voice hoarse. But it was her gaze that concerned him. Bold and direct as always, her eyes were filled with a rawness that unsettled him right down to the bone.

"Theo's dead, isn't he?"

Chapter 10

Every part of him wanted to lie. Look her in the eye and blatantly withhold the truth.

"Why would you ask me that, sweetheart?"

Her blue gaze was direct, and clearer than it had been since that awful day. Evie had used some of her magic potion on Imogen as well, apparently. "I feel it. I can't tell you how, but I know he's not with me anymore, at least not in this world."

That was impossible. Nonsense. Yet Mac's heart skipped in response. He'd had a similar feeling when Evie left him. Of course he knew she was still alive, but he felt her absence before anyone had the nerve to tell him she was gone. They'd lied to him then, told him she was with other patients, or that she was on assignment, but he knew. Even as friends looked him in the eye and told him otherwise—just so he'd want to live—he'd known that she wasn't coming back. Whether he gave up or went on was up to him.

And it should be up to Imogen. To hell with the Wardens. The information Imogen carried was not more important than the truth. Her husband had died for that information. Mac had almost died for it as well. He'd married a woman he didn't even love to protect it.

He didn't even know what it was.

He was done lying to protect it.

"He's gone, Genny. I'm sorry."

She nodded—one last moment of stoicism before tears filled her eyes. She began to weep, great racking sobs that came from the bottom of her soul and shook her entire body. It had to pain her to cry like that. Every tear had to feel as if it were ripping the wound in her torso wide-open.

Mac took a cushion from another chair and pressed it against her front. He didn't have to say anything. She wrapped her arms around it, holding it tight as she turned to her side, her breaths coming in ragged gasps.

Nell woke up, turning a startled and horrified gaze to her brother. Mac shook his head. Nell's shoulders slumped briefly. Then she got up and left the room. Mac followed, giving Imogen the privacy to mourn her husband.

In the corridor they encountered Evie. She was rumpled, dark braid mussed and loose, hair curling wildly around her head. She had sleep wrinkles on her left cheek. "What's wrong?" she demanded.

"Mac just told Imogen— Ow! Bloody hell, Gav!"

He refused to feel guilty. He hadn't punched her that hard, and it was only in the arm.

Evie's eyes narrowed. She was alert now. "Told Imogen what?"

"Something she deserved to know," he replied.

She stared at him.

He stared back.

"Really?" Dark brows knitted and rose. "You're not going to tell me?"

"No. I'm not." It wasn't because he was particularly cruel, though there was a certain satisfaction in knowing something she did not, no matter how awful it was, but he wasn't about to tell her that Imogen's husband was dead, because then she'd want to know why he had married her so slapdashedly and then he'd have to tell her that he was working for W.O.R., and he'd rather eat his own liver than tell her he sometimes worked for the very people he blamed for tearing them apart. He especially wasn't going to tell her after all that hero rubbish she talked.

"She's my patient," Evie insisted. "I have a right to know—"

"No," Mac bit out. "You don't." She seemed surprised by his reaction. "Maybe you like to pick and choose which patients are your responsibility, but not on my ship. When we dock in London you'll walk away from Imogen and never see her again. Do you really think that gives you the right to know something private that was shared between husband and wife? Something deserving of that anguish?" He pointed at the cabin door as he spoke.

Evelyn stared at him, as though seeing him for the first time. "What did you do to her?"

His jaw was clenched so tight it was a wonder his teeth didn't crack. "She asked me a question and I told her the truth."

"Yet when I ask questions I get obfuscation and lies."

"She's my wife. I don't owe you anything."

"Except for saving your life—twice. Is it your fault she got hurt, Mac? Did you rush in, guns blazing, and almost get her killed?"

Oh, he'd had quite enough of this. "You hate me for taking risks—fine. Hate me as deep and long as you want, Evie. Imogen risked her life for the man she loved, something you know nothing about."

Her fist connected hard to his jaw, turning his head to the right. Stars exploded behind his eyes, but he shook them off. He'd been hit by stronger people, and a lot harder. At least she hadn't gone for the nose.

"You're a bastard, MacRae," she growled.

He smiled—smirked if he was truthful. "Strike a nerve? Both times you saved me I was hurt trying to protect you. I willingly would have died for you twice. What do I possibly owe you?"

"I never wanted you to die for me. I wanted you to *live* for me!"

Her outburst gave way to stunned silence. Mac stared at her. She stared at him. Poor Nell looked back and forth between them. "I'm going up top," his sister said, and practically ran up the stairs.

Finally Mac found his voice. "I did live for you. Everything I did was for you. Every mission was to

protect what we believed in, in service to the agency
to which *you* swore loyalty. I busted my arse for the
Wardens trying to get enough money together to
buy us a house, so we could have the life we always
talked about. Christ, Evie. I had the ring."

She recoiled as though he had struck her. He'd
admitted too much, but then he'd never been very
good at keeping his feelings inside where she was
concerned. He had loved her, and that meant shar-
ing everything. And now she stared at him in horror.
Was that guilt or pity in her eyes?

Did it even matter?

Mac scrubbed a hand over his face. On the other
side of the door, Imogen's sobs had quieted. He
needed to talk to her. She was more important than
him and Evie taking jabs at each other. He was too
tired for this.

And there was the realization that she was right—
at least partially. He did put himself in harm's way a
lot. He was right as well—it was almost always for
her. Or it had been once upon a time. If she stayed on
the ship, she was a prime target for the traitor who
would know what she once meant to him. He should
have thought of that before snatching her, but he'd
been desperate to save Genny.

Well, now he was desperate to save Evie. In the
past that meant putting himself between her and
danger. Now it meant sending her as far from danger as he possibly could.

"Collect your things," he ordered, wincing at how
hoarse his voice was. "Dash will take you on to Lon-

don. Thank you for all you've done for Imogen, but
you have a life to go back to. The Wardens need
you."

She looked . . . confused. There were probably very
few—if any—men who had ever sent her away. Mac
turned, hand on the knob of the door to Imogen's
cabin. He paused long enough to glance over his
shoulder. She stood there, watching him. He opened
the door.

"Good-bye, Evie."

It took her longer to pack than it ought to have.
Trembling fingers and shaking knees finally drove
her to take a deep swallow from the bottle of whiskey on Mac's desk, just so she could pull herself—
and her luggage—together.

She hadn't put any of her items away, so it was
just a matter of making certain anything she had
taken out was put back in its spot. After a lengthy
embrace of Napoleon, which included a few tears
shed into his thick coat, Evie locked her trunk,
picked up her toiletry case and medical bag and left
the cabin.

Pliny met her in the corridor. "Nell says I'm to
take your baggage aground, miss."

He looked almost apologetic, dear thing. "Yes,
thank you, Pliny. That would be grand." She managed a small smile before moving past him to climb
the steps. It felt like climbing the gallows.

This was good. Mac was letting her go. She could
go back to London and back to her life. He could go

about his heroics and they'd continue on as they had been the last three years.

Miserable.

She didn't want to leave him. It made no sense. In fact, it was dead mental, but her heart didn't care. He made her angry, weak and too happy to see straight. It was madness and good God, she had missed it!

He told her she had broken his heart. That he had done it all for her. That he had bought a ring.

She put a hand on the railing to catch herself as a wave of nausea rolled through her. Too much whiskey. Yes, that was it.

Up top the sun was shining. Dash's workers were doing a final test on the new balloon canopy to make certain the *Queen V* was air-worthy once more. Evelyn took one last look around. She liked this little ship, even though she sometimes used to feel like a mistress in comparison. This pile of wood and steel was Mac's real wife. She hoped Imogen MacRae reconciled herself to that.

Why had Mac married her? What were the real circumstances around her injury? Mac never used to keep secrets from Evie, and she hated that he was doing so now. Maybe he had good reason.

Or maybe he trusted her as far as he could throw her. Honestly she wasn't certain she could blame him for it. In his eyes she was a selfish bitch who ran out on him when he needed her most.

There was a lot of shame attached to that. She

would take responsibility for it, but it was a little late for that. The damage was done.

"Evie."

She stopped—mere feet away from the stairs to the dock below. She'd almost made it. *Sigh*. Slowly she turned to face the music, so to speak.

Nell stood maybe eight feet away from her, legs splayed, fists on her lean hips. She looked like a fearsome lady pirate, with a blue bandanna around her head and her tanned skin. "You weren't going to run off without saying good-bye again, were you?"

"Thought I might, yes," Evie admitted. "I'm not very talented when it comes to good-byes, Nell."

"Not enough practice maybe."

Evie flinched. She deserved that. "Indeed. It was good to see you again, Nell. Take care of yourself." *And your brother*.

Before she could take a step, Nell was right there in front of her, grabbing her up in a fierce hug that threatened the very integrity of her ribs. "Don't hate him, Evie," she whispered. "He's never loved anyone but you. It's hard for a man to get over that."

That was not what she wanted or needed to hear, not if she was truly going to make it off the ship. She didn't hate Mac. She could never hate him.

"You have to let me go, Nell," she murmured. "He wants me to leave. I owe him that, I think."

Reluctantly the strong arms around her middle let go. A faint squeak made her smile. "I think you need to oil that," she said, nodding at the other woman's brass arm. The dull metal didn't even glint in the sun. That was a good thing. Made it harder for enemies to spot you. What little vanity Nell had was in that hand. The brass might be flat, but it was beautifully etched with images of the moon and stars.

"I reckon I do," the older woman replied. Were those tears in her eyes? No. Nell never cried. "I hope our paths cross again one day, girl."

"If they do, I'm not letting you within arm's reach. Either that or I'm searching you for chloroform first."

Nell grinned. "Fair enough."

The rest of the crew had drawn close as well. Evie managed to say good-bye to all of them in one attempt, and somehow managed to keep from crying as well. How had she never realized before this how much she missed them?

By the time she descended to the dock below, her throat was tight and Pliny had appeared with her belongings. Eli took her toiletry case, and Barker took up the other handle on her trunk. Every one of them seemed eager to help. How could Mac possibly believe one of them was disloyal?

The thought made her look at the hands of each and every crew member present. Not one of them appeared to have suffered any serious injury. A bite from a dog the size of Napoleon would leave a sizable wound. It wouldn't be terribly easy to conceal. But if the person had medical knowledge, he'd be all the better off for it.

She'd begin to suspect Dash was involved, were it

not for the fact that he was with Mac and the rest of them when the dog bit Imogen's would-be assassin. It would almost be easier to imagine he could be in two places at one time rather than believe one of these people would betray Mac.

Speaking of Dash, he was outside when Evie and her entourage descended upon him. The deck had been washed—though blood always managed to leave a stain—the bodies cleared away, and the corpse of the monster wrapped in a tarp and crated in ice for transport.

As W.O.R's medical director she had access to the Minotaur. It would be interesting to study it—if I.T. didn't push her aside. They had their own doctor who was also a chemist and a scientist. Their unique situation demanded as much. She'd seen some insane things in her life, but while she could be horrified by a man whose feet resembled hooves, she couldn't figure out exactly how or why anyone would do that to another person. How could you make such a terrible creature? It should never have happened at all.

Then again, if she'd learned anything from the Wardens, it was that "never" did not apply.

Pliny and Barker put her trunk just inside the door of the small office building. Eli set her case on top of it. They tugged their caps at her—Pliny went so far as to pat her on the shoulder—and then walked away without a word. They wouldn't ask her to stay even if they wanted to. That would be a blatant disregard for an order by their captain.

Evie folded her arms over her chest and leaned against the doorframe to watch them walk away. Her gaze followed them back to the ship. Mac had yet to make an appearance. He probably wouldn't.

"You wouldn't happen to know anything about the latest advancements in reanimation, would you?"

Evie frowned and turned. Dash stood by a large, scuffed antique of a desk. He was a gorgeous man. His dark hair caught gold highlights, as did his eyes. He had what was quite possibly the most perfect mouth she'd ever seen. No man deserved those lips.

She had no carnal interest in him whatsoever. She blamed Mac for that.

"Am I correct in assuming you refer to cadaver revival?"

Now he frowned. "Is there any other kind?"

He had a point. "I know a fair bit about it. Why?"

"I want to reanimate this human guard and find out what he saw."

Postmortem science was a burgeoning field. Evelyn had of course studied it in medical college, but the legitimacy of the practice was caught up in a religious debate. Some insisted it was a sin against God. Others argued that it only proved the theory that Aetheric energy was the "Breath of God."

And then there were those who simply believed it was disrespectful to the dead. Evie didn't know where she stood on the subject. She didn't believe it was a sin, but neither did she feel completely comfortable with the process.

"You do realize that the reliability of the process

depends on how long the subject has been dead and the nature of death?"

Dash looked at her as though she were an amusing child. "Of course. We are within the twelve-hour window, and I've made certain the body was kept as close to optimal temperature as possible."

She didn't ask how he'd managed that. I.T. was known as the division of the Wardens that dealt with the "bizarre" and often macabre ramifications of modern science.

"Should I assume you have all the necessary equipment on hand as well?"

He nodded. "You should."

"You probably know more about the process than I do. I doubt I'll be of much help."

"I know it in theory, and I've seen it done, but I haven't done it myself. I've heard of you, Dr. Stone. I know what you managed to achieve in Paris."

Evie swallowed. That night had unsettled her greatly. She'd reanimated a corpse, and also used an invention of Arden Grey's so that not only could the audience of Wardens and trusted alliances hear the corpse say what happened, but could also see the last few moments of the man's life through his own eyes, projected onto a large silk screen.

Of course trouble came when the wife of the corpse barged into the room and dissolved into hysterics at the sight of her husband. The situation further escalated when the man remembered that he was supposed to be dead.

After that the practice of postmortem reanimation

was shelved by W.O.R. as potentially too "risky." Also, the Church of England denounced it, as did the Roman Catholic Church. Panic rose amongst the devout—did this mean the soul didn't leave the body? Were they playing God? Only Christ had been resurrected. It went on for several weeks. Evie gave up her private practice at the same time because of verbal and physical attacks against her person and office, but also because of those poor souls who came to her begging her to bring back their dead loved ones.

When a mother showed up on her step with a dead four-year-old girl in her arms, Evie thought she might well go mad.

"If you know about Paris, you must know about the rest of it," she said in a low, measured tone. "I am not keen to assist you, Mr. Evans."

"Call me Dash." He smiled, not at all perturbed by her reluctance. "I need to know who did this, Doctor. Don't you want to know who released a murderous monster so that it could kill so many people, including Mac?"

It appeared he knew about her history with Mac as well. Not as though it was any secret.

But damn him for turning her conscience so quickly. "Fine." She did want to know—and not just to protect Mac, but to protect Imogen and Nell. She tried to ignore her mother's voice in her head, cautioning her against losing her immortal soul.

"Lead on, Dash. Let's raise the dead."

*   *   *

He had failed. That was inexcusable.

He should have killed the dog, but he didn't have it in him to do such an awful thing. Napoleon was only doing what loyalty dictated. He was a fierce protector, but a good boy. The bite had bled a fair bit, but that was his own fault for trying to yank his hand free. The dog would have let him go eventually, but he couldn't risk being found in the room. He'd had no choice but to retreat.

It was bad enough his superiors questioned his loyalties. After all these years of faithful service, they wondered if he had begun to sympathize with this crew, with its captain.

Captain MacRae was a good and honorable man. He respected him despite the fact that he was in league with the Wardens. He'd even had some good memories of being on this ship as part of this crew.

But this was not his life. Not his duty. Those were back in Russia, where he longed to be. He would do what his country needed him to do, and then he would go home, hug his wife and children, play with his dogs, eat proper food. Yes, that was all worth what they asked of him. Worth the blood on his hands.

The others believed MacRae that nothing was afoot, that he'd brought Dr. Stone on board for his own amusement, that there was nothing of interest in that small guest cabin at the base of the stairs. He'd only had to sneak into it when they were all busy on the dock—unfortunate business, that was— to discover the truth.

He slid the long, wooden-handled pick into the special sheath strapped to his forearm. It was unnoticeable beneath the coarse fabric of his shirt. Now he just had to wait for the right moment.

Then he would take back what the woman and her husband stole.

And then he'd kill her.

Chapter 11

"How did he die?"

Mac sat on the chair beside Imogen's bed, his hands linked between his spread knees. This was one of the most difficult conversations he'd ever had.

"He was shot in the back."

"Did he die right away?"

Damnation. "Yes." He hadn't. In fact, Theo had seemed to take forever to die, but Mac wasn't going to tell his widow that her husband had suffered.

She eyed him carefully. "I think you're lying."

He tried again. "It was over quickly, Genny. His last words were asking me to protect you."

Tears shimmered in her red-rimmed eyes, but she blinked them away. "And our baby?"

Mac froze, as though captured in a vise made of solid ice. "What?"

"Our baby. Did I lose the baby?"

How the hell was he supposed to know? Wait, Evie once told him about the miscarriage she'd treated. She talked about how difficult it had been emotionally as she tried to comfort the woman, but she also mentioned blood and . . . other things.

"I don't think so," he replied. If only he'd waited an hour before sending Evie away. He could probably get her to come back.

No. She'd done enough. More than enough. And he wasn't going to chase after her demanding she do more. He couldn't put her in any more danger.

And after all the things she'd said, he'd rather cut off his bollocks than ask her to come back.

"There hasn't been any blood in . . . that area." He frowned. "Not that I've looked there. I've seen nothing on the sheets." His cheeks felt hot. Wonderful. He was blushing. Was he a pirate or an eleven-year-old boy?

"No," she said with a sly smile. "He's still with me." Above the blankets her hands settled over her stomach. "A part of Theo is still with me."

And now his eyes burned. He wasn't an eleven-year-old boy; he was a bloody girl. Nell would punch him for the comparison, but then again his sister was more of a man than he was. She certainly had more honor.

"I tried to save him, Gen. I need you to know that."

"I know. You'd save the world if you could, Mac."

"I'm sorry for lying. I didn't want you to give up."

She nodded.

"I'm bringing him home with us. You can bury him."

A tear slid from her eye, into her hair. "Thank you." She sniffed. "I'd like to be alone for a bit if that's all right."

It wasn't. But he could hardly deny her. He rose to his feet. "I'll lock the door." He didn't have to say anything else. Imogen was a spy, and a spy's wife. She knew that there was always danger, especially when there were government secrets involved.

"Mac."

He paused at the door, about to exit. "What, sweetheart?"

"What does this look like to you?"

He leaned toward her, so he could see the flesh revealed by the open neck of her shift. There was a drop of blood on her pale skin, with a bruise forming around it.

It was right over her heart.

"I don't know." But he had a suspicion. The location made him think of puncturing instruments used by Russian agents and a handful of anarchist groups scattered around Europe.

She'd come close to dying. If not for Napoleon she would have—and he would have been none the wiser, playing matador to a man-made Minotaur.

The crew of that ship, and the creature itself, dead for the sake of a diversion. An unsuccessful diversion at that. The traitor had to be pissed about that.

Mac sure as hell was. How could anyone have such a blatant disregard for life?

Imogen wasn't stupid. She'd been a spy for years as well as a spy's wife. She knew the value of the information she carried even if Mac did not.

Imogen pulled the covers up over the mark. "If anything should happen to me, the information is in my belongings. Make sure it gets to Director Withering."

"You can give it to her yourself when we get to London." He wasn't going to tell her about their sham marriage. There was no point. It only made a difference if she died, and that wasn't going to happen.

He left the room, took the key from inside his coat and locked the door. When Nell returned from walking Napoleon, he'd have her put the dog in the room. With any luck they'd be airborne within the hour, and finally en route to London. He would never be so glad to see a journey come to an end as this one.

Up on deck the sun was shining—a lovely day to be in the sky. The clouds were few and far between. The northwest flight path would keep the sun port side, and if the breeze kept up they might even gain some extra speed.

He looked up. Dash's men had set up a lattice-work of ropes and ladders in order to install the new balloon canopy, and now had it inflated for testing. It would rest above the sails, so that if they lost the wind they'd maintain altitude. Very important when hundreds of feet above the earth.

"Looking good, isn't it, Captain?"

Mac turned his head. "It is indeed, Eli. Has Nell returned yet?"

"She's coming up the boarding stairs now. Shall I tell everyone to man their stations?"

"Not yet, but advise the crew that we'll be departing within thirty minutes." High overhead, the workmen were already lowering their equipment as well as themselves as they dismantled their spiderweb of ropes.

"Aye, sir." The smaller man went off to spread the word. Mac moved his gaze from above to below. Two men carrying what appeared to be a sheet-covered body on a stretcher entered the building on the dock. What the hell was Dash up to? I.T. were morbid bastards at times. To be part of the organization you had to have unshakable nerves, and next to no feeling. Or perhaps you just had to be rather adept at turning off your humanity. Regardless, too many of them in one room made Mac's flesh creep.

Whatever Dash had planned he didn't want to know about it, and he certainly didn't want to know if Evie was involved. With her steady stomach and scientific curiosity, she'd probably think it bloody brilliant.

"What are you looking at?" came his sister's voice from behind him. Napoleon nudged his hand with a wet nose.

Stroking his dog's head, Mac turned his head. "What the hell's he doing down there, do you know?"

"Mm. Ran into him on our walk. Apparently he's going to try some postmortem . . . something or other. Evie says it's something scientific to get information out of corpses."

Mac made a face. He'd heard of it. And he knew Evie had done it before. She used to dream about it. "She's doing it willingly?"

"You ever know her to do something against her will?"

Not really, no. If Dash could charm Evie, then he was a talented man indeed. No doubt the two of them would celebrate later on. Get naked and do some biology experiments.

He'd rip Evans apart. He really would. It didn't matter that he had no right to be jealous; he was. This was why he was going to start going to parties as soon as he returned to London. He needed to meet people. He needed to meet women. Surely he could find at least one who liked the look of him and shared a few interests? Preferably one who looked nothing like Evie, but was still pretty and laughed at his jokes.

And really, she needn't be all that pretty provided she found him interesting and vice versa. Surely that wasn't too much to ask.

"You're jealous."

He might have scowled, but he wasn't in the mood. "Yes." Why deny it? She'd know he was lying. Her surprised expression was more than a just reward for being truthful. "I am, and it doesn't matter. She hasn't been mine for three years and she'll never be mine again. She's made that clear."

"No, *you* made that clear. At least for the part of it I heard."

"It doesn't matter, Nell." He turned to face her too

fast, causing the healing flesh of his side to pull sharply. He clenched his jaw to keep from swearing. "Her opinion of me couldn't be any lower if it was buried at the center of the earth, and that's fine. If she can't accept me, I don't want her."

His sister smiled, but it was an unsympathetic smile. "Liar."

He shrugged. "Like I said, doesn't matter." He patted Napoleon, ruffling the big dog's ears, which earned him a whack on the leg with a tail as big around as a tree limb. "Come on, gorgeous. What do you say we get this bird in the air?"

The dog chuffed, and that was a good enough answer for Mac. Getting into the air and making their way to London, getting Imogen to safety, those were things that mattered. The only things.

At least that's what Mac was going to tell himself.

Evie was not, in a word, spleeny. However, sticking conductive pins into a cadaver's brain through the nasal cavity filled her with the same sense of unease as sticking her hand in a lion's mouth.

In fact, she'd prefer the lion. At least it would be alive. She didn't mind dead people, at least not when they behaved as dead people ought. This sort of thing and Arden's invention for viewing the last moments of a person's life seemed like violations of some kind. Of privacy. Or perhaps dignity.

"You're not going all religious or something equally superstitious on me, are you?" Dash asked—rather mockingly, she thought.

She shot him a sharp glance as she reached for the second pin. "I happen to believe the doctrines of science and religion need not be mutually exclusive, sir. God can be found in an arc of lightning as well as the pulpit."

He rolled his eyes. "You and MacRae are made for each other. He's always spouting that kind of rot."

Surprisingly she wasn't the least bit offended. Dash Evans was indeed a charmer if he could insult her to her face, and she didn't want to stab him with a scalpel.

Or at least any more than she wanted to stab most people.

"Perhaps Captain MacRae isn't as intimidated by an intelligent and spiritual woman as you are."

A wide grin spread across his face. Dear Lord, but he *was* beautiful. And he knew it.

"A smart woman is as attractive as she is annoying, Dr. Stone."

"I have a suspicion you don't wait around long enough for her to annoy you." Carefully she slid the pin into the cadaver's nostril. "Would you ready the auditory cylinder recording station?"

The "experiment" would be recorded—etched into a small brass cylinder—not only to preserve what the dead man had to say, but also to prove that no harm befell the corpse during the interrogation, just in case any findings had to be used in a court of law.

"I'd feel better if we had a visual recording device as well," she remarked as her companion set the cylinder into place. At least he was familiar enough with them to take care not to leave any smudges from his fingers on the recordable surface of it. They were more . . . finicky than the cheaper wax cylinders, but retained their integrity much longer.

"And we would have one had our 'Manotaur' not destroyed it."

"Poor creature."

He slid a disbelieving look in her direction. "Sympathize for the man it once was, not for the thing it became. There was no more humanity in that beast than there is life in our friend here."

With the second pin in place, Evie couldn't keep from smiling—smirking, actually. "Why, that sounds almost philosophical."

"I'm more than just a pretty face."

"Now I see why you and Mac are made for each other—both of you are humble and self-effacing." She pried bloodless lips apart and stuck a finger inside. Dry as a bone. "Do you have any glycerin on hand? His mouth needs to be lubricated."

Dash pulled a face. "That's disgusting."

"Out of this entire enterprise, the poor man's dry mouth is what unsettles you?"

He tilted his head. "Huh. When you put it like that, it does sound odd. I have an aversion to mouths, especially those belonging to dead people. You never know what might crawl out."

"Dear God!" If a glare could be incredulous, then that's what Evie bestowed upon him. "What is wrong with you?" And what was wrong with her

that she actually took a step back from the corpse?
Nothing was going to "crawl out" of it.

The blighter was actually *laughing*. Where was her
scalpel? She was going to stab him after all.

"Sorry, Doc."

"Please don't call me that." That was Mac's pet
name for her. It felt wrong hearing someone else say it.

He bowed his head. "Apologies. Sometimes I forget that not everyone has the same buggered-up job
that I do."

"I think you like it."

"You've figured me out." His gaze fell upon the
dead man. "Are we ready? He's not going to stay
fresh for long."

Honestly it was no wonder the man was a bach-
elor. "As soon as you give me the glycerin, we can
begin."

He opened a cupboard and removed a brown bottle. This small room being the lone medical laboratory
in the building, she wasn't surprised to find that he
kept the liquid here. It was excellent for keeping skin
supple and soft as well as for forming a thin barrier
on the skin's surface.

Evelyn dipped a swab into the bottle. After ensuring that it was good and coated, she withdrew the
swab and placed it in the cadaver's mouth, swirling
it around to moisten the tongue and surrounding tissue.

Dash watched with an expression akin to biting
into a lemon. She hid a smile. So he could be unsettled after all.

"How did this man die? He doesn't appear to have a mark on him."

Dash leaned over the body and opened the man's coat. There, directly over his heart, was a blood stain. "If you look under his shirt, you'll see the entry wound."

Evie peeled back the coarse, damp fabric and used a square of gauze to wipe the area. There was a small diamond-shaped wound.

"It went straight through, didn't it?"

Her companion nodded, watching her in a manner she thought might be complimentary or wary. "It did. You've seen this sort of thing before?"

She nodded. "A couple of years ago a Warden was killed in a similar manner in St. Petersburg."

"It's a method used fairly often by Bears." "Bears" was a term used amongst those in the espionage business to refer to Russian operatives who called themselves *Medved*, which in their language also meant "bear."

"Is it significant?" she asked carefully. Because of her friendship with Dhanya, the director of W.O.R., she was perhaps a little more up-to-date on what faction was doing what in the great game of power being played across Europe—across the world.

"Not to me. Could be involved in Mac's business."

Paranoia prickled at the base of her skull. "What do you know of Mac's business?"

"Nothing needs to get tied in a bunch, Doc . . . *Doctor*. If I wished your boy harm, you'd know it and so would he."

"He's not my boy."

"Mm." There was a lot of meaning in that little sound. A lot of insinuation Evie didn't like.

"Why cause so much death?" she wondered aloud.

"Our friend here is the only one killed by such an instrument. The others were ripped apart by the beast once it was released."

"But the person who let it out seems to have escaped unscathed."

"Unless it was one of his own crew aboard that ship."

Maybe that's what it had been. Maybe it hadn't been one of Mac's after all.

No, that was wishful thinking. It was a little too convenient that while the beast was running wild, and everyone was distracted, someone sneaked into Imogen's room and got bitten by Napoleon.

She placed small pads on the man's cheeks and connected more wires to them. These would stimulate facial muscles to help the corpse better communicate. Depending on what stage of rigor the body was at, talking could often prove difficult.

Finally, after a few more adjustments, they were ready to begin.

The process of reanimation differed depending on the conductor. A more religious person might describe it as filling the conductee with that elusive "Breath of God"—awakening the body and infusing it with life for a brief time. It wasn't that simple. Aetheric energy was everywhere—the wondrous emission and sustenance of all living creatures. It wasn't tangible and it couldn't be seen, but it could be measured, and it could be harnessed.

The energy stimulated necessary systems and organs within the corpse to give it a brief return to a lifelike state. But it was not living, and though duration depended on how long the person had been dead, it didn't last. She'd heard of people experimenting with ways to make it last longer, but Evie was convinced nothing good could come of it. Had no one read about Frankenstein's monster? Mary Shelley was right to caution man about playing in God's toy box.

"Ready?" Dash asked as he moved into position by the control box.

Evie took a step back. "We're good."

He flicked three switches, dialed the operation code and then threw the main lever. A loud hum filled the air as the body on the gurney twitched.

Dark eyes opened wide, lenses covered by a milky film. Then the mouth opened, the jaw stiff and slightly off center. It was a ghoulish sight, but worse was the noise that came out of the body's throat.

"Harungaaaaaah."

A chill slithered down Evie's spine. She really didn't like this. "What is your name?" she asked in a loud voice, following protocol.

"Hharr . . . Oli . . . ver Nels . . . on."

"Occupation."

"Irrrrreguuulaar Trans . . . transpirations."

"Do you remember the night you di . . . were attacked?" She cursed herself under her breath. She had to be careful. One wrong word and this poor man could seize the reality of his situation. That would not be good.

"Guuuaarding the M . . . M . . . Minotaur. My t . . . turn at watch." His lips and tongue were remembering how to work. "A man approached me. Said he was on the other ship. Asked me if I had a pocket flint to light his pipe."

The "other" ship was the *Queen V. Damn.* "Did you?"

"Yes, of course. My wife gave me an engraved one for my birthday this year." He patted his front, searching his coat. "Where is it?"

Oh, hell. "It's fine, Mr. Nelson. It's on the table next to your bed." Someone was going to have to tell his widow not only that her husband was dead, but that the killer had most likely stolen her last gift to him as well.

"I can't turn my head. Did I hurt my neck?"

"Yes," she lied. She wasn't going to tell him that he was strapped in place on the table, his head intentionally held still by metal posts so he couldn't look at himself. "Can you describe the man to us?"

"Of course," replied the corpse of Oliver Nelson in a most indignant fashion. He was dead, not a simpleton. "He was medium height. Older than me. I'd say in his late forties or early fifties. Salt-and-pepper up top. Wore a tweed cap. Bit of a limp. Not many teeth."

No. Evie could feel her heart shatter against the cage of her ribs. It couldn't be. He had to be wrong.

But he wasn't.

"I took out my pipe and we smoked together, talking about our travels. He told me he would be returning to Russia as soon as he finished this last run." The dead man frowned. "And then he apologized, which I thought rather odd because he hadn't done anything to offend. Then there was this pain in my chest and I looked down. Oh God!"

"Turn it off!" Evie barked.

Oliver Nash tried to look down at his chest, and when he couldn't, began to struggle. When he realized he was restrained, he began to scream.

"Let me go! My chest! Lord Christ, my chest! Blood! I'm dead! I'm dead!"

Evie turned on Dash. "Turn the goddamn thing off!"

Wide-eyed, Dash finally did as she commanded, shoving the large lever back into position and slamming his hand down on the switches.

The humming stopped. Oliver Nash fell limp on the table like a rag doll tossed aside by a bored child. Dead. Again.

"That's going to stick with me for a bit," Dash commented, but the lightness of his tone was forced.

Evie nodded, pressing the heel of her right hand into her forehead. It was all right. She hadn't just killed a man. He hadn't been alive to begin with.

"You have to get Mac," she said.

"That's going to be difficult." Dash pointed out the window.

The spot where the *Queen V* had docked was

empty. Mac had left without saying good-bye. Correction, he'd left without her getting a chance to say good-bye.

He was on his way to England with a killer on board, a killer who . . . just drove by in a steam carriage. Pliny saw her at the window and waved sadly at her as he passed at what seemed like an abnormal rate of speed for such a vehicle.

How could he? So many years with Mac, and were they all a lie?

"Hey!" Dash cried. "That bastard stole my carriage!" He ran from the room. He'd be back, though. There was no way he could catch Pliny.

But if Pliny was the villain, and on the ground, that could mean only one thing.

"Oh no."

Evie ran for the door.

Chapter 12

When Mac found Imogen's body—after a communique from Dash via the telegraph machine—he sank to his knees by the bed, pulled down by a feeling of abject hopelessness.

Nell was in tears—said she'd left the room for only a moment to get a bite of lunch. Eli had taken Napoleon for a walk before their departure, and Nell had put the dog back in Imogen's room after she finished her sandwich. When Mac walked in, Napoleon was sitting by the bed, his chin resting on the mattress, nose against Imogen's hand.

She'd been left pinned to the bed like an exotic butterfly on a collector's board. Her cabin had been torn apart in a frantic search that would have proved fruitless since he'd had all of her things stored in a hidden compartment behind his own armoire. He would have hidden Imogen herself in there if she hadn't been shot.

The poor thing had suffered so much. Had made the ultimate sacrifice for her country. He wasn't much of a religious man, but he hoped that there was indeed an afterlife, and that Imogen and Theo were reunited in it.

Pliny did this. It was too mad to believe, but the old man was gone, and Dash claimed to have a witness.

Pliny, the friend who had been with him for years, was a damn Bear. Mac had thought of the man as something of a mentor in many ways. Pliny always seemed loyal to a fault.

He hadn't been loyal at all—at least not to Mac.

He pulled the diamond-shaped pick from his friend's chest—he couldn't bear to leave it in her, but he laid it on her torso so the Wardens would have it to examine.

Then he wrapped her in the sheets from the bed and carried her to the room where her husband waited on an icy berth. When he returned to the deck, the entire crew waited on him.

Nell and Eli were up front. His sister's face was as stoic as ever, but he could see the concern in her eyes. She would never offer comfort, but he knew it was there if he wanted it. That was the way they'd always been. He also knew she blamed herself for this. In another life he might have blamed her as well, but Imogen had been his responsibility. Ultimately, he was the one to blame.

"Is it true?" Eli asked. "Pliny's a traitor?"

Mac nodded. "Looks that way. Wardens are looking for him now." They wouldn't find him, though. A man that good at hiding his real self from people he spent day after day with wasn't going to be tracked so easily.

"Guess we've no right to be put out that you hid the lady from us. She'd been done in a lot sooner if you had."

Another nod. Damn, but he was tired. Right down to the bone, he was exhausted. And finished. He was so very, very done. He couldn't do this anymore.

"Captain?" It was Barker. "We've an incoming bird. It's hailing us."

Mac frowned. "Bird" was the common term for most small flying vessels. Sparrows were the smallest and most common, though some folks had slightly larger personal vehicles that were good for somewhat longer flights.

He looked in the direction the man pointed and saw a sleek, pretty raven-class ship headed straight for them. He recognized it right away and his heart gave a thump. That was Dash's flyer.

"Bring it in," he directed. Without thinking he moved closer to the rail. He couldn't see if there was just one passenger or two, but somehow he knew Evie was coming for him.

It was tricky business, bringing a small craft close to one the size of the *Queen V*. Fortunately the raven didn't have the top propeller blades that sparrows used. Ravens had propellers in the front and back, and wings for stability; both of these things made getting close enough to board difficult. However, ravens were also very good at gliding. A few moments before interception, the raven's propellers cut off and its wings shifted, allowing it to pull alongside the larger ship on the port side of the stern.

Several crew members quickly tied the two crafts together. The door lifted up and a trunk came out. Eli took it and set it on the deck. Next was a dilapidated old leather bag that had to be one of the prettiest things Mac had ever seen.

Another small case followed, and then the woman herself. She accepted Barker's hand and leaped down onto the deck like any seasoned sky rat. Her black hair was slipping free of its braid—tendrils blew against her face in the wind. She pushed them back, smiled and said something to Eli as she petted an enthusiastic Napoleon, and then . . . she looked up.

There are moments in a life that stand out as meaningful even as they're happening, though a body would be hard-pressed to say why. Oftentimes they are fairly commonplace—a sunset, a letter from an old friend, a particular line from a song or poem.

Or perhaps looking into the eyes of the only woman you ever loved as she stands on the deck of your ship because she came back. To you.

They stepped forward at the same time—he with his left foot and she with her right—and kept moving until there were no more steps to take. He didn't speak and neither did she, but their arms opened in unison and each drew the other one in.

"I'm so sorry," she whispered against his ear, holding him tight.

Mac squeezed her back.

His crew, tactful lot that they were, busied themselves with sending Dash on his way. Mac looked up from Evie's hair long enough to raise a hand in thanks.

The other man saluted him before shutting the door. A few seconds later, his raven dropped away, only to rise when her propellers and wings were engaged once more.

"Let's have a drink," Evie suggested, pulling back. Instead of releasing him completely, she wrapped one arm around his. Mac followed her lead; he would have been happy to stay on deck and just smell her hair.

They left her luggage. They'd get it later if the crew didn't deposit it outside his cabin door.

At the bottom of the stairs, she paused, attention turning to the room where Imogen had lived her last days. He'd left the door open, and the bloodstained mattress was easily visible from the small corridor.

"I can't believe he was a traitor."

Mac wiped a hand over his face. "I can't believe he was Russian. He never once smelled of cabbage."

She smiled faintly at his poor attempt at humor. "Makes you wonder who else you can't trust, doesn't it?"

"No," he replied. "I won't let that happen."

"I don't see how you can avoid it, but perhaps I'm paranoid."

He shrugged. "Sometimes you trust the right people and sometimes wrong." Lord knew that he had good friends who weren't considered the top of society, but he'd put his life in their hands.

"Where is she?"

"Cold storage."

Evie nodded. Of course that wouldn't seem strange or revolting to her. As a doctor she had undoubtedly seen people who had died in any manner of ways, and kept in perhaps not so great conditions.

"Did you want to examine her?"

"What for?"

"W.O.R. She was an agent. She often hired me to get her into places—or out." He smiled a little at a particularly happy memory.

Evie shifted beside him, glancing away. Was she uncomfortable because she thought he was having a private moment or because she was jealous? "I'd rather wait until we're in London. If we're going to go after Pliny for the murder of a Warden, I want to have every scrap of evidence I can get."

The murder of two Wardens, but he didn't say that. Telling her the truth now would be the right thing. The good thing. But ... he was tired. He didn't want to fight, didn't want to think about what he could tell her and what he couldn't. Director Withering would have his head if he gave away sensitive information, and she didn't like him much anyway, as she had some foolish notion that he had hurt Evie and not the other way around.

"Come," she said, guiding him into this cabin. "You need to rest."

Time alone inside his head was the last thing he

needed—or wanted. "I need to fly this bird to London as fast as she'll go."

"Nell can do that. Lie down."

Arguing with her required more energy than Mac possessed, so he did what he was told, because it was easier, and she would be quiet about it. He stretched out on the mattress.

"Feet."

Automatically he raised his left leg. Years ago, when he would be tired or ill, she'd mother him and take off his boots. When she grabbed hold of the worn leather, he moved his foot in exactly the right way to facilitate her tug. It was as though they had done this only yesterday. When the boot came off, he put that leg down and lifted the other to repeat the process. Then she untied and removed her own boots and stretched out beside him. She didn't touch him. This wasn't an attempt to force him into intimacy, he realized. This was her falling back into old habits as easily as he.

"Are you all right? I know that's a rubbish question, because how could you possibly be all right when you've lost someone you care for?"

Mac smiled. "I'm all right. Thanks, Evie."

She rolled onto her side to face him. He resisted the urge to do the same. He was still, waiting for her to speak as she stared at him. He raised a questioning brow.

"Did you love her?"

Hadn't they already talked about this? He seemed to recall they had. "Not in the way I loved you." He turned his head toward her. "That's what you really want to know, isn't it?"

He waited for the slap, or the denial. "Yes. I'm an awful person for wondering, but that's exactly what I want to know."

"Then I have no problem telling you that you ruined me for other women. I've never loved anyone like I loved you. I don't expect I ever will." Why not be honest about this at the very least?

"She was lucky to have you."

"No, she wasn't. I tried to protect her and she was killed. I think you're right, Evie. I need to stop trying to be the hero. I'm rubbish at it."

"Your wife would probably argue that point."

"The dead can't argue at all."

A strange expression settled over her face. "If I said I could make it possible for you to speak to her again, would you do it?"

"If you're talking about reanimation, then no, I wouldn't do it."

"But you could say good-bye."

"I don't need to say anything." Except maybe how sorry he was, but that wouldn't change anything. "I appreciate the offer, though."

"That's how we knew it was Pliny. The dead guard told us who killed him."

Mac gave in and rolled onto his side as well. They were less than a foot apart, but it wasn't their proximity that made this moment intimate. What made it intimate was just how right it felt to be there with her.

"Are *you* all right?"

Evie shrugged. "It was unsettling, but worth finding the truth. I would do it for you, if you wanted."

"You don't have to make up for leaving me, Evie."

"I'm not!" She was all indignant.

Mac studied her face—the big dark eyes, full lips and flushed cheeks. She seemed completely sincere.

"Did you ever love me?" he asked. How very pathetic.

"What sort of question is that? Of course I loved you. I wouldn't have been with you if I didn't love you."

"But you weren't with me—at least not after a fashion."

"I didn't walk out the door and immediately fall out of love with you."

But she had fallen out of love with him—that was what she didn't say. She didn't need to say it. Part of him even envied her for being able to get over him. Maybe she'd tell him the secret if he asked, so then he could get her out of his blood once and for all.

She obviously mistook his silence for something it wasn't, because she started explaining herself. "I left you because I loved you."

"That makes no sense."

Evie sighed. "You almost died, and that terrified me. I couldn't bear the idea of losing you, of letting you become my world, maybe having a family with you, only to have you taken away."

It was a rather romantic statement, and mostly utter bollocks. "Evie, everybody dies. You of all people should know this. I could live to be ninety."

"The odds of you living to see forty are slim."

"And you could fall down a flight of stairs and break your fool neck. Life doesn't come with a guarantee. Why don't you just admit that you left not because of me, but because you were afraid to love? You were afraid you'd end up like your mother." A low blow, but Mac reckoned it was truth. Evie's mother had been a wealthy man's mistress, and even though he took financial responsibility for the mother of his child and his daughter, he hadn't really been anyone she could depend on, though he seemed sincere in his efforts.

"I am not afraid of love," she retorted.

"How many times have you ever felt the emotion for someone who wasn't family? The kind of love you feel in every part of you?"

He could tell from her expression there had only been one time, and that it had been with him. Discovering this was as sweet as it was painful.

"Do you think your mother would like knowing you won't let anyone love you?"

"Leave my mother out of this. She loved too much. She devoted herself to a man who was only half hers."

"And she was happy with it." He'd met her mother—a lovely woman with a sweet face who loved life and wasn't afraid to live. Evie called her weak—broken—but that wasn't how Mac had seen her.

Evie's gaze narrowed sharply. "She used to cry over him."

"I've seen you cry over baby animals. Shedding a few tears never killed anyone."

"What do you want from me, Mac? What do you want to hear?"

"I want you to tell me the truth."

"Fine." Her eyes snapped with emotion. "I left because I loved you so much the idea of a world without you in it made me want to curl up in a ball and die. I would have traded my life for yours in an instant, and I was terrified that someday I wouldn't be there to save you. Most of all, I was afraid that your love wouldn't last, that it would dry up and you'd leave me. I was afraid that I would continue to love you even after you were gone, that you would possess more of me than I ever had of you. I was afraid of *you*, Mac."

That was a powerful confession; it made his chest tight, as though his heart were too big for it. "Did it work?" he asked calmly. "Did leaving make you happy? Did it make you stop loving me? Because it sure as hell didn't work for me."

Her eyes widened. "No."

That was all the answer Mac needed. A rush of emotion spurred him to action. If he didn't kiss her now, he'd explode.

He reached out and cupped the back of her head in his hand, pulling her close so he could claim her mouth with his own. As soon as their lips touched, the pressure in his chest erupted. It was like a drink of cold water after a month in the desert, a warm fire after nights of damp cold, a sunset after a month of endless day.

Evie's hands clutched at him, bringing them even closer together so that her torso pressed against his and their legs entwined. Trousers made it so much easier to slip his thigh between hers, to press his hips into hers.

Her lips parted—familiar yet all the more exciting for it. God, he had missed this: the feel of her, the taste.

Her hands slipped beneath his shirt to stroke his back. Tingles—little pinpricks of pleasure—danced so spritely along the base of his neck and spine that he shivered.

When she pulled his shirt up, he didn't protest. In fact, he reached back, grabbed a handful of fabric and pulled the damn thing over his head and tossed it to the floor, breaking their kiss.

Evie's mouth brushed against his throat, pressed against his collarbone before traveling down the blade-thin scar that bisected his chest. The tingles spread.

Mac's fingers found the buckles on the front of her waistcoat and began loosening them, muscle memory making it a surprisingly easy task. He pulled the fabric off her shoulder. She moved her arm so it slipped right off, then lifted the other side of her body to shuck it completely.

He then set to work at removing her shirt. There was no hesitation on either of their parts. It was as though they'd known this would happen, or at least their bodies had, and now that they were together, memories of other such encounters came rushing back. He remembered with perfect clarity that she liked to have her neck kissed, and she remembered that he had sensitive ears.

Their breathing was the only noise aside from the rumble of the engines, punctuated by gasps, little moans and breathy laughter.

Her nipples were hard beneath the fine lawn of her shirt, pebbling against his palm. God, she felt good.

Mac bunched the front of her shirt in his fist and shoved it up, baring her breasts—café au lait skin with rosy-brown tips that hardened even further when he closed his mouth around one, then the other. His tongue swirled, his lips sucked. Evie arched against him, pressing her pelvis hard against his. His cock, already hard and eager, pulsed in joyous response.

He was going to bury himself to the hilt inside her and stay there.

Strong fingers ran down his back, gripped at his hips, pulling at him as though the layers of fabric between them didn't exist. Her hips moved rhythmically—press, release, press, release. He ground his erection against her softness. He could come right then and not be ashamed. She'd make him hard again in seconds.

Her shirt was yanked over her head. With that obstacle gone, his trousers and then hers quickly followed. He was done being patient. He'd been waiting for this for three years. There were so many things he wanted to do to her—bury his face between her thighs and lick her until she screamed, stroke her deep inside with his fingers and make her come again and again until she begged for him to stop. And he wanted to feel that beautiful mouth around his cock. Her fingers closed around it and stroked, drawing a low groan from deep inside him.

Suck it, he wanted to beg, but then Evie pushed him onto his back and rose over him, her round, strong thighs straddling his hips. His hands came up to the curves of her full hips and small waist. She was an artistic blend of firm and soft, strong yet feminine.

One hand splayed across his chest as the other slid down and took hold of him, guiding him into place. The head of his cock pressed against the humid notch between her legs. Slowly she pushed down, taking him inside by slow degrees.

Mac groaned, fingers digging into her hips. She was hot and wet and so incredibly tight as her slick flesh parted just enough to accommodate him. Her internal muscles seized him all the way, until the back of her thighs rested on top of his. He was fully inside her, drenched and clenched by her sweet quim.

And then she began to move. Another groan broke free of his throat as Evie moaned in unison. This was not going to last long; he just knew it. Both of them would see to it that it didn't.

He arched his hips in time with hers. Her fingers wrapped around his biceps as she dug her knees into the mattress. His jaw clenched, head tilted back. Just a little bit longer . . .

Her movements increased, became frantic and rough. Her breasts were just above his face and he drew one nipple into his mouth, nipping at it with his teeth as he sucked.

Evie cried out and drove her hips down, all the while making little noises of pleasure that brought him closer and closer to the edge. He wanted to erupt inside her, fill her, but he also wanted to stay inside her forever.

The muscles in her thighs quivered. He could feel the tension mounting in her in the grip of her fingers, the clenching together of her knees. She thrust herself up and down on him, lowering her torso so that he could more easily suck at her flesh and she could grind her pelvis into his, increasing her pleasure.

"*Oh.*"

That simple sound acted as a trigger. She always made that sound when she was close. Mac dug his fingers into her flesh and pulled her down as he thrust faster and faster, and then . . .

There was no thought, no words, nothing but their bodies joined in mindless pleasure. He came hard, muscles twitching, spine tautly bowed. If this was what the French thought death felt like, then it wasn't a wonder they didn't all commit suicide.

He wanted to spend the rest of his life dying with Evie.

As the spasms in his own body died, he was aware of just how hard her legs gripped him, of her cries of release as her body shivered on top of his. Her internal muscles gripped and squeezed as climax rippled through her.

It was the closest thing he'd ever had to a religious experience, and Evie was his angel.

She collapsed on top of him, breath coming in gasps that matched his own. He wrapped his arms around her, so that even when she eventually slid off him, releasing him from the warmth of her body, she had to stay close. She didn't put up a fight, but snuggled against him just as she always used to do.

Mac didn't think about how long it would last, or when she would leave. He didn't think of the other men she'd been with or might be with in the future. He didn't think of Imogen or secrets or guilt. There was only Evie, and how good it felt to have her beside him.

For the first time in days, Mac fell asleep peacefully, and not afraid of what might happen before he woke up.

Chapter 13

This was usually the point at which she skulked away. Her lover was sound asleep and she could get up, get dressed and leave without him waking. She could do all three things silently.

But Evie didn't want to leave. Never mind that there was no place to run to while sailing through the open sky, she was completely and totally content to stay exactly where she was. The realization should have frightened her, but it didn't. She might not always be completely honest with herself or anyone else, but there was no point in denying just how utterly right it was to be with him.

She never should have left in the first place.

Maybe it was just the sweet lull of climax that brought her to this realization, or perhaps she no longer had the energy to deny what she'd known for the last three years.

It was definitely the lovely gloss of climax to

blame. That old fear and urge to run away would return in a little while, but for now she was content to not be afraid, and to snuggle next to the only man she ever cared enough about to be afraid for or of. He would never hurt her intentionally, but he had the power to hurt her greatly, which was what made her antsy.

Her father was not a bad man. He simply was a selfish one. Evie had inherited much of that selfishness, she realized. She would not be content to be a man's second love, even if the first was something as awe-inspiring as the heavens. She wanted to be first. She demanded to be first.

Unfortunately, unlike most demanding women, she also wanted to respect and love the man she was with. That posed a conundrum, as anyone worth respecting wasn't about to give in to her demands.

Rock, meet hard place.

Such thoughts threatened to snuff out the warmth of her afterglow, so she pushed them aside. Right now she was going to live in the moment and stop thinking of the future, as Mac always suggested she do.

And at this moment, what she wanted was more of Mac.

Carnal pleasure was not difficult to achieve. She was more than adept at pleasing herself, or taking pleasure when with a partner, but it was different with Mac. Perhaps it was because she had loved him, or maybe because he was the least selfish lover she'd ever known. His enjoyment seemed to depend on hers, and he wouldn't give up until she was as limp as a dishrag with about as much capacity for thought as one as well.

Had she ever shown that much consideration to him? Of course she knew what he liked and what to do to make the situation enjoyable for him, but if she was honest she wasn't nearly as generous. If they were going to go their separate ways in London, shouldn't she give to him as he gave to her? Give him something to miss when he was sailing through clouds being chased by pirates?

Smiling, Evie slipped from bed and went to the small attached bath. She tidied herself up and then collected a washcloth, some soap and a basin of warm water, all of which she brought back to the room.

Slowly she peeled back the covers. Mac didn't stir. She took a moment to enjoy the sight of him. He was all golden, lean and muscled. Fine golden hair trailed down his abdomen—and farther. The penis always struck her as a tragic organ, comical, vulnerable and at times pathetic. It was surprising, however. How could anything that retreated into itself be seen as the symbol for strength and masculinity? Men would be better off putting their pride in their hearts and brains rather than a little bit of flesh between their legs.

She actually liked Mac's, though. When erect it gave her a sublime amount of pleasure, and more important at this moment, it gave him pleasure as well.

She put her hands in the warm water and lathered up the sandalwood-scented soap. Then she applied her slick hands to him, pushing back the foreskin to massage the head.

It took perhaps two seconds of this for him to begin to grow in her hands. She stroked him in her fist, the soap providing an easy glide. Another few strokes and he was bigger still—and stirring in more ways than one.

She wet the washcloth and quickly wiped away all the soap, letting the warm, wet cloth provide more stimulation. His eyelids fluttered as she set the basin and cloth aside. He woke up just as she lowered her head and took him into her mouth.

He groaned, and she smiled, slowly taking him as far into her mouth as she could.

"Evie." It came out of his mouth like a sigh as his fingers tangled in her hair. Had it been anyone else to use such a reverent tone, she would have gotten up and left him there hard and wanting. But this was Mac, and she never should have left him in the first place.

She continued this erotic torture a few moments longer, until the hands on the back of her head became insistent. Then she drew away, looking into his face to see the need there.

"I'm selfish," she told him, on her hands and knees beside him. "I want you inside me."

She didn't have to ask twice. He rose onto his knees and moved behind her. The hair on his thighs tickled the backs of hers as he slipped inside her.

Her body opened eagerly and easily. Evie dug her fingers into the mattress as he filled her. Nothing had ever felt so incredibly good.

Last time she had been in control, so she let him take the lead this time. He teased her with long, slow strokes that sent ripples of tense pleasure through her entire body with every thrust.

She lost track of how long this exquisite torture went on before Mac began to quicken his strokes. Evie's own need built in tandem with his, until she finally reached out one hand, grabbed the headboard and pulled her torso up, changing the angle of her hips.

Mac sucked in a breath and thrust harder. Evie grabbed the headboard with both hands and met his hips with hers. She bit her lip and tried not to cry out as the tension inside her coiled tighter and tighter. So close. Release was . . . so . . . very . . . close. . . .

She came hard—spine-bowing, brow-furrowing, openmouthed-incoherency hard. The fingers of one of Mac's hands dug into her hips, the other into her shoulder, holding her tight against him as he gave one final thrust. A raw groan tore from his throat as he dropped forward over her back. Her shaking legs refused to hold them both, and they slowly collapsed to the mattress.

"That was the nicest wake-up I've had in a long time," Mac remarked a few moments later, as they curled up together.

"I thought you might like it."

"Feel free to wake me up in a similar fashion every day until London."

Only until London? Did that mean he thought of this as a short-term arrangement?

No, she wasn't going to do that. She wasn't going to make up her own meaning for his words. She wasn't going to think too far ahead or make herself mad, and she certainly wasn't going to ruin this moment by demanding that he clearly state his intentions. They were both adults, and more than capable of figuring this out as they went along.

London would bring complications for both of them. For one thing, Mac was a pirate. Granted he'd been aiding a Warden, but they might still have ideas about taking him into custody. She'd go to Dhanya if she had to. She'd use blackmail if she had to in order to make sure Mac avoided rotting in a cell.

But for now they didn't have to worry about any of that. London was still a couple of days away, and she and Mac had three lost years to make up for. She snuggled closer to him, wrapping an arm and leg around him as she buried her face in his neck. The stubble on his jaw scratched her cheekbone and she didn't care.

Evie placed her hand over the scar on his chest. A second later, Mac's fingers entwined with hers. Below her palm she would feel his heartbeat and the slow, steady rise and fall of the bellows she'd put inside him. Both rhythms were strong and certain—comforting—and she fell asleep secure in the knowledge that both would still be there when she woke up.

The next two days passed faster than Mac liked. He thought they would drift on as they always had—slow and leisurely. Instead, they picked up a lovely wind that bolstered their speed and pushed them onward. The skies were clear, and there wasn't a Jolly Roger in sight.

The crew took it as a sign. A horrific journey was coming to a quick end and the gods were smiling upon them once more.

It was an omen. Mac was certain of it. His time with Evie was being cut short—a reminder that he was not to get comfortable with their current arrangement. This amounted to spending as much time in bed as they possibly could.

It wasn't enough.

If he thought screwing her six ways from Sunday would get her out of his system, then he ought to be hung by his ankles and horsewhipped for being a bloody fool. Sex with Evie wasn't like drinking yourself stupid, waking up in a pool of vomit and swearing you'd never do it again—and meaning it for at least a good month. No, Evie was a puff of opium, sweet and potent, and the more you had, the more you needed.

She was going to bolt once they landed in London. Not that she had said anything to that point, but he was prepared for it.

They were the reverse of what he had been taught to believe was the usual way of things. *He* was supposed to be the one who shied away at the thought of being tied down. She was supposed to be the one who wanted a less than extraordinary life. Evie was all the extraordinary he needed, or wanted. He was done being shot at and not knowing who to trust. He wanted a house that didn't move, fields for Napoleon to run through, maybe even puppies. He wanted to be a gentleman of leisure and get fat and gouty.

Maybe not gouty, but fat might be nice. He wanted a steam carriage and one of those velocycles he saw speeding through the streets of most big cities. And a family. A family would be nice.

These things would frighten Evie, who had a hard time believing in happy endings. He couldn't make her trust him, couldn't force her to take that chance. All he could do was live and hope that she might want to live her life with him.

And if that didn't work, kidnapping her again was always an option.

An hour outside London, he sent word to Dhanya Withering that they would be arriving soon. The Wardens would want to collect Imogen's and Theodore's bodies, as well as all their belongings.

Genny had told him that the information was in her things, but he had yet to find it. It had to be hidden in a manner with which he wasn't familiar. Even with Evie's help the search turned up nothing.

He was beginning to worry that Pliny had found it after all.

There was nothing he could do short of hunting Pliny down, and while part of him wanted to do just that, another part just wanted to wash his hands of the whole thing.

Imogen and Theo were dead. He'd been shot and gored by a monster, and would have died if not for Evie. How many people had to die or be hurt for this information?

Once he handed everything over to W.O.R., he could walk away. He needed to do that if he was ever going to have anything.

"My turn, Nelly," he said to his sister as he approached the wheel.

"I can take her in."

He fixed her with an I-don't-think-so gaze. "This might be our last dance, but she's still my girl. Now step aside."

She saluted him—rudely—with her mechanical hand. "Aye, Captain. Brat."

"Witch." He grinned at her, though.

Mac's hands settled on the wheel, as familiar as his own face. He gave a cursory glance at the instrument panel in front of him before making the rest of the journey by sheer instinct. He knew exactly when and how much to turn, when to tell Barker to start easing off on the sails and the balloon.

London drew closer, until they floated over the Thames, the sooty East End of coal smoke and steam—a black film that covered those who lived and worked there. This gave way to the cleaner, but still steamy West End, where the upper classes resided. He had to skirt north of Mayfair, despite its close proximity to their destination as the richies and peers didn't like the noise of air traffic to disturb them.

The *Queen V* drifted to the docking station in Hyde Park as gracefully as a feather, slipping easily into the magnetized landing bay that clamped and held the ship in place.

A young man at the station shoved hard on a lever that released the automatized stairwell. The wood and iron structure sat on a rail, and was guided to the side of the ship by a small, steam-driven engine. Once it was in place, stabilizing "feet" came out of the bottom of the steps and locked into the wooden dock, securing the structure so it wouldn't move when used.

Eli had just tethered the ship and prepared it for disembarking when the director of W.O.R. and several of her minions reached the top of the steps.

Dhanya Withering was an exotic woman—coldly beautiful—with a complexion that was English rose by way of Bombay, glossy dark hair and clear amber eyes. She was rumored to be an illegitimate grandchild of Her Majesty, but Mac had never seen proof, though she certainly acted as if she thought she was royalty. As it was, she stared down her nose at Mac despite having to look up at him.

"Captain MacRae."

"Director."

"I've come for my agents."

He nodded. "I'll take you to them."

"I'll take their possessions as well. Unless you've managed to recover the information they obtained."

Maybe he was overly sensitive, but it almost sounded as though she thought him incompetent, or a liar. "I haven't, and you are welcome to all of it."

"I wasn't asking permission."

Mac met her gaze and shrugged. "I'd never assume you were."

They stood there, staring at each other. Both her people and his exchanged uncertain glances.

"Are you going to show me where they are?" the director asked finally.

"Not until you say the magic word." He was poking a shark with a stick and he didn't care. He was not her subject, nor was he beneath her socially. She was the leader of an organization he'd left years ago, but she did not own him.

Her jaw clenched. "Please."

Mac smiled mockingly. "That wasn't so hard, was it?" He turned on his heel and led them down to the bottom of the ship and the storage room where the bodies were kept.

Collapsible gurneys were unfolded and a sheet-draped body placed on each. While four men carried them out and up, three more went to the cabin for the couple's possessions.

The Wardens immediately took everything to the

steam carriages they had waiting on the ground, leaving their director with Mac.

"This is the end of our association," Mac told her. "I've done everything you asked for the last six months. I'm done."

"You'll be done when I say you're done, Captain."

Mac's temper rose. "That was not our deal."

"I made charges of piracy go away for you, Mac-Rae."

"In exchange for six months of service. You told me this would fulfill my debt."

She shrugged. "If I don't recover that information, our arrangement will not be completed as discussed. I can't just let you walk away and return to a life of crime."

He clenched his jaw. This woman was a ballsy bitch; he'd give her that. "I—"

"What arrangement?" came a voice from behind him.

Mac groaned inwardly. Could this get any worse?

Withering turned her head, her face lighting up when she saw Evie. She looked positively human when she smiled. "Dr. Stone."

"Director Withering." Evie was decidedly cooler to her friend. "What's going on?"

Mac opened his mouth, but Withering cut him off. "Captain MacRae was arrested for piracy several months ago. He was given his freedom in exchange for service to the Crown. He thinks he's done enough." That hard amber gaze swung back to his.

"The director seems to think the terms of our agreement are subject to her whim."

"Why didn't you tell me about this?" Evie asked, her brow puckered.

Wonderful, now he was going to get it from both women. He should have been a priest as his mother wanted. "It wasn't your business. I didn't want you to know I'd had charges laid against me, and it was supposed to be over with this trip, so I didn't think it mattered. Does it?"

She looked at him for a moment. "No." She turned her head toward her friend, but the director was all business.

"Dr. Stone, you'll have to excuse us. Captain Mac-Rae is going to accompany me back to my office to continue our conversation, and I believe you will have two bodies waiting for you at yours. I'd like a full postmortem by tomorrow afternoon. Coming, Captain?"

Evie's cheeks were flushed. She obviously was not accustomed to being talked down to. "I'll be sure to deliver the results as soon as possible, ma'am."

Meaning Withering would be lucky if she got them in the next month.

"Excellent." The woman responsible for the safety of the entire empire flashed a false smile. "Come along, Captain. Please."

He could have chuckled, but his heart just wasn't in it. He started to follow her, but a hand on his arm stopped him. Evie.

"Will you come by the medical ward when you're done?"

"If I'm not in a cell." He kissed her forehead. "Don't fret, Doc. It will be all right."

But even as he said the words and turned to follow after the woman who held his future in his hands, he wondered if maybe he wasn't a liar after all.

Chapter 14

Evie's hospital ward in the secret Warden complex beneath the Downing Street area of London was her sanctuary. Despite often having grievously injured bodies to work on, or brutally murdered corpses, she found it easy to hide there, away from the world.

The dead didn't pull rank on her, and patients didn't walk away when she wanted an explanation.

She understood why Mac didn't tell her the truth about his "marriage" to Imogen. She understood the need for secrecy under such terrible circumstances. Rationally she knew it was none of her concern. Of course Dhanya wouldn't tell her, but that didn't make it any easier to swallow. Regardless, her heart insisted that Mac should have told her. She would have been prepared then, when one of her closest friends acted like a coldhearted bitch.

To Dhanya, Mac was just a pirate. An outlaw. He certainly wasn't to be trusted, yet she had trusted him with two agents. Did she blame Mac for their deaths? Because Evie couldn't imagine how Mac could possibly be held accountable when he'd done everything he could to protect and save them.

The poor husband—Theodore—was a terrible sight. He'd been shot not only with scatter shot, but with Aether pistols as well, so in addition to his being full of holes, some of those holes were rather large and burned. The smell of scorched human flesh was not one a person ever became accustomed to— at least not in Evie's estimation.

She thoroughly examined the body, collected samples that might be useful when studied and then washed it. Any debris loosened by the water would catch in the mesh cup she had set into a drain beneath the table. It was in the center of a slightly concave circle in the floor, so all fluids ran downhill rather than pooling across the floor.

Then she moved on to Imogen and repeated the procedure. When that was done and the bodies were as clean as they were going to get, she took out her photographic equipment and took photographs of each body from several different angles. She was able to get quite close to the wound in Imogen's chest where the Russian stiletto had pierced her flesh.

How awful it must have been for her to see her husband shot and then find out that he had died while she lived. Though it was probably macabre, Evie almost envied Imogen for not having to go through life without her husband.

People did manage to go forward with life after such losses, and some even found love, and happiness, again. Evie just couldn't imagine it.

Isn't that what you're doing now? she asked herself. Her hands stilled on the camera. Wasn't it? She had pushed Mac away because she couldn't bear to lose him, but by leaving she had done just that—lost him.

"You look like you just bit into a crab apple," came a familiar voice.

Evie's heart leaped. It had been only a few hours since she last saw him, but part of her—that not so practical part—had worried that perhaps he would slip away when he had the chance.

He looked lovely, of course. His gold-touched hair was mussed, his eyes glinted as his lips curved into that smug little smile. His unbleached linen shirt pulled across his shoulders. His tan leather waistcoat matched his trousers, which were a little on the snug side. Good thing he had on a long great coat or she'd be concerned with other women looking at his behind.

"Just thinking," she told him, and then, because she cared about him, "Mac, you might not want to come any closer. Let me cover the bodies."

"Please don't." He moved toward her with quick, long strides. "I want to see them and say good-bye. They were my friends and I want to remember their deaths when I find Pliny."

A hard lump pressed against the inside of her throat. "Of course."

He came to stand beside her, his gaze going from

Theodore's ruined form to Imogen. They were both nude, but Evie had covered what she didn't need to photograph. Just because a person was dead didn't mean she had to disrespect him or her.

"Thank you for taking care of them," he said softly.

Evie forced herself to look at him. His expression hadn't changed, but she could sense his pain. Mac always felt everything so keenly—joy, anger, grief. Sometimes she envied that.

This was not one of those times.

She put her arm around him, and he put his over her shoulders so that the length of her pressed against him. He kissed her temple. They stood there for a few moments, silent for the couple laid out before them.

Evie let Mac pull away first. When he did she directed him away from the bodies.

"Did you find anything with Dhanya?"

Mac rolled his eyes. "A sharp pain in the arse, that's what I found. I know you're friends with the woman, and maybe that's why she hates me, but by God, she's a harpy."

She almost smiled, but he was trying to be nice. She knew full well what a cow Dhanya could be if she put her mind to it. Evie had seen the director reduce full-grown men to tears.

It was her job. That didn't mean Evie had to like it. "Were you really arrested?"

Mac walked over to the counter, leaned against it with his legs stretched out in front of him and crossed his arms over his chest. He managed to look both re-laxed and guarded at the same time. "Nell was. They grabbed the ship when she was making a run. As soon as I found out I joined up and took responsibility."

Evie's brows rose. "You took responsibility for something your sister did?"

"You're an only child, aren't you? Yeah. My ship, my responsibility. I was captain, so your director and I made a deal to keep Nell and the crew from prison. We agreed Theo and Imogen would be my last mission for the Wardens. Now she's saying I broke our agreement because she can't find the in-formation."

Was it foolish that she could kiss yet slap him for being such a good brother? His loyalty to those he loved was boundless, which must make Pliny's be-trayal all the more raw.

"You told her about Pliny, right? She does know that there's a chance he found what Imogen was car-rying?"

"I told her. If Pliny has the information, then I'm expected to retrieve it, especially since I was the one duped by him."

"We were all duped by him."

His lips twisted. "Yes, but, darlin', I'm the one with his balls in the director's palm."

That was an image she didn't like at all—literally or figuratively. If Mac went after Pliny, he'd be com-pletely out of his league. The Russians would know him, but he wouldn't know them. Sending an agent already undercover with the Russians would be a much better plan; then Mac could intercept from there.

Dhanya might as well put him in front of a firing squad of precision-shot automatons.

For the first time, Evie felt anger at her friend. Not just that, but she felt . . . possessiveness. Mac was being threatened, and her first thought was to protect.

She didn't admit that out loud, however.

"Obviously we have to find that information," she said instead of ranting.

Mac looked dubious. "We?"

Were her cheeks actually flushed? They were suddenly quite warm. "I thought I'd help. If that's all right with you."

His eyes twinkled, making them look a brighter blue. "I suppose I could put up with you for a little while. It might involve a trip to Brackenhurst, though."

His family home in England. There was one in Scotland as well, but that belonged to his cousin, who was an earl. This one had belonged to his mother and father. Mac had inherited it upon their deaths. It wasn't a huge monstrosity, but she remembered it being pretty and bright and homey. Returning there might not be such a good idea.

"That would be lovely," she heard herself say. "It would be nice to see it again." And it would be nice to be there alone with him, despite her misgivings. Yes, it would make leaving all the more painful, but she found she didn't care much about that, which was odd.

"Nell's on her way there with the *Queen V*." He must have seen the disappointment on her face, because he smiled. "She won't be staying. She's off to Scotland in a day or two. But if we can't find the information in Imogen's things, I'll have to go up and search the ship."

"How will we travel if Nell has the ship?"

"How do you feel about steam carriages?"

He actually bought ground transportation? Why that should make her heart speed up she didn't know, but it did. "I like them quite well."

Mac's smile widened. "I thought as much. Look, I have to go, but I'm staying at Claridge's if you want to meet me later."

A hotel? She supposed she should be grateful Dhanya didn't keep him in one of the cells. "You could always stay with me."

He shifted his weight and stood up a little straighter, arms uncrossing so his hands could grip the counter on either side of his hips. "At your house?"

"No, in a circus tent. Of course in my house."

"What would the neighbors say?"

"That probably depends on how loud you are."

Their gazes locked. A tingle began at the base of Evie's skull and ran all the way down her spine to buzz seductively deep inside her.

Mac straightened, and closed the scant distance between them. He tipped her chin up with one finger and then kissed her. A slow, deep, wet kiss that not only increased the tremor inside her, but started one in her knees as well.

He pulled back, leaving her dizzy and longing for more. "What time should I come over?"

She wanted to say now, leave the ward and take him home so he could finish what he started. "Seven?" Her voice was a rasp.

Mac smiled. "See you then."

He left her there, twitchy and needy. She watched him go with a mix of lust and annoyance. *Brat.*

She glanced at the clock. It was almost four. Only three hours until she saw him again. Surely she could wait that long. Couldn't she?

It was going to be a *long* afternoon.

Mac, valise in hand, stepped out of a steam-belching hack in front of Evie's Chelsea town house at a few moments before seven o'clock. It was just as he remembered it—redbrick with wrought-iron work and a heavy oak door with a shiny brass bellpull to one side. It was located close enough to the Chelsea Embankment to afford a lovely view of the Thames, but just far enough away to avoid much of the stench.

When the city of London finally finished the "Reclamation and Purification of the Thames Waterway and Its Environs" project started two years ago, the river would be much cleaner. Sewer systems were being redirected by the city, who had determined that human waste made better fertilizer than river sediment. They'd even started supplying homes all over the city with waste containment devices, or as some called them, "shit chutes," so those of the lower orders might not be so tempted to empty their chamber pots in the gutters or out of windows.

As the cab rattled away, leaving a trail of warm, moist air in its wake, Mac noticed another carriage approaching. This one was sleek and obviously expensive. The man driving wore a tweed cap and driving goggles and the lady had a bright scarf about her head and wore goggles as well. Maybe he'd purchase something similar now that he was ready to stay on the ground for a bit.

That was if Director Withering didn't force him back into service. Wretched woman.

He continued on to the front door. He was just about to ring the bell when he noticed the man and woman had stopped their vehicle, gotten out and were headed straight toward him. Habit made him calmly set down his luggage and reach a hand nonchalantly behind his back, underneath his coat where he'd secured an Aether pistol and holster on the waist of his trousers. His fingers closed around the jet inset handle.

The gentleman had a walking stick that he carried in one hand. His companion sported a fan in one of hers. Neither seemed to have any intention of using either for their intended uses.

Bloody spies.

"Good evening," the gentleman—who was something of a ginger with gray eyes—said. "Are you here to see the doctor?" Bit of a rugged character. His companion was incredibly beautiful, but there was an edge to her Mac found a little . . . abrasive. She looked as though she might slit his throat and then have tea.

She looked familiar.

"If you mean Dr. Stone, yes, I am."

The man looked from the arm Mac kept behind him, to the scuffed valise on the step. "Come for an extended visit, have you?"

Mac smiled, knowing full well the look didn't meet his eyes. "I'm not sure that's any of your business, Mr. . . . ?"

"*Lord* Wolfred. This is my wife, Lady Wolfred."

Now he remembered. "You were on my ship," he said to the woman. "I flew you back to London the night Stanton Howard was apprehended." He also remembered that the spy ended up being the lady's brother, but it would be rude of him to point that out.

Her eyes brightened—and not in a friendly way. "So you must be Captain MacRae."

"I am." He extended his hand. Neither took it. Undaunted, Mac lowered his. "She did tell you that she left *me*, right? I didn't do anything."

Sharp brows arched even more. She was a haughty-looking piece, that was for certain. "That's the point, Captain."

Everyone was a bloody wit. Mac forced a smile. "How could I do something I didn't even know was expected of me? Besides, I'm here because she invited me."

The two exchanged glances. "So are we."

Well, that was going to make seduction tricky,

now, wasn't it? The only thing that would make this moment more awkward would be if he said that out loud.

"Then I'll assume Evie wanted us to meet." Mac raised his hand and pulled the bell.

"*Evie*, is it?"

He turned his attention to the woman. "Calling her doctor would be a little formal considering we're sleeping together."

That was certainly not the reply or tone she expected if her expression was to be taken as sincere. Behind her, her husband turned his head and raised a finger to scratch his temple. Mac couldn't be certain, but he thought the earl was smiling.

The door opened and a small woman with graying blond hair, brown eyes and a figure like a plump hen stood before them. She wore a tidy dark gray gown and a pristine apron over top.

"Good evening!" she chirped. "Dr. Stone is expecting you. Won't you please come in?"

Mac gestured for the couple to precede him, and didn't move his hand from his back until both of them had crossed the threshold. Then he plucked up his luggage and stepped inside.

The housekeeper beamed up at him. "You must be the captain. I'm Mrs. Ferguson, but the doctor calls me Addy, and you may as well if you like. You can leave your luggage here and it will be attended to."

She had a charming Scottish accent that reminded him of his nan. "Thank you, Addy," he said with a smile, then added, *"Beannachd Dia dhuit,"* which was an old Gaelic blessing that wished God's favor on the person.

The older woman beamed at him. He had no doubt she would have started jabbering away in Gaelic had there not been other people present. Cold as they were, he was grateful for their presence; otherwise he'd be forced to admit just how little of the language he actually spoke.

Earl Wolfred's expression was neutral—perfectly so—while his wife shot Mac a look of disdainful disbelief. He smiled at her. It was obvious she thought of him as the enemy, and if that's what she needed to do, so be it. He wasn't here to impress her; he was here for Evie. She had protective friends, and that was good, but he wasn't about to let anyone treat him as though he wasn't wanted.

Mrs. Ferguson led them to a small parlor decorated in chocolate and cream. It was inviting and totally lacking in pretention. He remembered this room— and the medical paintings on the wall. The sight of those somewhat macabre images made him smile. He used to tease her about them, and she would threaten to perform each and every one of the procedures depicted on him if he didn't stop.

Evie sat at the large, dark-stained desk near the large bow window. She had the front of her hair pinned back, the rest cascading down her back in thick curls. She smiled at the three of them and rose to her feet.

Mac's wasn't the only jaw that dropped.

She was wearing a dress! A gown, even. It was a

rich, dark plum velvet that hugged her tightly from the waist up, and flared out in a simple drape to the floor. It even had a little bustle. Had he ever seen her in such feminine clothing before?

Good Lord, she was showing cleavage. If he caught Wolfred looking . . . No, it was good. The man seemed surprised by Evie's appearance, but he only had eyes for his wife. It had better stay that way.

"I'm so glad you could join us," she said to the couple, kissing them both on the cheek. "I invited Arden and Lucas, but she's so close to her delivery they decided to stay in."

"Wouldn't it be more convenient if they were here when she needed you?" Alastair remarked.

Evie turned to Mac. "Friends of ours are expecting their first child very soon."

"I figured that out." He couldn't keep from smiling. He was a smiling fool. "You look beautiful." He didn't kiss her on the cheek, but lightly on the lips. Let the countess stew on that for a bit.

Evie beamed at him. It was akin to being punched in the face by the sun. "Did the three of you properly meet? I'm sorry to be so rude."

The countess actually softened—wonders would never cease. She was attractive when she didn't look as if she wanted to tear out your spleen with her teeth. "We met outside." The light in her eyes faded as she looked at Mac. "It's so nice to finally have a face to put to the name."

Mac rolled his eyes, and didn't care if she saw.

Her husband—Wolfred—put his hand on the

small of her back. The loosening of her spine was actually visible.

"Would you like a drink?" Evie asked.

"Yes," Mac and the countess chorused in unison. He laughed; it was absurd behaving like this.

Apparently Lady Wolfred agreed, because she chuckled as well. When she smiled she was downright radiant. Not as striking as Evie, of course, but lovely all the same.

Once everyone had a drink in their hands, they sat. If Mac had been worried about small talk, he needn't have been.

"That's quite the vehicle you have," he said to the earl.

Wolfred grinned proudly. "She is. I got her for a steal from a fellow in Germany. I made some modifications—mostly to the engine—and now she purrs like a kitten."

"Do you hear how he talks about it?" the countess said to Evie with mock gravitas. "I swear, I'm the other woman where that carriage is concerned."

"You made the modifications yourself?" This was a conversation Mac could get into. He wanted to find good ground transportation, and the earl was a man who knew his steam carriages. The two of them discussed various manufacturers and the pros and cons of each, plus what sort of changes he could make on his own if he was of a mechanical bent. In his youth he'd taught himself about dirigibles and flying machines by trial and error starting with an old sparrow of his uncle's. Mechanics were something he understood.

Despite interesting conversation, his attention strayed to Evie several times during drinks. He had to remind himself that she was real. It had been only a few days since he nabbed her in Vienna. A short few hours to go from hurting to feeling . . . whatever this was.

It wouldn't be smart to feel too much too quickly, but what if he never stopped feeling it? Had three years of resentment also been three years of love?

Yes, they had been. He could admit that to himself easily. But what of Evie? She was terrified of giving herself to someone, terrified of what might happen. How could she love him when the very notion of it scared her?

If her father were alive he'd love to introduce the bastard to the sublime pain of a broken nose—and possibly a few fingers. And a knee.

Mrs. Ferguson came in to announce that dinner was ready at half past seven, and the four of them made their way to the dining room. Rank didn't matter; they walked together and sat together—the earl and countess across the table from him and Evie. They served themselves from the various platters and dishes, and poured their own wine.

It was good food—actually good company—and a relaxed atmosphere. It was nice, reminding Mac a little of gatherings at his uncle's estate in Scotland.

"I heard you speak Gaelic to Mrs. Ferguson," Wolfred said, pouring another glass of wine. "You wouldn't happen to be related to William MacRae, Lord Kincargin?"

"He's my uncle," Mac replied. Wolfred didn't look surprised—as though he already knew the answer. "You're familiar with my family?"

"Some, yes. They've had ties with W.O.R. since its inception."

Oh, wonderful. Now he got to talk about the Wardens. *Huzzah!* "That's true, yes."

"But you aren't a Warden?"

Mac met the level gray stare. "Not for some years now."

"Would you consider coming back?"

His wife shot him an exasperated look. "Are you really trying to recruit him over dinner?"

Honesty was generally the best policy in such situations, unless he wanted to have this conversation again someday. "Not if Withering got down on her knees and begged. Not even if she stepped down and her successor got down on his or her knees and begged."

Wolfred guffawed as he lifted his wineglass. "I'll take that as an empathetic no."

Mac smiled. "Please do." He glanced at Evie, who had a strange look on her face. "What?" he asked.

She shook her head. "Nothing important."

"Uh-oh," Wolfred said. "That usually means it's *very* important."

His wife shot him a very pointed glance.

Mac didn't need to be a mind reader to have an

idea of what Evie was thinking about. She was worried about the future, about whether W.O.R. would let him, if he would continue to be a pirate, or something else she could use as an excuse not to be with him.

He wasn't going to give her an excuse to run, but he wasn't going to pander to her anxieties, either. Either she would believe him when he told her he was done with a life of intrigue or she wouldn't. She would either have the balls to give them another shot or she wouldn't.

But by God, she wouldn't be able to blame him for its not working this time.

Chapter 15

After Alastair and Claire left, Evie tried not to think about what might happen if Dhanya refused to let Mac out of their arrangement. She refused to think about what might happen if he ran, or if he didn't. And she tried very, very hard to ignore terrible thoughts of him ending up like Imogen, or worse, like Theodore.

If Mac ended up on her table one day, past the point of her being able to save him, it would be the end of her. She didn't want to let him go, but she couldn't ask him to give up everything he ever loved to stay.

Well, she could, but how long before he started resenting her for it? How long before she started wondering when he'd get bored and leave?

To stop this fruitless cycle, which was pathetic and foolish, she poured herself another glass of scotch. She poured one for Mac as well.

"Are you trying to get me drunk and seduce me?" he asked before taking a drink.

Evie smiled and sat down on his lap. "Yes." Being this close to him, feeling his warmth, smelling that clean, spicy scent of his skin, was more powerful than any aphrodisiac she'd ever tried. She was desperate for his hands, for his mouth, for the feel of him inside her. Those were the only things that could ease her fears.

They each took another drink from their glasses, and then Mac set his on the table beside the sofa. He took hers and set it there as well. Then he reached up and pulled the combs from her hair so the front fell down around her face.

"I like you in dresses," he said, sliding an inquisitive finger into her cleavage.

"Do you?" It was all she could think of to say when that finger brushed her nipple. One touch and he reduced her to a simpleton.

"A very accessible article of clothing," he replied. "Much more so than a shirt and waistcoat."

"I don't know." Her own hands made short work of the buttons on both his waistcoat and shirt. Then she moved on to his cravat. "I don't have any problems with accessibility."

That was the end of polite conversation. They shucked off layers of clothing as they made their way to the rug in front of the fire. Mac explored every inch of her by the firelight, using his hands, mouth and tongue to tease her, stroke her and ultimately reduce her to a boneless heap. Then, when he was done, he slid inside her with one deep thrust.

Evie arched up, wrapping her legs around his flanks, angling her hips for the best friction. Holding his head, her fingers tangling in his hair, she licked at his face, not caring that it was her own juices she lapped like a cat. Mac growled low in his throat and reared back, so that he knelt on the rug, thighs beneath her hips. As he slid in and out of her—and Evie could see every wet stroke—he licked his thumb and then applied that to the sensitive, swollen knot of flesh between the lips of her sex.

Heat crawled up Evie's chest and neck. Mac's free hand slid up her rib cage to find her breasts. He squeezed one of her nipples in time with the rhythm of each stroke, adding to the glut of pleasure churning within her. She writhed and gripped and met his every thrust.

Climax hit her once more hard and without warning. She made a low keening noise as she tumbled into the abyss again. Mac's movements increased to a pounding, one she eagerly embraced and kept the sparks of sensation rippling through her. Then he stiffened, held her hips tight as he emptied himself inside her with a groan.

They stayed on the floor longer than they probably should have, but neither of them seemed to have the energy required to move. Finally, as the fire banked in the hearth and the room grew a little too chilly for naked flesh, Mac staggered to his feet and pulled her to hers.

"Come on, you wanton wench. Off to bed with you."

She giggled. She never giggled. Oh dear, she was quite drunk. "I'm not sure I can make the trip." A trickle of wetness made her clamp her thighs together. How unromantic.

Mac had to be mildly intoxicated as well, because he grabbed up some of their clothing, wrapped her gown around his waist like a kilt and held it there with one hand, while he pitched her—in his shirt— over his shoulder.

Thank God the staff was gone for the night, or else poor Mrs. Ferguson might have had a heart attack.

Evie wasn't drunk enough to be ill, which was good because she would have vomited down Mac's back and all over her pretty dress. The journey was bouncy, and a tad unsteady, but finally he kicked the door to her bedroom wide-open and deposited her on the bed like a sack of potatoes.

"Ah, hello, bed," she murmured against her pillow. "Did you miss me?"

She was just slipping off to sleep when she was jostled around some more. She started laughing when Mac tossed her under the blankets and crawled in after her—without her gown wrapped around him.

"Is that what I think it is?" she asked as something poked her bottom.

"It's your own damn fault," he replied.

"I like it when you swear," she muttered. "It's so rough and manly." She giggled again, but that turned into a gasp when he lifted her leg and slid into her once more. "Mac!"

"Think of England, Doc. I'll just be a moment."

When was the last time she laughed during sex? When was the last time it had been such fun? These were rhetorical questions because the answer to both was when she'd been with Mac the first time.

She soon stopped laughing, and enjoyed herself immensely. He was right—it didn't take long, but it was certainly delightful. He didn't even withdraw from her when it was over, just kissed the back of her neck. They fell asleep exactly as they were.

So it was no surprise to anyone when Mac "rose" with the sun the following morning. Not even a full bladder could deter either one of them.

"I'm done," she told him later as they shared the shower bath and his soapy hands got a little too talented. "I'm exhausted and I have to work today."

"One more and that's it."

And of course she laughed. He lifted her up and she wrapped her legs around him as he pressed her back against the wall, hot water cascading over them.

She left the house later than she should have, after a huge breakfast and several cups of coffee. Mrs. Ferguson didn't act as if it were odd at all to have a man in the house, God love her. Mac was the only man who had ever spent the night in her home, though he probably didn't know that. She'd fired the last housekeeper because the woman kept asking when Mac was coming back.

It hadn't been one of her prouder moments. But

then, she'd done many things where Mac was concerned that could be ranked the same. She wouldn't change a single one.

Hopefully she'd be able to say the same about what she was about to do.

Warden headquarters was located in Downing Street through a nondescript door. You had to enter a lift that could be accessed only by punch card, and even then you had to have another card that would take you into the inner sanctum. Not everyone had access to this particular area. Evie was one of the chosen few who did. Although that might get taken away very soon.

What she was going to do was very close to treason, and yet she could not talk herself out of it.

The sentinels at the door didn't question her, but she still had to use a punch card to gain entrance—a new security measure.

"Is she in?" she asked as she strode through the reception area.

The woman at the desk—a former prostitute who had helped catch a Jack the Ripper type of monster a few months ago—looked up. "Yes, but she's very busy."

"I don't care." Evie walked over to the woman's desk, hit the switch that controlled the outer locking mechanism of the door and then barged into Dhanya's office.

Right into the middle of sweaty, nasty sex involving her friend and a Warden agent. The agent's husband would no doubt be very surprised.

The women gasped. Dhanya came up onto her knees between her partner's thighs. "Evie, what a surprise."

Evie knew Dhanya was attracted to both men and women—it wasn't really a secret. She knew other things as well, and had assisted her friend with procuring a "procedure" some time ago that had resulted in her absence from office. However, knowing something and witnessing something were *quite* different.

"I don't have to ask for your discretion, do I?" Dhanya inquired.

Evie tore her gaze from Mrs. Ruckland's naked self—the woman had not only her nipples pierced, but her clitoris as well. The very thought made Evie squirm uncomfortably.

"Leave Mac alone."

Dhanya rose to her feet. She was a beautiful woman, with a beautiful body and no shame whatsoever. Even naked she was somewhat intimidating. "I beg your pardon?"

"He fulfilled your bargain. Now stand down. Let him go."

"You have a lot of nerve. I should dismiss you for this."

"Try to find a doctor as good as me." It wasn't bravado; it was truth. She was good at her job, and always made herself available when W.O.R. needed her. "I've never asked you for anything, and I've come running every time you call. I'm asking as a friend for you to let him go, and if that's not good enough for you, if you don't release him you won't have to dismiss me. I'll quit."

"You'd do that for a pirate?"

Evie shook her head. "No. I'd do it for Mac." And then, because it was true, "I'd do it for me."

Her friend regarded her narrowly for a moment. "Of course I'll release him, if that's what you want."

"It is."

"But he's your responsibility. If he's arrested again, I won't be able to help him."

That was assuming he lived long enough to get caught again. "Understood."

"Good. Now get out. And next time, ring me first."

She practically ran from the office.

"Are you all right, Doctor?" Peg, the secretary, asked.

That was not an answerable question at the moment. She wanted to scrub her brain with a scouring brush to get the image of Dhanya naked—Dhanya having sex—out of it. She also wanted to squeal with glee. Mac was free.

"Fine, Peg. Thank you. Have a good day."

She left the office and hurried back to the lift. She had to use her punch cards again to get the box forward and up to the floor where her ward was located—still somewhat underground, but closer to street level.

She had released Theodore's and Imogen's—she didn't remember their surname—bodies into Dhanya's care. Someone else would notify the next of kin of their deaths, and make up some sort of explanation for them if the family didn't know they were agents. Thankfully that wasn't part of her job, because Evie would never be able to come up with believable lies.

There was a new patient in the ward—a note from the nurse said the agent had been brought in with injuries from a physical altercation with a Company operative, who was also in the ward under guard. Wonderful; two patients and they wanted to kill each other. Another typical day with the Wardens.

Her smock hung on a hook behind the door. She put it on over her shirt, waistcoat and trousers, and washed her hands before going out to check on her patients. At least it looked to be a relatively easy day.

That was until the telephone rang. It was Lucas Grey. Arden was in labor.

The message was waiting for Mac when he returned to Evie's house later that morning. He'd gone out to visit the tailor, and to buy a little gift for Evie. He really should be on his way to Brackenhurst to meet up with Nell and give the ship one more ransacking before turning it over to his sister for good. But the search would wait. Nell would wait. The Wardens could damn well wait. He'd been waiting three years for Evie. He hadn't known it at the time, of course, but all he'd been doing was biding his time, going through the motions of life until she came back to him.

All right, so she hadn't come back to him of her own accord, but so far it was going pretty well, so he wouldn't complain.

But there was such a thing as keeping promises, and he'd made one to not only Theo, but to Imogen as well, that he would get the information they uncovered to the Wardens. He had to try once more for them. Part of him—the naive part, Nell would say—clung to the belief that he would find it. Imogen had been a top-notch spy, and not the kind of person who would leave something important where a killer in a hurry, such as Pliny, would be able to find it.

As he was unlocking the front door, it opened. Mrs. Ferguson smiled at him. "Captain MacRae, how lovely to see you again. Will you be wanting luncheon?"

As if on cue, his stomach growled. "That would be lovely. Oh, these are for you." He handed her a bouquet of flowers he'd picked up on his travels.

The old girl lit up like a drunk at a gin factory. "Oh, how lovely! What a wee charmer you are! You go freshen up and I'll have a nice luncheon laid out for you in the dining room when you come down."

Smiling, Mac watched her bustle away. Dear old girl. He missed this sort of thing. Charming older women had been a favorite pastime before the Wardens got their claws into him again. He rather liked making the old girls blush and smile. It made him happy. It was probably foolish, but there was no harm in it.

And it apparently got him luncheon, so it was all good.

He went upstairs to tidy up—washed his hands and face, and ran a comb through his mussed hair. He left Evie's present on the neatly made bed. Poor Mrs. Ferguson must have had a trial of it earlier given the state they'd left it in. He made a mental note to get her more flowers, or perhaps a trinket of some kind.

When he entered the dining room, there was a cold platter on the table for him—meats, cheese and bread. There was even ale to go with it. His dreams of growing fat suddenly seemed achievable.

There was an envelope beside his plate with his name on it. Frowning, he picked it up and turned it over.

It was the seal of the Warden director on the lip. So much for being in a good mood. The harpy probably wrote just to tell him how stupid and useless he was, or to give him his new orders. It would spoil his appetite to read it before eating.

But he couldn't ignore it and enjoy his meal, so he broke the seal and removed the letter from within.

Captain MacRae:
    You are hereby released of all obligation to the Wardens of the Realm. Please note that while your actions on behalf of W.O.R. have been greatly ap-

*preciated and of great service to the Crown, they are
no longer needed. Thank you on behalf of the British
Empire and Her Majesty Queen Victoria.*

It was signed by Dhanya Withering. Dated, too.
Mac stared at it. What had made this woman, who
just yesterday wanted him in shackles, change her
mind about using him?

Evie. Of course. Mac smiled. He knew he should
be put out that she interfered, running in to fix things
as if she were his mother or he were an idiot, but it
was difficult to be angry when he would have loved
to be a fly on the wall during that conversation. His
girl didn't like to be denied.

Still grinning, he put the letter aside and dug into
his meal. He was well past replete and working on
stuffed when he heard the front bell ring. A few moments later, Mrs. Ferguson swept in with the earl on
her heels.

"Lord Wolfred to see you, Captain."

One look at the woman and Mac had no doubt
that she'd pitch the peer out on his ear if he so de-
sired. "Thank you, Mrs. Ferg. Would you care to join
me, Wolfred?"

If the other man took offense to being referred to
in such a familiar manner, he didn't show it. "I'd
love to." Then to Mrs. Ferguson, "If it's no bother to
you, of course."

Not bad. A smile would have driven the courtesy
home a little more smoothly, but then again Wolfred
didn't strike him as much for teasing or harmless

flirtation. He probably didn't have to rely on charm or wit as weapons very often, either. It was a lot easier to catch an enemy off guard with a fist to the throat when he thought you nothing more than a witless lip-flapper.

"No bother at all, my lord." The housekeeper curtsied and scurried off. Wolfred set his beaver hat on the table and sat down in the chair opposite Mac.

"I find it interesting that you don't sit at the head of the table," the earl remarked casually.

Mac shrugged. "I sit at the head of the table on my ship every day. Sometimes it's nice to sit somewhere else."

"Rather like the days I can shuck off the responsibilities of my title and spend an afternoon working on a carriage engine or a velocycle."

"I imagine so, yes, only with slightly less mechanics."

"You should come to the house sometime. I'm building a new velocycle out of a mix of English and German parts. She's going to fly."

Mac raised an eyebrow. "Are you honestly inviting me to your home?"

"If you plan to stay around for a while, why not?"

He laughed. "Your wife sent you to spy on me, didn't she?"

The red-haired man grinned. "She did. And now that you've found me out, you really ought to come by sometime."

"I'd like that. How long I stay is up to Evie. I need

to make a trip to my estate soon to settle some business, but if she wants me to come back, I will."

"If?"

"I try not to take anything for granted where Doc's concerned."

"Probably safer that way with women in general."

"Amen."

Mrs. Ferguson returned with an extra mug and then collected a plate and silverware from the sideboard. She placed everything in front of Wolfred, bobbed a curtsey and left again after the earl thanked her.

The two of them ate and drank with a mix of companionable silence and good conversation. It had been too long since Mac had talked with a man with a background similar to his own, who had similar interests and was also in love with a headstrong woman. Not that Wolfred said as much, but a man had only to meet the countess to make that leap on his own.

They were discussing German engineering vs. English when something in the earl's pocket made a noise. He withdrew a small device not much smaller than a cigarette case from his coat.

"Is that a telegraph?" Mac asked. He knew about the latest innovations in communication, but he hadn't seen one up close.

"It is. Brand-new as of last week. A friend built it for me." Wolfred consulted the device and frowned.

"Is everything all right?"

"No. It's from Claire—my wife. She says that Arden Grey has gone into labor and that I'm to bring you to Mayfair with me."

Mac drew his shoulders back. "Me? What the devil does she want me for?"

Wolfred met his gaze over the top of the device. "It appears that Evelyn is going to deliver the baby and she wants you to help her."

Chapter 16

"You want me to do what?"

The note of panic in Mac's voice would have been humorous if Evie wasn't already feeling the stress of the afternoon weighing upon her.

"I *need* you to help me deliver this baby." Lucas, the father, was too close, too involved to be of any use if there were complications. Claire had practically no experience when it came to these sorts of things, and Alastair was . . . well, Alastair. He and his wife were much better suited to provide moral support for Lucas.

Mac, she knew, had delivered at least one baby in the past, and during the few years they had been together, he assisted her in several medical situations, some that were critical in nature.

He might sound like a hysterical schoolgirl, but when there was a crisis, when it came right down to it, he would keep his head. Above all else, he would do as she told him and do it well.

They were outside the room in which Arden had decided to give birth—a renovated room on the second floor with a small attached sitting room where family could gather.

Personally, Evie would prefer all friends and family to be on another floor—preferably in another house. However, Arden wanted Lucas close, and he wanted to be there for her, but both agreed it might be best if he remained a short distance away. The man's bones were plated with gregorite, an incredible strong metal. Usually he knew his strength, but in a stressful situation such as this, he might forget himself and break Arden's hand while innocently holding it.

An agitated father-to-be was bad enough, let alone one who could crush bricks with his hands.

Mac was pale, his hair mussed, but his jaw was set. As soon as she had told him she needed him, his spine snapped straight. He wouldn't let her down.

"Let's do this, then," he said. He'd already removed his coat and he always wore his shirtsleeves rolled up to his forearms. "What do you need me to do?"

Evie smiled. "First of all, Arden's water broke several hours ago. She's dilating as she should be, and I expect her to start feeling the need to push very soon."

He didn't look as though he wanted to hear any of this. "All right."

"I need you to help keep her as focused and calm as possible. I may need you to assist me in getting the baby out, and I will need you to help me with a few things such as cutting the cord. Most of all, I need you to look me in the eye and tell me I can do this."

Mac blinked. "Excuse me?"

"More than anything else, Mac, I need you in there with me. Arden is as calm as a rock and ready to do this. She's a very good friend, and I want this to go smoothly for her. Do you understand?"

One look and she knew he did. No, she hadn't much experience delivering babies and that was all right. She knew how to do it. She also knew what could go wrong. She'd seen it. Women died giving birth far too often in this modern day and age. If Arden wasn't her friend, she wouldn't be nearly so skittish.

He jabbed his thumb toward the door. "This is easy. She's going to do most of the work. All you're going to have to do is catch that little thing when it shoots out."

The image was enough to make her chuckle. The butterflies attacking her stomach weren't so agitated now. "Thank you."

Mac smiled and kissed her on the forehead. Her heart gave a little flip, but the rest of her relaxed. She knocked on the door and turned the knob.

Arden Grey had worked for several years for W.O.R. as an inventor, investigator, gadgeteer and weapon smith. She wasn't as well-known as her fa-

ther, who had had the post before her, but she was
damn good at her job, as the ladies who purchased
her mechanical "hysteria relief" devices could attest.
So it should have been no surprise that Arden would
have prepared for the arrival of her child in her own
way.

Only Mac didn't know Arden.

Evie glanced at him as they entered the room, just
to see his reaction. He stopped just over the threshold. His jaw dropped and he looked around in
amazement.

There was something like a barber's chair on a
high pedestal that could be raised or lowered using
a ratcheting foot pump. The chair could also be angled forward or back, with more or less tip. There
was an adjustable mirror suspended on a metal arm
above it.

A tray of instruments was laid out on a movable
table. The area was well lit, with the faint strains of
Beethoven coming from a cylinder phonograph in
the corner. There was a small incubator and a sink
with hot running water, thanks to a boiler.

It was a little hospital room, only with more
equipment—better equipment—than most hospi-
tals. Arden liked to be prepared.

Her friend had been pacing back and forth along
the plush carpet when Evie and Mac entered. Her long
russet hair was tied back with a ribbon behind her
neck. She wore a long, loose nightgown and wrapper
that draped over her extremely pregnant belly. She

had one hand on her stomach, and a pocket watch in the other. She looked up.

"Three minutes apart, Evie."

Sweet Jesus. "Arden, you shouldn't be up."

"Nonsense. Movement and gravity are the best ways to speed up the labor portion of any birth." She glanced at Mac. "Hello. You must be the infamous Mac."

He nodded. "In the flesh. Pleasure to meet you, Lady Huntley."

Arden smiled. She was one of those women whom pregnancy made even more gorgeous than she was before. Her hair had thickened and waved down her back. Her whiskey-colored eyes were wide and bright, and her skin was flawless and fair.

Most women would want to slap her for looking so good this far into labor.

"We'll see if you still think that in half an hour, dear man. Help me to the chair, will you, please? You look like a strapping fellow."

Mac went to her immediately. As soon as Arden gripped his arm, Evie knew what was happening— another contraction. Mac understood as well. He held Arden as she groaned in pain, supported her through the spasm and then picked her up into his arms and carried her to the chair. As soon as he deposited her, he reached into the basin on the instrument tray, wrung out the cloth there and placed it on Arden's forehead.

Evie beamed. The man should have been a doctor.

If nothing else he would make a brilliant doctor's husband.

She froze. No time to think on that.

"Is she going to give birth in this chair?" he asked, mopping Arden's brow.

Evie nodded. "Despite its not being a very lady-like position, it's been thought by many physicians that it is much easier for a woman to give birth in a vertical posture rather than horizontal."

"Did you build this chair, Lady Huntley?" he asked.

"Call me Arden. I think we're going to be far past formality in a very short time. And yes, I did."

"Are you extremely clever or just lazy?"

Both women looked at him in disbelief. Damnation. The man never knew when to stop teasing and joking.

Arden smiled. "Both. Very much both. I'll tell you what—why don't you climb up here and give birth for me, ambitious bastion of manhood that you are?"

The man was magic. That was all the explanation Evie's usually rational and logical brain could settle upon. No one else could say some of the things he said when he said them and live to be into his thirties.

"I wouldn't want to steal your thunder," he told her, eyes sparkling. "You've gone through all this trouble. You should reap the reward."

Arden laughed, but the sound was quickly cut off by another contraction. "Evie, I'm beginning to feel as though I should push."

This was it. Evie flicked the switch inside herself that cut off her emotions. It was something she had learned to do a long time ago. She couldn't think of Arden as her friend right now. She had to think of her as a patient, presenting a challenge that must be overcome.

"Feet on the rests, then, love." She made certain Arden was positioned just right, the stirrups at the right angle to give her something to dig into. Then she did a final examination. Everything looked as it should, thankfully.

"All right, my girl, it's up to you." She grinned. "Let's bring this baby into the world, shall we?"

Arden was nervous, something Mac seemed to comprehend. He stood by her, facing her so that she had someone to focus on. He even gave her his hand to squeeze.

I love you.

Evie froze. Had she said that . . . ? No. Mac wasn't looking at her and neither was Arden. She was safe. Now was not the time to go making declarations, especially not when in a situation that heightened emotions.

She turned her attention back to where it needed to be—and she didn't let it waver again.

It took a little over an hour to bring the Huntley heir into the world. Mac alternated between giving Arden encouragement, buoying her resolve, letting her abuse him both physically and verbally and helping Evie. The delivery was fairly easy for a first birth. Once the little man slipped into her hands, Evie made sure his mouth and nose were clear, tied off and cut the cord—with Mac's help—cleaned the baby up and handed him to his sweaty, tired and beautiful mama.

"Mac, would you go get Lucas?" Evie asked. As he walked away she smiled at Evie. "One more push, and we're done." She disposed of the placenta before Lucas came in. It was something that tended to send men into a tizzy if they saw it.

She had never seen a man as in awe as Lucas Grey was. The sheer love in his eyes for wife and son was humbling, and it made Evie extremely envious. She left the room so the two of them could have a few moments alone. She'd tend to Arden afterward—not that there was much to do.

When she joined her friends in the sitting room, Claire grinned at her. "Good job, Doctor."

"He's a beautiful boy." She turned to Mac. "Thank you for being there with me."

He smiled—there was a lot of that going on in this house at that moment. "Anytime. Although next time you hold the woman's hand. I think she broke two of my fingers."

Next time. Were there any two words in the English language with more hope and promise attached? Evie didn't know if there would be a next time, but there was one thing that occurred to her— the thought of it wasn't as frightening as it used to be.

"I will not return home a failure," Anatolii Veselov told his friend and fellow agent, Sergei. "I must find the information the English spies hid."

Sergei nodded. "I will do what I can to assist you."

They were in a little inn north of London, where it was safe for them to sit in private and talk in their native language. Most people would assume them travelers. There was very little risk of Anatolii being recognized as "Pliny."

He had shaved the scruffy beard he'd been forced to wear for years, cut his hair and put on a decent suit of clothes. He'd gotten rid of those disgusting dentures that made it appear that he had no teeth. His fingernails were clean for the first time in a long while, and his feet were back on solid ground.

As soon as he located and recovered the information, he would be able to return home to Russia, to his family. He could live out the rest of his days in peace and quiet.

He had few regrets in his life, but almost all of them happened during his time with Gavin MacRae. He liked the man. He liked the crew. Most of all he liked Nell. She was his biggest regret. He would have liked to share her bed. She would no doubt rather slit her own throat than have anything to do with him now.

No, he would be glad to return home and leave this life behind.

"MacRae's ship is at his home—Brackenhurst," he informed his companion. "If we are correct in the assumption that the Wardens do not have the information, that's where it will be. We need to move quickly."

"My associates tell me MacRae is at the home of the woman doctor. With that sort of distraction, he may not give us the trouble you expect."

Anatolii regarded him. "You do not know the man, my friend. It is better if you have no expectations of him, for he will almost always do the opposite. How soon can you get me to this Brackenhurst place?"

"We can leave in the morning."

"That is good." He eyed the mug of ale on the table. "I cannot wait to taste good vodka again." Vodka was not as popular in England as it was in Russia. It would look odd for him—supposedly a British sailor—to be an enthusiast. The English liked their warm ale and disgusting gin.

And no one even ate black bread, let alone knew how to make it.

"We will meet here at seven and depart shortly after."

Anatolii nodded and took another drink of the dreadful ale—he was thirsty. "*Da.* I think I will retire now. Good night, Sergei."

His fellow Russian wished him a good rest as he rose to his feet. It was late and there was a nice soft bed waiting for him that would be a decadent pleasure after sleeping on a ship. That was just one small reason why he would have liked to lie down with Nell—she had a real bed. He would never know all the delights in which they could have indulged while in it.

He climbed the stairs to the first floor where his

room was located—overlooking the yard so he could see who came and went—and removed the key from his pocket.

Creak. Someone was on the stairs behind him.

Anatolii turned the key in the lock and pushed the door open with one hand as his other went to the blade strapped to his trousers. He had barely crossed the threshold before garrote wire slipped over his head. He managed to get his hand up, protecting his neck, as he pivoted from the waist and shoved his knife forward.

Sergei seemed surprised to have a dagger shoved into his throat. It wasn't the quickest or cleanest way to kill someone, but then, Anatolii wasn't trying to be quick or clean; he meant to send a message.

Traitor. The Medved would not have him killed this way. The Medved would not kill him after such a successful career. No, Sergei was the one who had betrayed his country.

As the other man slowly collapsed, Anatolii followed him down to the floor, holding the blade so it couldn't be pulled out—that would just make far too much mess.

He dragged Sergei over the threshold and shut the door. He locked it and then squatted beside the man. Gurgling noises and blood escaped the wound.

"When the Wardens find you they will know I killed you. They will know they failed. And they will know they cannot stop me. They will learn all of this much later than they would like. And by the time they know it, I will be gone. You should not have betrayed me, Sergei. You should not have betrayed Mother Russia."

The man stared at him, the life leaching from his eyes. Anatolii saw the question there. There would be no harm in answering it. "I have pretended to be a friend to my enemies for years. Did you think I would not know when someone is pretending to be *my* friend?"

Then he let his weight fall back on his heels, and stayed there, staring into the other man's eyes until there was nothing there but his own reflection. The gurgling noises had stopped.

Sergei was dead.

Anatolii was not squeamish, and it wouldn't be the first time he'd slept in the same room as a corpse, but he wanted the body out of the way, and where it would make the least amount of mess when he removed the knife.

He carried the body to the adjoining toilet and put him in the tub. Then, after double-checking to make sure that Sergei was indeed dead, he pulled the blade from his throat and wiped the blade on each of the traitor's cheeks before cleaning it.

It was sad—not that he had killed Sergei, but that Sergei had turned on his country. It was not the first time something like this had happened; people betrayed their countries every day, but he wished he hadn't been the one to discover Sergei. He did not enjoy killing his own countrymen, but he'd rather be the killer than the victim.

And he would much rather kill than end up a

Warden prisoner. There was no dishonor in killing a traitor, or in protecting oneself.

He closed the toilet door behind him with a yawn and lay down upon the bed, the dagger beneath his pillow. After a few moments he toed off his boots and pulled the quilt from the bottom of the mattress up over him. It was every bit as comfortable as he hoped it would be.

He was asleep within minutes.

Chapter 17

"What is this?"

Mac grinned at the look of disbelief on Evie's face. "It's a Daimler steam carriage."

"I know what it is. Why is it here?" Here being the street in front of her house.

"I bought it." If he told her he'd just pulled it out of his backside, he didn't think she could look more surprised.

"Just now?"

"About an hour ago, yes."

"From whom?"

"Wolfred. He's rebuilt it. Sold it to me for a song." And was all too happy to have someone else to talk to about mechanical things and driving.

"I've heard you sing. He got the sharp end of the stick."

He patted her on the head. "Look at you, being a wit. I'm so proud." It was a good comeback.

Evie braced her hands on her hips and studied the vehicle.

"She's gorgeous, isn't she?" If the thing was a woman, she'd be the most expensive and celebrated courtesan in the world. A little polish and she might even be as beautiful as Evie.

"It is lovely—I'll give you that." She turned her face toward him. "I thought you preferred to do all your traveling by air."

He shrugged. "People change. Do you want me to bring the luggage out?"

"That would be wonderful. I have to stop by Arden and Luke's before we leave."

"Of course." He wouldn't have thought otherwise. She'd want to make certain mother and child were doing well before going away. "I rang Nell and told her to air out the master bedroom. You know I haven't been back there in over a year?"

"A pitfall of being a pirate—it involves a lot of travel."

Former pirate, he wanted to correct her, but there was little point—she wouldn't see much difference between the two. "That's why I'm staying on the ground for a while."

She blinked. "You are?"

Maybe he was a fool to read so much into it, but her surprise pleased him. She still cared. "Why not? Even birds have to land occasionally."

"I suppose they do." She looked perplexed. He'd be damned if he told her that he was grounding himself. She'd think he was giving it up for her, and that wasn't the case, although he'd be lying if he didn't admit that she had something to do with the decision.

"I'll get our bags and then we'll check in on the new parents. We can leave for Brackenhurst right from Mayfair. Go get ready."

"Being a wee bit bossy, aren't you?"

"I learned from the best."

Evie chuckled and shook her head. He knew she thought him a fool, and he didn't mind. At least she was still smiling and laughing. How long before she got either bored or frightened? He knew her, knew how her mind worked. She was going to spook on him soon, and there was nothing he could do about it except try not to fall in love again.

Problem was, he didn't think he'd ever fallen *out* of love with her. He could thump his chest and tell himself that this time he wouldn't let her go, but how could he possibly make her stay? He wasn't about to beg—that was just pathetic.

So he was just going to ride it out, see where the wind took them. In the meantime, he was going to take them both to Brackenhurst, which was to the west, between Bristol and Glastonbury. Wolfred told him the Daimler could get them there in about three and one-half hours. Mac wasn't so sure he believed that. He also wasn't so sure if Evie would appreciate driving that fast.

He ought to have known better. An hour later they were well into their journey, the Daimler tearing cross-country at a fantastic speed, Evie grinning the entire way.

How could a woman so fearless in almost every way be so utterly terrified of love?

They made the trip in four hours—including a stop for food and one to answer the call of nature. The glossy lacquer of the carriage was splattered with mud and dust, but they'd had the collapsible canopy to keep the dirt from their clothes.

Brackenhurst was a large gray stone house set upon acres of green rolling hills that were attended to by Mac's tenants. The entry door jutted out from the front of the house, and was flanked by gently recessed walls that extended on along the front and then came out again, so that each wing lined up with the front door. It was an interesting design, but an old one. The house had been in his family for centuries. He had spent a fair bit of time here as a boy— when not in America or Scotland.

His family were great travelers, all of them, but Mac looked forward to putting down some roots.

The *Queen V* was moored out back in the docking bay his father had built almost thirty years ago. It was easy to travel when you had your own flying machine.

His family had never been incredibly wealthy, but his father was smart, and now Mac had more than enough to live out the rest of his life in comfort—not counting the money he'd earned during his years at W.O.R. and as an "import/export facilitator."

"Nice to see the old girl's still standing," he remarked as they climbed out of the car—Evie didn't wait for him to get her door. She never did.

"Just as lovely as I remember," she added. "Roof looks a little dodgy, though."

It was intact, but a little saggy in places. "I'd better have it replaced before winter." There was already a bit of nip to the air, that signal that autumn wouldn't last forever. It was a sin, really, because everything looked so much brighter and more colorful at this time of year.

Nell met them at the door—a fact that must have the housekeeper, Mrs. Lily, in a tizzy. Very big on keeping up with tradition was Mrs. Lily.

His sister had her hair down and was grinning like a madwoman. She was wearing a loose tunic and trousers that he remembered her buying in India because they hid her scars and most of her arm.

These days she seemed to have accepted her mechanical appendage as part of her, because she never took pains to conceal it. She'd lost her arm the same day Evie gave him back his breath. The Company—a worldwide agency devoted to chaos and anarchy—had decided to blow up one of their ships rather than allow the Wardens to take it in. Mac had been chosen to pilot the thing back to London. His sister was with him. Thank God he'd made Evie and Napoleon remain on the *Queen V*.

The ship he'd been on exploded twenty minutes outside London. Forty people had been injured by debris, but none seriously. Their altitude had been low, and somehow the balloon sail managed to slow their fall; otherwise he and Nell would have been dead when they hit the ground.

Instead, he had a small cannon—really, was there such a thing as a "small" cannon?—on his chest, and Nell's arm was pinned under the anchor. He'd wanted Evie to take care of Nell first. She refused.

He'd come here after she left him. He'd planned out a vacation of sorts for them. He was going to bring her here, spoil her rotten and then give her his grandmother's ring.

That never happened. She saved his life and then walked out of it. At the time, he wished she had just let him die.

"You're here!" Nell cried, throwing her arms around Evie. His sibling never made any secret of the fact that she thought him an idiot for not trying to woo Evie back. He didn't think his sister knew what it was like to have her heart broken. He hoped she never did.

When she hugged him, the metal of her arm bit into his ribs—on purpose, he suspected.

"We won't take long," Mac assured her. "We just need to see if Imogen left anything behind."

"It's no bother. I was planning to muck about for a few extra days anyway."

"Are you planning to leave again so soon?" Evie asked. Maybe it was his imagination, but Mac thought her voice cracked on "leave."

"I am," Nell replied. Mac shook his head, but she

ignored him—*meddling cow*. "You're looking at the new captain of the *Queen V*."

"*What?*" Evie looked to him, but before he could speak, his sister pounced again.

"Although I think I'll have to rename her, seeing as how she was named for you." Nell just let that little tidbit fall where it needed.

Poor Evie looked lost.

"I'm going to take our bags up to the master suite," Mac announced, edging past them both. Normally there'd be a butler or at least a footman to help, but there hadn't been a full staff in the house for years. He'd have to remedy that, he supposed.

Unfortunately escape was not an option. Evie was hot on his heels as he practically ran upstairs carrying two heavy suitcases and her doctor's bag. She never left the house without the bloody thing, it seemed.

She followed him into the suite, shutting the door behind her. He was trapped.

"I never knew the ship was named for me."

He set the bags on the rug. "I never told you."

"Why?"

He shrugged. "Seemed silly maybe. You never suspected?"

She shook her head. This seemed to bother her. Frowning, she lifted her gaze to his. "You're giving her to Nell?"

Squatting down, Mac opened his suitcase and removed his shaving kit. Maybe she'd start unpacking as well and get distracted. "I'm not going to need her anymore, and Nell deserves her own ship. She'll be a good captain."

"Of course she will. Why didn't you tell me this?"

"Does it make any impact on your life?"

She stared at him as though he'd started talking Gaelic. "What does that mean?"

"I mean, does my giving up flying affect you?"

He could literally see her squirm. "I don't know."

"You should, don't you think? Given that you helped make it happen."

"What the devil did I do?"

He pulled the letter from Dhanya out of his coat pocket and shoved it at her. He'd been waiting to talk about it. "Are you going to deny having anything to do with this?"

She took the paper and opened it, reading it quickly. She thrust it back at him. "I know nothing about it."

"*Evie.*" How much of an idiot did she think he was?

She threw her hands up into the air. "All right, fine! I went to see Dhanya."

"And?" Seriously, he didn't know whether to shake her or kiss her. Laughing was out of the question—unless he wanted to lose an eye.

Her fingers fiddled with a figurine on the dresser as she avoided his gaze. "I might have coerced her into letting you out of your agreement."

Not one, but both of Mac's brows shot up. She could have lifted her skirt and revealed herself as a man and he wouldn't have been any more surprised. "You blackmailed the director of W.O.R.? Damnation, Evie that's treason! That's a hanging offense. That's . . ."

"Lovely?" she suggested drily, finally dragging her gaze to meet his. "Brilliant, perhaps? The nicest thing anyone has ever done for you?"

He crossed the distance between them and took her face in his hands. She wrapped her fingers around his wrists.

"It is the most insane, dangerous, reckless"—she tried to pull away, but he held fast—"most *amazing* thing anyone has ever done for me."

Her eyes widened. "Really?"

Mac grinned. "Shut up." He kissed her before she could possibly say another word.

As their mouths were otherwise employed, it was a long time before either of them spoke again.

Evie and Mac didn't attempt to search the ship that night—it was too dark, and given that the ship's engine was what generated power to the lights, they'd be dependent on torches and lanterns. Starting the engine would be loud and a waste of fuel.

They had a simple but delicious supper of meats, cheese and bread, with fruit for dessert. Some of the evening was spent with Nell in the library, where they each curled up with a book. Mac reclined on the sofa, his feet across Evie's lap. They shared a glass of port. It was all terribly domestic.

Evie liked it. There was nothing fearsome about it,

nothing that made her twitchy and unsettled. It was incredibly comforting, soothing. As she read her book—*Tom Jones*—she slipped her hand up the leg of Mac's trousers and absently stroked his shin and calf. It wasn't sexual, just something she was compelled to do. She needed to touch him.

Just before midnight they headed off to bed. Nell wished them a good night from her chair by the window and went back to her book—that was the extent of her interest in their affairs.

In the privacy of their chamber, Mac and Evie shared a bath, where their casual touching quickly ignited into something more. By the time they crawled into bed, Evie was languid right down to her bones.

Mac left the drapes open so they could look at the moon as they drifted off, and so they'd rise with the sun.

They did get up early the next morning, but not obscenely so.

They threw on clothes and slipped downstairs for breakfast. Nell wasn't up yet, but Mrs. Lily had coffee and warm bread waiting for them, and soon produced a hearty breakfast that could have fed a small army.

"I love that woman," Evie remarked around a mouthful of fried bread.

Mac grinned. "She's taken, but I'm sure she'd share her culinary secrets with you."

She tore off another bite and reached for the molasses. "I'd have suitors lined up all the way to Hyde Park once that got out."

"I suppose you would. I'd have to fend them off with pats of fresh butter and strawberry jam." Both of which he slathered onto his own bread.

"Forget the suitors. If you've got jam and butter, you'll have to fend off me."

"I doubt I'd put up much of a fight." He gave her that little smile—the one that always made her heart skip a beat.

"You're so easy," she teased. God, she could get used to this. *Careful, Evie.* But none of that old fear rose to the surface. She was content just to enjoy every moment with him.

Was it because he was giving up the *Queen V*? He wasn't doing this for her, was he?

"Mac, why did you give your ship to Nell?"

He wiped his mouth with a napkin. "Because I've seen the sky over practically the entire world and I'm ready for a change of scenery."

She raised both brows. "Really?"

"Cross my heart. I might miss it someday, but for now I'm looking forward to getting my land legs back."

There it was—a little tingle of anxiety in the pit of her stomach. What did this mean for her? For them? Did he have expectations? Did she?

"I think I might get fat," he announced, almost as an afterthought.

She stared at him and tried to picture him with a big belly and jowls.

Evie burst out laughing.

Mac put on his "mock indignant" expression that she knew all too well. "I think I'd look rather stately if I was a little portly."

"Do you?" The words spilled out wrapped in a chuckle. "You ought to think again."

"Would you still want me if my thighs visibly quivered?" he asked, all fluttering eyelashes and puckered lips.

"Oh God!" She shuddered.

"Would you let me rest my belly on you when I got tired of hauling it around?" He drew closer, breathing hot breath and foolishness against her neck. She squirmed, laughing. "Would you nestle my chins between your bosoms?"

"Stop it!" She was crying and her stomach was beginning to hurt.

He nipped lightly at her neck. "Would you like to spank my doughy, white arse?"

"Mac, stop!" She pushed him away, laughing and cringing at the same time. "You awful man!"

He grinned and returned to his chair. He caught the napkin she threw at him and tossed it back. "I guess that answers *those* questions, then. You know, I'd still want you if your thighs visibly quivered."

She frowned. "I think they already do."

"Hypocrite." He took a sip of his coffee and consulted his watch. "Shall we get this over with?"

For a moment she sat there, wondering what the devil he was talking about. Them?

"Searching . . . the . . . ship?" he intoned at her bewildered expression. "Shall we? The sooner I find what Imogen and Theo died for, the sooner I can tell Dhanya Withering to go swiv herself."

She clucked her tongue. "Such language." Dhanya was her friend, but Evie knew how difficult she could be—it came with the job of director. It wasn't a position you were given for being weak or considerate. "Let's go, then. Can I be there when you tell her, though? I want to see the top of her head come off."

"Of course. I might need to hide behind you."

One of the things she adored about Mac was that he was more than willing to be the fool, the butt of the joke. Sometimes people thought him foolish, but that was the point. Always relaxed, always charming and witty—until it came time to knock your teeth out.

"I'll protect you," she quipped.

They climbed the stairs to the docking platform and walked onto the ship. Evie stood on the deck and looked around. "I suppose it's not bad for a namesake."

Mac patted the scuffed wooden rail. "She's been a good friend all these years."

"You're going to miss her, aren't you?"

"Maybe. Probably. She'll be in good hands." He turned then and started for the stairs to belowdecks. Evie followed.

He was really going to give up his ship. Give up his life of adventure. Perhaps there was a chance for them after all. Or would he grow bored of a quiet life? Worse, would he get bored of her? That was always the fear, wasn't it? That she wouldn't be a good enough wife, a good enough doctor, a good enough lover. That she just wouldn't be *good enough* for him to stay.

What if he left her?

The thought sent a sharp, cold pain straight to her chest. She was terrified of that. What if she gave herself to him totally and completely, and like her mother with her father, she wasn't enough?

What if he did get fat? What if she got fat? What if he lost his hair and decided he wanted a younger woman?

What if monkeys flew out of her arse?

Jaw set, Evie followed after Mac. Fretting over what-ifs led to madness. Her mother never did this to herself—not that she knew of. Of course, look where her mother had ended up: abandoned by the man she loved.

Oddly enough, she didn't remember her mother ever blaming herself for her lover's betrayal. She pined for him, but she never accepted blame. It was Evie who took that on.

Look at her, being all reflective.

She followed Mac into the cabin where Imogen had died. The bed had been stripped of its sheets and mattress. Only the frame remained.

"How about you start here and I'll start with the storage room where the rest of her things were kept?"

"I can do that if you want," she suggested.

Mac shook his head. "It will be easier for me to tell the difference between what belongs on board and what doesn't."

"All right. Any idea what I'm looking for?"

He smiled tightly. "None whatsoever."

Evie surveyed the room with her hands on her hips. "That ought to make it easy, then. I'll yell if I find anything."

"Likewise."

Evie began looking in one corner of the room, checking under furniture and in drawers and cupboards. While she found a fair bit of dust, and a lady's stocking, there was nothing out of the ordinary.

Wait. What was she doing? Imogen had been too badly injured to hide anything in this room. She rubbed her forehead. How could she have been so dumb as not to remember that?

That meant that the information had to be in something she had with her when she came aboard the ship—even before that because Imogen had told Mac that she had it, not that her husband had.

Every woman knew there was the chance that she might lose her bag—or have it stolen. And spies knew that keeping information on your person was the best choice. Better still was concealing the information in something mundane and innocuous.

Mac said he had gone through Imogen's clothing and found nothing. He'd had the forethought to keep the clothing she'd been wearing the night she'd been shot, and there was nothing there, either.

Evie looked around. If she was Imogen—a sea-soned spy—where would she hide something where no one except perhaps another female spy might think to look?

She crossed the small cabin to the armoire, her boot heels clunking on the smooth floor planks. The heavy wooden doors opened with the slightest groan. Inside were a few items of gentlemen's clothing that she patted down just to be thorough, and a woman's coat, skirt and pair of boots. She passed her hands over the coat and skirt, feeling for lumps, unusual seams or hidden pockets.

Nothing.

There was nothing inside the boots. She tipped them upside down and even slid her hand inside, searching out hiding spots. They were nice boots—Italian if she wasn't mistaken. Too bad they were a size too small. That was awful and she knew it. They were gorgeous.

Well, perhaps not too gorgeous. One of the heels was slightly misaligned. That was shoddy work-manship.

She bent to put them back and then froze. Slowly she straightened, bringing the boots with her.

No one who crafted boots so lovely would ever let one go out with a dodgy heel. Evie turned the boot over, wrapped her hand around the heel and twisted.

It loosened, and then finally let go.

Inside the hourglass heel stem was a tiny brass cylinder—smaller than the ones used by the general populace to listen to music or stories. This was

Warden tech—and crafted by either Arden or her father.

This was what they had been looking for.

Her throat dry, heart pounding, she put the cylinder in her inside coat pocket and put the heel back on the boot. She had to show this to Mac.

She yanked open the door.

"Oh, look what I"—she looked up— "found." The bottom fell out of her stomach.

"Hello, Dr. Stone," said the man she knew as Pliny. Only he didn't look much like Pliny now. He looked like an ordinary middle-aged gentleman, who spoke with a Russian accent. And he had a rapid-discharge pistol in his hand. It looked like a fairly normal weapon, but it automatically loaded ammunition into the chamber from a containment unit in the hand. If the person firing kept the trigger pulled, the gun would fire until it was empty, and it would do it incredibly fast. "What did you find?"

Evie held up the boot. "There's a secret compartment inside." Then she tossed the boot at him. He staggered backward to catch it, and she pushed past him into the corridor. He turned on her almost immediately.

"Hey, asshole!" It was Mac. He ran toward her.

"Pliny" raised his weapon. "I do not want to hurt you."

Mac didn't stop. He had a dagger in his hand—she had given it to him four years ago on his birthday. He pulled back his arm as if about to throw it.

Pliny pulled back the hammer as he gazed down the barrel. He pulled the trigger.

Evie didn't even think; she just acted. She threw herself between Mac and the gun.

White hot pain exploded in her chest. She crashed to the floor screaming soundlessly as her lungs fought for air. Dear God, she was going to die.

And then there was nothing.

Chapter 18

"Evie!" Mac's shout came too late. She had fallen before the words could even echo in his head.

The fool woman got in the way, and Pliny shot her. At least the bastard had the grace to look horrified at what he had done, but that faded as he raised the gun again.

He never got to fire another shot. Mac was on him like a lion on an old stag, catching the spy's wrist and jerking it upward with a snap he'd learned from the Wardens that broke the wrist. His other hand shot forward, hard and true.

He buried the dagger deep in the older man's gut and then jerked it upward. It was a fatal wound, but it wouldn't end quickly for the bastard. The traitor fell forward as Mac yanked the blade from his flesh, his knees hitting the floor as he tried to stanch the flow of his own blood with his one usable hand.

Mac had both the dagger and pistol as he fell to his knees beside Evie.

The front of her shirt and waistcoat were covered with blood that splattered her neck and face, but she was breathing, and that was what mattered most at that moment.

Boots thumped on the steps. It was Nell. "Mac, what the . . . Oh, Jesus."

Mac glanced up at her. "Get me Evie's medical bag and send for the Wardens."

His sister nodded once, then ran back up. Nell could run like a cheetah, and she usually kept her wits about her when things exploded out of control. He just had to keep Evie alive until she returned.

"Evie? Can you hear me, sweetheart?"

She moaned softly, eyelashes fluttering. A few feet away wet, squelching noises combined with ragged breath and gasps of pain.

Good. He hoped the bastard took a good long and excruciating time to die. If he weren't so concerned about Evie, he would go stick his fingers in Pliny's gut just to make it hurt a little more.

"Evie." He pushed hair back from her face. "Evie, open your eyes."

She did. The dark depths were clouded by pain and confusion, but they focused on him. "Mac."

He smiled. "Hi."

She frowned and lifted her hand to her chest. "I got shot, didn't I?"

"You did. Why'd you go and do that?"

"Couldn't . . . I couldn't let him shoot you."

"So you had to play the hero." He tried very hard not to let how angry he was at her show in his voice. Or his fear—he couldn't let that show, either.

Her lips curved slightly. "I thought it was my turn."

Mac blinked, willing the tears away. "Nell's gone to get your bag."

She nodded. "The gun, was it a normal pistol?"

"It was."

"If the bullet didn't go through, you have to take it out."

There wasn't any blood seeping out around her, but he slid his hand beneath her just to be sure. She made a small sound of distress at the movement, and her jaw tightened.

"It didn't go through."

"When Nell gets back you need to use Listerine on it and your hands. Pour some over the long tweezers in the instrument roll and use them to extract the bullet."

"I will." He'd removed bullets before, but never from the woman he loved.

Evie licked her lips. Was that blood on her tongue? "I may pass out. Once the bullet has been removed, you need to inject me with the fluid I used on you. Inject it right into the wound."

He nodded. "Then what?"

She placed her hand over his, which lay on his knee. Her fingers were sticky with her own blood. "Bandage it up and hope it works. I can't tell how bad it is, but I know it's not good."

The shot had missed her heart, but not by much. It was one of the few times that "almost" counted for anything.

"You're going to be fine," he told her.

Another tiny smile. "Which one of us is the doctor?"

"Ah, but which one of us has been shot the most?"

She chuckled, then winced. "I found the information. It was hidden in her boot heel."

Ingenious. Of course she would be the one to find it. "That doesn't matter right now."

"It does." Her fingers squeezed his. "I hear something. Is that Pliny?"

Mac's jaw tightened. "Yes."

"You didn't kill him."

"Oh no, I did. He just hasn't gotten there yet." Above his head he heard boot falls. Nell was coming back. Thank God she could run like the wind. She flew down the stairs and dropped to her knees on the other side of Evie. She thrust the bag at Mac.

"W.O.R. has been notified. What else can I do?"

"Assist Mac as he removes the bullet," Evie told her. Her voice was getting weaker.

Mac's fear was getting stronger.

"You may have to hold me down, Nell. Don't be afraid to do that. I need to keep as still as possible during the procedure. If I pass out from the pain, all the better."

"I will. I promise." Nell took the scissors Mac offered her and began cutting away Evie's shirt.

Mac grabbed the tweezers and the Listerine. He

cleaned his hands and the instrument. Once the wound was exposed, he cleaned that as well. Evie hissed. "Damn, but that burns."

He didn't apologize. If he thought about how he hated to hurt her, he'd never do the job. "Hold her shoulders, Nell."

His sister did so immediately. She was a tall, strapping woman with muscled arms and strong hands—much physically stronger than Evie.

Mac picked up the tweezers and a wad of gauze to wipe away blood as he worked. Thankfully it was daylight, and Evie had fallen into a convenient patch of sunlight that wouldn't last for long.

He kissed her on the forehead. Her skin was damp. "Here we go."

Evie nodded, took a breath and steeled herself. He could see the determination and focus in her face. That was his girl. She never did anything without a fight.

A ragged cry tore from her throat as he prodded the jagged hole left by the bullet. Mac's stomach lurched. Damnation, the last thing he needed was to puke. He clenched his jaw and pressed on, searching as gently as he could for the ball of metal.

There was a lot of blood. He mopped at it as he worked. He couldn't see a damn thing, which made it like searching for a penny in the dark. He had to go solely by feel.

Tears leaked from Evie's eyes, trickling into her hair. He couldn't do this. He couldn't hurt her like this.

He didn't have a choice. Evie was depending on him and he needed to fix her.

Was this how she had felt when she gave him new lungs? When she patched him up at Dash's? Had she felt this helpless? This angry? He wanted to scream at her for putting herself in harm's way, and he wanted to beg her not to leave him.

This was a kind of fear he'd never experienced before, and he never, ever wanted to feel it again.

The tips of the tweezers hit something solid. His heart leaped. "Did you feel that?" he asked.

"A little," she replied from behind clenched teeth. "That was bullet, not bone. Now get it the hell out."

Carefully Mac opened the pincers until he felt them close over the sides of the bullet. Then, with a tight grip, he began to pull.

Evie screamed.

He froze. She went limp.

"She passed out," he told Nell. Terror squeezed at his chest. "Right?"

His sister nodded. "She's breathing." She took the gauze from him and took over wiping away blood. "Get that damn thing out of her."

Mac used his free hand to stretch the wound a little so there was less suction on the bullet. Blood and raw tissue were like glue, folding around the shot and holding it close.

Sweat dripped down his brow, but he ignored it. Just a little more. His fingers and forearm cramped under the tension, tightening as he willed himself not to tremble. He'd never held on to anything as

tightly as he held on to those tweezers and that goddamn bullet.

Almost. *Almost.*

The bullet came free with a wet pop. He'd done it.
Oh God. He could weep.

But he wasn't done yet. He set the ugly bit of metal
and the bloody tweezers on the floor and wiped his
sticky hands on his trousers. He washed the rest of
the blood away with Listerine, and irrigated the
wound once more. Then he took up a syringe and the
bottle of familiar pink goop. He filled the syringe to
the top and then eased the needle deep into the hole
in Evie's chest. Blood welled up around it.

He depressed the plunger as he slowly pulled the
needle out. The empty syringe was put next to the
bullet and tweezers. Then he poured a little of the pink
stuff right onto her skin for good measure and placed
a thick padding of gauze over the top and pressed
with his palm, putting pressure on the wound to
ease the bleeding and keep the healing liquid inside
her.

"Is she going to be all right?" Nell asked.

"She has to be," he replied. It wasn't the answer
his sister wanted. It wasn't the answer he wanted,
but it was the only one he could give. And then, because Pliny was to blame for this—and for Imogen
and Theo—he took a scalpel from Evie's bag and approached the dying spy.

He held up the blade so Pliny could see it.

"Time for you and me to have a little chat, old
friend."

*   *   *

Evie loved her work, and she loved her ward. She did not, however, like being in her ward as a patient, having someone else look after her.

Especially when that someone was Franz, her Austrian bedmate who lived with his mama. *Lived*, actually, since he'd taken great pains to inform her that since their ill-ending tryst he'd accepted a better position with the Germans and had taken his own apartment.

How wonderful for him. Now if he would just hand her a scalpel, she'd use it to rupture both eardrums so she didn't have to listen to him any further.

He acted as though the ward were his, not hers. Thankfully her nursing staff didn't agree with him. Also, thankfully Mac used the healing compound on her, so she wouldn't have to be his patient for long.

Mac had saved her life, and she had yet to see him to thank him for it. They'd arrived a few hours ago from Brackenhurst via a Warden airship. She'd been mostly unconscious for the short trip, but now that her body was healing, she was stuck listening to Franz and wishing Mac would come see her.

It wasn't that he didn't want to—she knew that. But Dhanya would have questions about Pliny, about what happened. And Mac would have to give her the cylinder she found in Imogen's boot.

She still thought that was a rather ingenious hiding spot.

The door to the ward opened and in sauntered Claire. Evie didn't miss the expression on Franz's handsome face when he saw the American woman. Most men had a similar reaction. Claire was gorgeous—to the point of being intimidating. She also looked as if she could be a stone-hearted bitch when she wanted.

Fortunately that wasn't the side of her that Evie saw most often.

A big grin parted Claire's full lips. "There she is. You're part of the club now, darlin'."

Ah yes, the club. That bastion of womanhood to which she thought she would never be admitted. Arden and Claire had started it because they'd both been shot in the line of duty.

"I can't say that I'm happy about it," she replied as her friend sat down on the side of her bed. "Do you have boots with hollow heels for hiding things?"

Claire looked insulted that she would even ask. "Of course. You don't? There's a fellow here at W.O.R. who makes them. You should get a pair."

"I think I will. Have you seen Arden? How is she?"

Claire rolled her eyes. "Insanely happy, tired, eager to get back to work on some gadget, convinced the baby looks just like Luke, when it's a ginger if I ever saw one—and I *know* ginger." She waggled her eyebrows suggestively.

"Poor Alastair," Evie lamented with a sigh. "He'd flush right up to his hairline if he knew you talked about him like that."

"Please." Claire made a face. "The man thinks he's the best lover in all of Europe."

"Is he?" She couldn't help grinning as she asked.

"Of course he is, but I'm not going to tell *him* that. He sends his love, by the way. How are you feeling?"

"A little sore, but it's healing. I have a newfound sympathy for my patients, I think."

"As well you should, heartless cow that you are. I heard what Mac did to the traitor." She shook her glorious head. "You can tell a lot about a person by how he reacts to someone who has hurt someone he loves."

Evie stared at her. Perhaps it was the laudanum she'd been given for pain, but she didn't even question the notion of Mac loving her. Of course he loved her, and she loved him. It was how to live with that love, how to hold on to it, that gave Evie heart palpitations.

Then again, they'd both managed to hold on to it for three years without each other.

"What did he do?" she asked, unwilling to follow that train of thought any further. It made her heart pound, and her insides—that was the medical term, of course—were opposed to that.

Claire's expression of surprise quickly faded. "Of course you wouldn't know. You were most likely out cold when it happened. He gutted the man. I don't have to tell you how long gut wounds take to kill."

No, she didn't.

"And then he apparently tortured him until he gave up what the Bears are up to."

"Mac tortured Pliny?" That was hard to believe.

Actually, on second thought it wasn't. Mac had a ruthless side. It didn't come out often, but it was there. Pliny betrayed him, and had tried to kill her. Mac wouldn't take that lying down.

"Did a fine job of it, too. Anatolii Veselov was the man's name. He'd been with the Bears for more than twenty years. This was supposed to be his last mission."

"How do you know that?"

Claire leaned forward conspiratorially and whispered, "Alastair looked for him in W.O.R. files and found all kinds of information. He was known to the Wardens, but no one had any idea that he had infiltrated to that degree."

"But Mac wasn't with W.O.R. anymore. Why stay with him?"

"Apparently your gorgeous captain stayed in contact with many of his Warden friends. He made his ship available to them when needed. Plus, as pirates they often stumbled upon jobs and information along the way. There's no knowing how much Veselov fed to his superiors. We have to assume all of it."

Evie let that all sink in. She was still having a hard time accepting that Pliny wasn't Pliny. He'd always been so good to her. So good to Mac.

"Don't you want to know what they're up to?"

"Hmm?" She turned her attention back to Claire. "I'm sorry, what are we talking about?"

Her friend grinned. "They gave you a cartload of laudanum, didn't they?"

"Enough to take down an elephant from the feel of it."

There was a glass of water on the stand by the bed. Claire took it and held it for her. "Here, take a drink. I was talking about the Russians."

Evie had never tasted sweeter water in all her life. The dry interior of her mouth rejoiced at the influx of moisture. "Tell me."

"This is directly from Alastair, who was present when Dhanya and the council debriefed Mac. He said that Veselov confessed to Mac that the Russians had gotten their hands on ancient technology— Egyptian—that could drastically upset the balance of power in the world."

Evie frowned. "Egyptian technology? Sounds dodgy to me."

"Not at all. These people were advanced, Evie. You know they were. Explorers have brought back items from tombs that we have no idea what they were used for. Two months ago a researcher for the Royal Society was killed by an Egyptian artifact he had been studying. It mummified him."

"That's ridiculous." She knew enough about the process to know how it was done, and it had nothing to do with a strange device.

Claire shrugged and held up her hands. "I'm just telling you what I know. Regardless, the two Warden agents that Mac helped escape got access to the information and made a copy. It's all on that cylinder you found. Nice work, by the way."

"Thanks." Evie was still frowning. There had been

quite a few discussions and essays about ancient Egyptians in the scientific societies and journals in recent years. There were those who theorized that the pharaohs were actually beings from Mars or some distant planet. Of course, recent exploration of Mars turned up no sign of life, but that didn't mean there hadn't been some there a thousand years ago or more.

She believed that there was life on other planets—most learned scholars did. Everyone in the spy game knew that the Americans had actually found a vessel that had crash-landed in California, and that there had been life-forms on board. Unfortunately the creatures had died in the crash. Their bodies and their vessel were kept in a secret facility known as Area 13 by the American equivalent of Irregular Transpirations.

Maybe the notion of ancient Egyptian technology wasn't so implausible after all.

"At least Imogen and her husband didn't die in vain," she remarked. Damn, she was tired. She yawned. It hurt to do that as well.

Claire smiled and patted her on the leg through the blankets that covered her. "I'll let you get some rest. When you're back on your feet, come to dinner with Alastair and me. Bring Mac."

Evie returned the smile, but quickly lost it to another yawn. "I will. Thank you for coming by."

After Claire left, Franz checked up on her. To his credit he didn't ask about her gorgeous friend. He stayed very professional, even though he looked at her as if she were a syphilitic leper with influenza.

She wanted to sleep, and there was no fighting it, so she let the laudanum do its job. The more she slept, the more her body could heal without her feeling every ache, twinge and ping. It wasn't as though she was going to miss anything. Mac would wake her up when he came to see her.

Evie woke up three hours later. Mac wasn't there. She asked Franz if anyone had come by, and was told no, as though he'd be surprised that she had friends.

She drifted off again. This time for two hours, after which Franz said that her healing elixir had done its job and there was no reason she couldn't go home.

She was still a little wobbly from the drug, and didn't have a vehicle anyway, so she arranged for a Warden driver to take her home. She'd changed into a shirt she had in her office, so at least she didn't have to go out in public with blood all over her.

At home, Mrs. Ferguson fussed at her as if she were a sick child, and Evie let her. She curled up in her bed with a book, a cup of tea and fresh scones with jam and cream. She'd just read and rest until Mac showed up.

She woke up the next morning with crumbs in the bed and her cheek smushed into the pages of her book. She was alone.

Mac hadn't come.

Chapter 19

"Are you going after him?"

Evie tried not to stare as Arden breast-fed her son, who had more names than she could remember and more than something that tiny should have. She'd seen the human body naked, clothed, smashed, cut up, decomposed . . . but there was something about breast-feeding that unsettled her. It seemed a deeply private, tender moment between mother and child, and yet here was her friend, sitting across from her with her boob out. Of course, they were in Arden's private rooms, but that only made it more intimate.

She focused on Arden's face instead. "You think I should?"

Claire, who was pouring tea for the three of them, frowned at her. "Yes." She said this as if a simpleton could have figured it out.

"But won't that make me seem desperate?" She'd never chased after a man before. She never had to.

Usually she just had to smile and express interest. She should have remembered that Mac wasn't like most men. He had his pride, and sometimes he was more vulnerable than she realized.

"You are desperate," Claire reminded her as she handed her a cup of tea. She delivered the other to Arden, who was buttoning her gown, and took the baby from her to burp while his mama enjoyed her refreshment. "Don't you want him back?"

"Yes." It was hard to admit that, even to her friends. "But what if he left because he doesn't want me?"

Her married friends exchanged a glance that seemed to say, *Poor Evie, the little mite knows nothing about men.* They would have felt the same uncertainty with their husbands not long ago, the hypocrites.

Arden took a sip of tea before taking a small bite of cake as she held the baby with one arm. "It's obvious that he left to protect himself."

"Protect himself? I was *shot*. Shot protecting *him*. A thank-you might be nice." Seriously, she couldn't be the only one who thought that, could she?

"You left him because his life was too dangerous and you couldn't stand to see him hurt. You saved his life twice, and now you've been shot while helping him. How do you suppose a man like Mac feels about that?"

Evie really didn't have to think about that at all. "Like it was his fault." Of course he would blame himself. He was a man who took care of his—it was something they had in common.

"He always has to be the hero," she muttered. It wasn't said with any sharpness. She was beginning to understand.

"Pot, have you met kettle?" Claire asked.

"What?" Evie blinked. She didn't get it.

The American rolled her eyes. "How can you, the person who puts people back together, who will operate under the most dire of conditions and dare God to defy her will, possibly comment on anyone having to be a hero? Hell and tarnation, woman. I've never met anyone with more of a need to be a hero than you."

Oh. That was something of a slap in the face. "Really?"

Her friends chuckled. Baby Ian chose that moment to belch loudly, adding his opinion on the subject, which made all three women laugh.

Evie was reflective, however. Claire hadn't meant her words cruelly, but there was enough truth in them to sting. She was just as guilty of taking risks and breaking rules to save people as he was. True, there was less danger in her line of work, but how could she condemn him for risking injury when she had jumped in front of a bullet meant for him? She was skilled at putting people back together. Despite some medical knowledge, he must have been terrified.

Operating on someone you love is not easy.

And now he'd left, just as she'd left him. Only, he hadn't left because he was afraid she'd die. He left because he thought she'd blame him for her getting shot. He left her so she couldn't leave him.

Again.

Lord, she'd made a mess of things. Part of her wanted to rage that she was right—things got tough and he ran away just as her father did, but she was too old to do that now. She'd been too old to do it three years ago, but love was new and terrified her.

Now . . . love had endured. Love didn't just switch off because it was difficult and frightening. If anything, she loved him more now. There was no reason for them not to be together. He didn't want to fly anymore, and she'd heard that Nell left earlier today with the *Queen V*.

God, he'd named his beloved ship after her. When he needed help, he came to her. Perhaps the kidnapping hadn't been his most shining hour, but she was who he wanted by his side during that ordeal.

The man would die for her. There weren't many people she'd do that for. She wanted to think that three of them were in this room, but the only one she was certain of was Mac. That was why she'd stepped in front of Pliny.

She loved him. He was not her father, and she was not her mother.

Because she was going to go after the man she loved. Her mother pined for her father, but she never once tried to get him back. What if he left only to see if she would follow him? Evie wasn't about to make a saint out of the man, but she'd been afraid of love her entire life because she thought it made a person weak.

Weak people did not risk their lives for other people. Weak people watched life pass them by. Weak people spent their lives alone because they let fear control them.

She was *not* weak. And she was not afraid. Not anymore.

She set her cup and saucer on the table in front of her and rose to her feet. "I have to go."

Arden and Claire exchanged glances again. "Ohhh," Arden said, "I wish I could go!"

Claire made a face. "She has to do this on her own."

That seemed to ease the redhead's disappointment somewhat. "Take my steam carriage. It's faster than a hack and four times as comfortable."

"Thank you." Evie hugged both of them, and kissed little Ian on his pink forehead before hurrying downstairs and out to the stables. Arden had rung ahead to tell them to give her the carriage, and the groom had just driven it out of the building when she arrived.

"Here you go, Doctor," he said, holding the door open for her.

Evie slipped into the vehicle. The top was up, so she didn't need goggles. As she engaged the motor and started off down the drive, she glanced up to see her friends watching from the window. They were grinning like idiots, waving at her as though she were about to embark upon a wondrous journey.

She supposed she was.

Mac never thought of himself as being overly dramatic unless it was for a laugh, or to cast enemy suspicion off himself, but as he rode the train out of London the next morning, he realized that he was being *quite* dramatic.

But not cowardly. And anyone who disagreed was liable to get a punch in the face.

He was trying to be honorable. He was trying to do what was right. He was trying to do both things miles away from London, and from Evie.

He couldn't fly off on the *Queen V* because she belonged to Nell now, and he didn't want the sky. He couldn't hang about London because people would expect him to go see Evie. He would expect himself to go see her.

But he couldn't. What would he say? *Sorry you got shot because of me. What do you say we get married?* Sorry was inadequate, and suggesting marriage might be a bit premature, especially when he suspected she'd tell him to go swiv himself.

Who could blame her if she did just that? Not only had he scared her by getting injured, but he'd dragged her into a situation that almost got her damn well killed. That had to piss her off. Why would any sane woman want to be with a man who seemed to be a trouble magnet? Never mind that he was going to be land-bound now. Pliny had shot her while they were grounded.

Pliny. Veselov. Whatever his name was, he had died slowly and painfully and Mac didn't much care. He'd gotten secrets out of the man, who apologized to him while blood bubbled on his traitorous lips.

He had apologized as Mac cut him. That was something he'd have to live with for a while. He'd taken no pleasure in torturing the man who had used him for the last several years, though there had been satisfaction in it. He got the Wardens more information on the Bears, and turned over the cylinder Evie found. What a brilliant hiding place.

But Evie wasn't an agent and never had been. He should have known better than to have her with him when he went to Brackenhurst, despite thinking it would be a wild-goose chase. He should have expected Pliny to follow him—or at least prepared for it. He would have done the same were the situations reversed. He should have been on guard, but he wasn't and Evie got shot. Because of him.

And he didn't want to hear her tell him that she never wanted anything to do with him ever again.

Maybe he was a *little* cowardly.

He was just giving her space—breathing room. Time to think. Time for him to think. Would being grounded make a difference with her? She was still Evie, the woman who believed she was doomed to her mother's mistakes, which was bullshit, but there was no telling her that. For a woman who lived so fearlessly in some areas, she was more of a coward than he when it came to love.

But she wasn't the one hiding out in the country. There was a part of him who insisted that he was spineless—weak—for not going after her, for not *making* her be with him.

Because that always ended so very well.

It wasn't weakness; it was pride. There was no way he was begging. No damn way.

Maybe.

He'd found the ring he intended to give her before. It was his grandmother's. It wasn't too flashy and it wasn't a gaudy size. It was a square-cut ruby so dark it was almost black. The band was delicate, patterned gold that looked like intertwined vines that curved up to form the setting as well. It was the perfect ring for Evie—elegant but a little untamed.

It was still in his pocket, though he would never even attempt to explain why.

He was in the outbuilding he had taken over specifically for the Daimler. It was near the stables and carriage house, but intentionally on its own so he could work there without being in anyone's way or anyone being in his. Despite his having grown up with privilege, it was odd having people about who wanted to do his every bidding. On the ship he'd been in charge, but it was understood that they were in it together. No one did anything for him unless he asked them to.

He paused under the Daimler's bonnet. Nell would have rendezvoused with the rest of the crew

by now. Had she told them about Pliny? It would be
a hard betrayal for all of them, especially Barker and
Eli, who had been with them the longest.

It was a bright day, temperate with the sun high
in the sky. A good day for flying.

He was very glad to be on the ground. Only one
thing—one person would make it better.

Mac shook his head and applied himself to the
engine once more. Thinking about Evie was only
going to make him morose and then drink too
much.

The distant sound of a hell-bent steam carriage
made him duck out from the bonnet. Through the
open doors he could see a shiny, sleek machine tearing up the drive. A few seconds later the engine died
and he heard a door shut.

Who was it and what did they want? He wasn't
exactly in the mood for callers. Still, curiosity got the
better of him. It was a nice-looking car, and the urge
to inspect it was strong. He wiped his hands on a rag
and left the building, starting down the path that led
to the back of the house.

He was halfway there when one of the terrace
doors flew open and a force of nature burst through.

Evie.

What was she doing there? More important, why
wasn't she still in the hospital, or at least at home?
She might have a miracle in that pink goo of hers,
but after a person was shot, sometimes the mind
needed to heal more than the body did.

She stopped on the edge of the terrace, her hand

shading her eyes. When she saw him—and he could feel her gaze fall upon him as tangible as a blanket around his shoulders—she smiled. It was a hesitant smile, but it was all he needed. He smiled back.

She ran toward him. Sweet God, the woman was going to injure herself further, or . . . oh, hell. He broke into a run as well, racing toward her with a smile on his face that got bigger and bigger as they drew together. She was smiling, too.

They met halfway, both coming to a complete stop just a few feet from each other. What did they do now?

"You shouldn't be here," he blurted.

Her smile died. "I shouldn't?"

He had a reputation for being charming, he reminded himself. At the moment he was not living up to it. "It's good to see you, but shouldn't you be resting?"

Her gaze locked with his. Her eyes were so dark, so bright. "I thought I might rest here, if that's all right with you."

Did this mean something or did she just like the countryside? No, she wouldn't be here just to recuperate. "Uh, sure."

"Oh, good. Although . . . I don't really have any clothes or things with me. I didn't think to pack."

"Your things are still here." From before he got her shot. He didn't add that.

"Ah, right. Guess I won't need to borrow anything from you, then."

He might not be the brightest star in the sky, but

even he knew that when a woman talked about wearing your clothes, it was a good thing.

"You can if you like." Very seductive reply.

She took a step toward him, then another, until finally she was right in front of him. "I didn't come here for rest or to raid your closet."

"No?" Maybe he was cruel, but he wasn't going to make this easy on her. Whatever "this" was.

She shook her head, gaze locked with his. "I came here for you."

Mac's heart punched him hard in the ribs. "You did?"

She laughed. "You don't look like you believe me."

"I don't. I mean, I do, but I'm not sure why. I got you shot, Doc. Aren't you upset about that?"

Evie shook her head, curls slipping free of her braid. "Not at all. I'd get shot once a week if it meant saving you."

This was certainly not something he had been expecting. Jumping up and down would not be manly. "That sounds a bit like playing the hero."

"I suppose it does."

"Now that you know something about having to be the hero, do you still think I do it for my own gratification?"

"Not at all." The toes of her boots were right against his. "I think you do it for the same reason I did."

"Which is?"

She reached up and placed her fingers on his cheek. Then she smiled as though she knew the secrets of the universe, if there was a heaven and where that one sock disappeared to every time he did his laundry. "Because you love me."

The smart-arse side of him wanted to ask if she loved herself, too, but common sense kicked in. "And you love me."

She nodded. "I do, Mac. I always have. I thought I could run away from it—that I had to leave you before you could leave me, but I . . . I don't want to run anymore. I don't want to waste any more time. I don't want to be so afraid of losing you that I don't realize how lucky I am to have you."

"You *are* extremely lucky."

"Immensely," she agreed with a grin. "I know you feel guilty about what happened with Pliny, but it wasn't your fault any more than it was mine when you took a bullet for me three years ago. We each made the decision to protect each other. That's what love is."

Mac didn't know what to say.

Her smile faded. "Now would be a good time for you to say something."

Right. He grabbed her hand. "Come with me." He pulled her toward the building where the Daimler was and gently pushed her inside before closing the door. The stable hands didn't need to see this.

"You wanted to show me a carriage?" There was no denying the disappointment in her voice.

Mac found the coat he'd removed earlier and dug into the inside pocket. He smiled as his fingers closed around the ring box. "No. I wanted to show you something else." He walked the few steps it took to stand before her and held out the box on the flat of his hand.

Evie stared at it, eyes wide.

Since she wasn't going to do it, he opened it for her. She gasped at the sight of the ring. Her fingers trembled as she reached for it.

"Your grandmother's ring."

"I was going to give you this ring three years ago—I had it with me when I got hurt. I was going to ask you that night."

Were those tears in her eyes? Yes, they were. "You were going to propose?"

He nodded. Oh, what the hell? He lowered himself to one knee. "Marry me, Evie. For God's sake take pity on us both and say yes."

Tears streamed down her face as she dropped to her knees. "Yes! A hundred times, yes."

Mac slipped the ring onto her finger. Of course it fit—he'd had it sized before. Then he wiped at her cheeks with his thumbs. He left a smear of dirt on one.

"I'm not going to let you run away again," he informed her. "Understood? I know it's going to be hard for you to trust in the future, but all you have to do is trust in me. In us. Can you do that?"

She nodded. "I can." Then she kissed him, almost knocking him over when she threw her arms around his neck. He kissed her back.

Somehow they ended up inside the Daimler. Even stranger, they seemed to have lost most of their clothes. They made love laughing and joking like idiots—as if they didn't have a care at all. He supposed they didn't.

As he slid inside her, strong limbs pulling him close, Mac realized that he might have given up the sky, but with Evie he had the whole world.

London, the Age of Steam

"You shouldn't go in there, ma'am. 'Tis no place for a lady."

Arden Grey, known in polite circles as Lady Huntley, and in less polite as "that poor woman," carried a small carpetbag in her gloved hand as she approached the factory door, pewter-colored skirts swishing around her matching pumps. Overhead the lights of a police dirigible swept across the scene, illuminating the night in a wash of glaring silver.

The veil attached to her tiny black top hat did nothing to shield her eyes, and Arden squinted against the intrusive brightness. "You will soon learn, sir, that I am not the usual sort of lady." She'd been born and bred to be one, even married an earl to maintain the illusion, but during her unusual life she'd seen and heard—*and done*—too many dark things to own such a gentle, ignorant title.

The Scotland Yard man tugged the brim of his hat at her in reply, and stepped back so she might pass. It was obvious from the tight set of his lips that he opposed her presence most vehemently, but knew his place well enough not to voice his disapproval again. In this thoroughly modern world there were still those who believed a woman ought to keep to home, rather than engage in any manner of business.

Tell that to Queen Victoria.

Sagging floorboards creaked under her boots as she entered B. E. Hammond & Sons, the varnish long since worn off this particular section of wood. The foyer was well lit and unassuming, and smelled vaguely of oil and metal. It was quiet now, but during the day this entire building would hum and vibrate with the sounds of working machines. The air would be humid and thick, tasting of steam and the sharp tang of industry.

She fancied she could smell blood, but it was most likely copper. When people used to oppose her father's support of the Automatization Movement, he would reply that it could not be a coincidence that the very life in a man's veins smelled like the same metal used to construct early automatons. He died in the middle of building what would have been his finest work, a piece that now sat hunched, gears gummed up, in the corner of his W.O.R. laboratory. Four years it had sat there, and despite all the brilliant minds the Wardens of the Realm—the mysterious government agency to which Arden herself belonged—set to work in that room, the project had yet to be completed. Arden had even provided them with the schematics of the machine, but to no avail. The automaton remained elusive, an example of her father's genius that would never come to fruition, though the Wardens would continue to try.

Then again, she was a fine one to throw stones, she who clung to a hopeless dream.

Another Scotland Yard man came through a set of double doors and paused there, holding one of them open. "This way, Lady Huntley—if you please."

No, she didn't please, but she walked past the man and through the doorway all the same. She'd rather be at home with a glass—or several—of fine Scotch whiskey, but she'd been summoned here instead. Granted, it had been a welcome rescue from insipid conversation and weak sherry with a group of females who would inevitably take her aside one by one and ask her if she might construct one of her "special devices" for them.

Few people knew the extent of her talents. To most of the world she was simply Lady Huntley, a woman who refused to accept that her husband was most likely dead. She wasn't the mechanical genius that her father was, but she had made a bit of a reputation amongst her sex for an invention she stumbled upon quite by accident. A device very similar—but far superior—to one sold by B. E. Hammond & Sons. It could have been quite scandalous, but since one of the Princesses Royal privately declared it a "miracle of modern medical science" in the field of feminine health, scandal became discreet acclaim. A treatment for "hysteria" that did not require the indiscretion of a trip to a sanitorium, but could be used in the privacy of a lady's boudoir.

The delicate silver chains that hung from the piercing on the side of Arden's nose across her cheek to her right ear quivered under the ceiling fans as she entered the large open room of the factory's assembly department. Recently she'd increased the number of chains from six to seven. One for every year her husband had been missing.

Missing. Not dead.

Two more Scotland Yard men—peelers as they were often called—stood with another man she assumed to be the senior Mr. Hammond, based on the distressed look on his face.

The policemen removed their hats when they spotted her. One of them was Inspector Grant, with whom she'd worked on several prior cases. Mr. Hammond held his fine, but worn, beaver top hat in his shaking hands. His graying hair stuck up in tufts around his head, as though he'd had his hands tugging at it. He had the countenance of a man who had seen—or done—something he should dearly like to forget.

As she approached, Arden withdrew what looked like a small lady's compact from her bag. She pointed the device in the direction of the factory owner and watched the tiny hand beneath the glass swing around like the needle of a compass, finally

coming to land on the word REMORSE. The senti-
mentometer was one of her favorites of all her father's work, even though he'd developed it when
she was but a child to determine whether or not she
had done something naughty.

She snapped the lid shut and slipped the brass
mechanism back into her bag. "Gentlemen."

"Lady Huntley." Inspector Grant greeted her with
a curt nod—his only deference to her station. "Thank
you for leaving your evening's entertainments to aid
us in this grim affair."

"No thanks required, Inspector," Arden replied in
her usual crisp tones that often sounded far too se-
vere for her liking. Lucas used to tell her she had the
voice of a governess. "What has happened?"

The inspector pointed his pencil at the pale gentleman to his left. "Mr. Hammond was working late this
evening in his office above stairs. When he came
down to check everything was as it should be for the
night, he found the body of a young woman." He gestured for her to follow him and she did. The factory
owner stayed behind, working the brim of his hat until it threatened to lose all shape.

"Did you take a reading of Hammond?" Grant
asked quietly as they maneuvered through the
jammed workspace of wooden tables littered with
tools, automaton parts and gears. "Says he was listening to phonographic discs as he worked and
didn't hear a peep from down here."

She shook her head, gaze wandering distractedly
over the tabletops. "I detected no guilt or malevo-

lence from him. But he does feel remorse. Could be a guilty conscious, or perhaps he is simply mortified that a crime was committed on his property with him being none the wiser." She stopped and picked up a rubber tube that was shaped like . . . a penis. She held it up with her forefinger and thumb, dangling it in all its flaccid splendor in front of the inspector's face. "I didn't know that the Hammonds had begun to incorporate rubber in their designs."

Grant flushed a deep red—the color of a cooked beet. He couldn't quite meet her gaze. "Er . . . yes. You may be aware that Hammond started this factory to make medical instruments to aid in the treatment of hysteria. He was one of the first manufacturers of automatons in England." He cleared his throat, as though he wanted to say more but didn't quite know how to word it, or how to justify it.

He didn't have to. Arden knew all about Hammond and his inventions. A contemporary of her father's, some of his earlier designs were rather ingenious, but it was his work in the field of mechanized human "marital enhancements" that had made him one of the wealthiest businessmen in the kingdom. Any man who dedicated his life's work to the carnal pleasure and emotional well-being of women couldn't be all that bad, could he?

But a murder certainly wouldn't be good for business.

A few steps on she spied a female automaton lying on one of the tables, its realistic limbs splayed, revealing a degree of anatomical correctness that would have made a bawd blush. Arden's lips tucked to one side in a caustic smile. Mr. Hammond obviously had decided to tackle the treatment of gentlemanly vigor as well.

Inspector Grant threw a tarp over the machine, but whether he did so to protect Arden's delicate sensibilities or his own was a mystery that she hadn't the inclination to pursue. Though it did not take even an ounce of emotional sensitivity to ascertain that the inspector was deeply mortified.

When they neared the end of the aisle, Arden detected a familiar, unpleasant odor, one she associated with murder: a mix of what she could only describe as fear, blood, and chamber pot.

Two more peelers and Inspector Grant stood between her and the source of that smell. Well, most of it.

The leg in the torn stocking and expensive silk pump looked like that of a burlesque automaton at first, so white and still was it. Were it not for the blood staining that stocking she might have been able to tell herself that it *was* merely a machine.

"I beg your pardon, Lady Huntley," Grant said in that faint northern accent of his. "But this isn't a pretty sight. You may turn back if you like."

She gave him what she hoped was a grateful smile and not a grim twisting of her lips. She'd often been told her smile could sometimes look a little . . . demented. "Your concern does you credit, Inspector. I assure you I shall endure whatever it is you wish me to see." She could do without seeing a dead body, particularly a bloody one, but if these men could look at it dispassionately then damn it, so could she. It wasn't as though it was her first corpse.

Inspector Grant's face was a resigned shade of pale beneath his muttonchops and heavy mustache. He nodded in acquiescence. "Pull back the sheet please, Mr. Fence."

An ashen-faced youth swallowed hard and bent down to do as he was instructed. Arden's confidence in being able to escape the viewing with the contents of her stomach intact diminished slightly.

The sheet—stained and wet with so much blood it was almost black in spots—pulled back with the resistance of the rind of an orange reluctant to leave the flesh beneath, to reveal the head of a pretty young woman wearing pearl earrings. Her neck was long, decorated with a matching pearl necklace, but beyond that . . . a pile of raw meat. Arden stared for a moment, her eyes not quite able to make her brain see reality. Finally, after a few moments—and a rather inspired bout of gagging from young Mr. Fence—she saw the scene for what it was.

Someone, or something, had torn this precious little girl apart. Her pale blue eyes were wide open, as was her Cupid's bow mouth. Her flawless skin, the pale robin's-egg waxy color of death, was dotted with freckles of blood. She was not a factory worker—a pair of fine silk gloves lay not far from her body. Nor was she a member of the demimonde, for she was far too fresh and sweet looking, and not nearly as fashionable. Her demure, ruined gown cost more than what the retching Mr. Fence probably made in a month.

She was a member of the upper classes, quite possibly of noble birth.

Dear God.

Mindful of her skirts, she lifted them as she moved around the clotted puddle to stand at the girl's head. She squatted down, tugging off her right glove so her fingers could touch the porcelain coolness of a stiff, delicate wrist. The girl had been dead for several hours—long enough for her body to lose all warmth and become fairly rigid.

A thin bruise spread like a stain beneath Arden's fingers. She glanced up at Inspector Grant. The older man was the only one of the three who didn't look ill. He was too experienced, too little shocked by humanity's capacity for violence to be sickened by it anymore. Instead, he looked resigned. And worried. A murdered debutante meant trouble on so many levels for a man in his position.

"She was bound?" she inquired, swallowing against the rolling of her own stomach.

Grant nodded, his shrewd gaze resting on the ravaged girl. "Most likely the bugger—pardon my French, my lady—brought the poor gel here by force."

It was possible, she supposed, but this bruise was purple and slightly yellow, not the usual raw red that one would expect if she had been recently restrained. This bruising was older and could have many causes.

The inspector jerked his head toward the entrance. "Fence, Brown, make use of yourself else-where." He watched as the two relieved young men walked away before navigating around the corpse to squat beside her. "Do you think you might . . . be able to use your apparatus on her?"

That was often why she was brought to such scenes. And dear Grant was always so considerate to never take her compliance as a certainty. It was her father who had come up with the general principles of the mechanism prior to his death, and Arden who completed the device. If he hadn't left so many unfin-ished projects, who knew what might have become of her? Mourning him and missing Huntley, she might have done something rash, especially without her mother to turn to, but instead she turned to cogs and gears and the reassuring hum of steam engines. Loss had given her more purpose than she'd ever wanted before.

"I will try," she told him, as she had every other time he asked. She rested the bottom of her carpet-bag on her bent knees and pulled the mouth of it wide open. She didn't have to rummage through a muddle of automata and tools as her father always had, because she had outfitted the case with internal straps and pockets to hold each and every item. She barely had to look in at all to find what she wanted— two pairs of specially augmented goggles, connected by coils of wires.

"Inspector, if you would be so kind?"

Grant's gaze jerked up from the mechanism. "Of course." He took the bag from her lap and placed it to his left, as far from the carnage as his reach allowed. "Explain to me again how these Aetheric Reminiscent Oscillation Goggles work."

Despite the smell and horrific visage before her, Arden smiled slightly as she placed the more ornate pair of goggles over the girl's open eyes. She had begun using the device two years ago and the inspector had yet to refer to it by the correct name. "Aetheric Remnant Oscillatory Transmutative Spectacles," she corrected. "You could use the acronym A.R.O.T.S. if you prefer."

He shook his head. "I'd rather not use the term 'rot' in any capacity given the circumstances, my lady—with all due respect."

Arden glanced at the girl's decimated torso and the decay that had already begun, as she carefully placed the small metal prongs of the headgear on the appropriate spots on the poor thing's skull. "Indeed. You are familiar, of course, with Aether?"

"Of course," he sounded vaguely affronted that she had to ask. "It's the Breath of God."

As a woman whose religion was more science than spirituality, it took considerable restraint for Arden not to argue with the inspector. However, she was not one to besmirch another's beliefs, no matter how ill-informed she believed them to be. "The energy of every living creature, yes," she said. "Some believe it to be the soul, while science argues that it is the result of an electrochemical process in living tissue that lingers even after we shuck our mortal coil."

Grant sniffed. "Sounds a bit far-fetched to me."

But the "Breath of God" did not? A god who took her husband away from her? Who killed her father and made her mother . . . what she was? If it was the breath of such a creature that gave the engine of her heart fire then she would rather suffocate on a cold hearth. For every religious zealot there was another who decreed the Aether as the playground of the Devil himself.

"Regardless," she continued through a clenched jaw, "there is no dispute that sometimes this energy lingers—around a body, or in a place where the person met their end. These goggles allow me to see the last things this young lady saw by utilizing that very energy." The dark lenses over the sightless eyes of the girl would prevent any light or new images from penetrating once the prongs stimulated the appropriate areas of her brain, essentially restoring them to life for a short period. Once engaged, the optical response would parlay those images to Arden's own goggles, where she would view the experience as though it were her own.

"Bloody amazing," Grant allowed. Then, with fresh pink suffusing his cheeks, "Beg your pardon, my lady."

Arden waved his concern away with a flick of her wrist. Then, something caught her eye. She frowned. "Inspector, did Hammond or your men rearrange her clothing?"

"No, ma'am. She's exactly as she was found."

Frowning, she leaned closer, and using the ear

wire of the goggles in her hand, lifted the edge of the torn gown. A small, bare breast, smeared with crimson, lay beneath. Elsewhere the fabric molded to the gore-soaked area, but not here.

"He took care to cover her," she murmured.

The inspector nodded, seemingly unimpressed by her keen detection. "I reckon the monster knew her."

Arden settled back on her heels. Her knees were beginning to ache from squatting so long. "Let's see if she knew him as well, shall we?" She wiped the ear wire with her handkerchief before placing the second pair of goggles on her own face. With them on she was practically blind, and would remain so until the image transfer began.

Then she would see things she would later regret seeing.

She wound the key protruding from the side of the small control box attached by even more wires to both sets of eye gear. The simple engine inside, attuned as it was to Aetheric energy—a vast resource Arden believed could rival steam and even the new wonder of electricity—whirred to life, sending a charge to the dead girl's mind.

Fuzzy images began to swirl before her eyes, dim and out of focus. She adjusted dials on either side of her goggles, making the images a little clearer. Sometimes, depending on how long the subject had been dead, she had to use all the lenses and settings she had to work with, and even then sometimes she only got a grainy, half-formed image.

She was not to be so fortunate that evening. She

had barely slipped the secondary lenses into place when everything came together in razor-sharp clarity.

The girl was running through the aisles of this very factory, the world jostled around her as a man in evening clothes chased her. She saw only his shoulder and part of his side, not his face, but she didn't appear to be running for her life, but with the lazy gait of a girl wishing to be caught. And catch her he did, turning her in his arms. A man's torso came into view— neither too broad nor too thin. His cravat was perfectly tied, decorated with an onyx pin in the shape of a horseshoe.

Arden's heart quickened, as it often did in these macabre situations. Everything was so keen, and sharp. If she could find a way to determine the emotional state and auditory memory as well, it truly would be an immersive experience.

The girl's arms reached for the man, whose face remained maddeningly out of sight. Slowly, her gaze lifted, past the cravat pin, to the throat and jaw of the man wearing it, then the mouth.

"Just a little further," Arden whispered as her heart pounded hard against her ribs. "Come on, dearest. Just a little more."

The world seemed to jump in front of her eyes. Her gaze dropped from the man to the space between their bodies.

Arden cried out.

Her chest was ripped open.

"Lady Huntley!" It was Grant. She could feel his warm hand on her arm. "My lady, are you all right?"

She shook her head, afraid that she would indeed vomit if she opened her mouth. Her hands clutched at the spectacles, and she wanted nothing more than to rip them off her face, but she held on until the images before her faded to blackness, signaling the girl's death. Only when she was certain there was nothing more to see did she remove the apparatus from her own head.

"My dear lady," Grant began, staring at her with wide eyes. "You look . . ."

"Like hell," Arden supplied, smiling at his surprise. Just as quickly her mirth vanished. "He ripped her open while she was alive. She felt it. Saw it."

The inspector turned his gaze toward the dead girl just as Arden did. He reached out and stroked the girl's hair, as a father might. "Poor thing."

"Indeed," Arden muttered, attempting to pull herself together. She raised the back of her hand to her nose and took a deep, calming breath. The bergamot she'd dabbed on her glove lessened the scent of death, reminded her of happier things.

"I didn't see his face, unfortunately. All I can tell you is that he wore expensive clothes and had an onyx cravat pin in the shape of a horseshoe." She sighed. "She knew him. They were lovers. If those marks on her wrists were made by him, they were done so with her consent, and before this rendezvous."

Inspector Grant went pale beneath the dark of his whiskers. "Knew him, you say?"

Arden met his gaze evenly, her typical tight rein over her emotions returning. "Yes. You are not wrong to be alarmed, Inspector. I'm fairly certain your madman is an aristocrat as well."

The inspector swore beneath his breath, and this time he did not apologize for his language. Arden didn't blame him. She'd curse as well, for the inspector's chances of catching this monster just dropped considerably, never mind the odds of actually bringing him to justice.

"If she'd only looked at him I might be able to identify him," she mused ruefully.

Grant shook his head and patted her shoulder one last time before he remembered his station and removed his hand. "Do not fault yourself, my lady. You have been of enormous assistance already."

As Arden removed the spectacles from the girl and used her palm to close her eyes, she didn't feel as though she'd been of much use at all. She quickly ran through the images in her mind once more. "He was older. Not elderly, but not a boy—perhaps in his late twenties or thirties."

The inspector wrote this down in his little leather-bound notebook.

"And, Inspector Grant?" When he looked up from his writing she said softly, "You should request Dr. Stone examine the body."

A soft flush flooded the lawman's face. The poor thing really had no idea how to handle such situations. He had more modesty than a fourteen-year-old girl. "I see."

Dr. Evelyn Stone was generally employed by Scotland Yard when a female victim had been molested in some way, but her talents were more extensively employed by the Wardens. The brilliant young woman had machines and formulas for making identifications and finding insights into crimes that baffled and impressed the agency to no end.

"She may find something that will aid in our investigation."

Inspector Grant's head snapped up. "*Our* investigation, my lady?"

Arden's lips twisted into a grim smile. "You're going to require my ongoing assistance with this one, sir. I travel in the same circles as our killer, and can therefore go where you cannot."

"Lady Huntley, I cannot allow you to put yourself in harm's way." He was clearly flustered. "To include you so thoroughly in a Yard investigation would be grossly unfair, not to mention ungentlemanly of me."

Not to mention it was terribly gauche of her—a lady—to engage in such horrid pursuits. No doubt that had much to do with her desire to do it.

"*You*, my dear friend, cannot prevent it," she informed him with a touch of warmth to her determined tone. She rose easily to her feet. "Now, do be a good boy and accept that you are powerless in this instance, and escort me back to my carriage."

Being the considerate gentleman he was, Inspector Grant could not refuse a lady's request—especially not the request of such a high-ranking lady as a countess. He also stood and offered her his arm, which she took with a faint smile on her lips.

Arden was all too happy to leave the awful vision of that poor girl behind, but she knew the memory of the sight, as well as what the girl had seen, would linger for at least a fortnight until she managed to put them away with all the other awful things she'd ever seen and buried. Or drowned.

Each peeler she passed tipped his hat and bid her a good evening. The transport team was there to collect the body, and the "cleaners" had arrived to ensure all evidence was collected and every trace of the crime erased. It was standard protocol when the details of a crime were to be kept undisclosed, and since the young woman obviously was of good birth, they had been brought in to save the family from being dragged through more unpleasant scandal than necessary.

Such precautions also kept the jackals of the press from plastering the tragedy all over the pages of the papers and sending the country into a paranoid tizzy that another Jack the Ripper was on the loose. They'd learned their lesson with that particular nasty piece of work.

"You have my gratitude for coming here tonight, my lady," Inspector Grant spoke, as he opened the door of her carriage. Two metal steps flipped down.

Arden turned to him, one foot on the bottom step. "That's very lovely of you to say, Inspector. Thank you." It wasn't as though she had a choice—it was her duty. Even though she did not answer to Scotland Yard, she reported to the Wardens—an organization higher up the clandestine ladder—and they would expect her to do all she could to aid in the apprehension of this monster.

Grant nodded, and closed the door once she was inside the vehicle. The driver started up the steam engine, and within moments the carriage jerked into motion, the comforting chug filling the interior.

Arden leaned back against the cushioned seat, a wave of weariness washing over her. She was just about to close her eyes when the dirigible made another pass overhead, illuminating the factory yard. Something—someone—on the roof of the factory made her sit bolt upright.

The factory was only two floors, so the distance to the roof wasn't that far, but when she looked up she swore her eyes were wrong, that they were deceiving her.

The man on the roof was dressed in black, so she couldn't tell if he had blood on him or not, and he dove out of sight when the bright light washed over him. However, his clothing wasn't what caught her attention, but his face. A face she knew as well as her own. A face she had once traced every inch of with her fingers, kissed with her lips.

It was the face of her husband.

ALSO AVAILABLE
FROM

KATE CROSS

TOUCH OF STEEL
A Novel of the Clockwork Agents

Reeling from her brother's death, beautiful spy Claire Brooks
has vowed revenge on the member of The Company who she
believes to be responsible. But when she chases him to London,
Claire is captured by the Wardens of the Realm and placed in
the custody of the dashing Alistair Payne. Seeing the prospect of
retribution slipping away, Claire convinces Alistair that she has
defected and will help him take down The Company. As they
travel, Claire can't deny the growing attraction she feels for
Alistair. But when revenge is finally within her reach, she will
have to decide if her true loyalties lie with The Company or
with her heart...

"Kate Cross is fabulous!"
—#1 *New York Times* bestselling author
Victoria Alexander

Available wherever books are sold or
at penguin.com

facebook.com/LoveAlwaysBooks

FROM
BETH CIOTTA

HIS CLOCKWORK CANARY
The Glorious Victorious Darcys

Simon Darcy has a daring plan to win Queen Victoria's competition to recover lost inventions of historical significance. His scheme draws the attention of the Clockwork Canary, London's sensationalist reporter. But, as the attraction between Simon and the Canary ignites, Simon realizes that this vixen has secrets that could be the key to his future...

Praise for *Her Sky Cowboy*:
"Pure charm...a must-read!"
—*New York Times* bestselling author Heather Graham

<u>Don't miss</u>
Her Sky Cowboy
His Broken Angel

Available wherever books are sold or
at penguin.com

facebook.com/LoveAlwaysBooks

LOVE

ROMANCE
NOVELS?

For news on all your favorite romance authors,
sneak peeks into the newest releases, book
giveaways, and much more—

"Like" Love Always on Facebook!

 **LoveAlwaysBooks**